BILLY CRAWFORD'S DOUBLE PLAY

Also by Brad Smith

All Hat
Big Man Coming Down the Road
Busted Flush
Cactus Jack
Copperhead Road
Crow's Landing
The Goliath Run
Hearts of Stone
One-Eyed Jacks
Red Means Run
The Return of Kid Cooper
Rises a Moral Man
Rough Justice
Shoot the Dog

BILLY CRAWFORD'S DOUBLE PLAY

A NOVEL

BRAD SMITH

JS NB

Published by James Street North Books
an imprint of Wolsak and Wynn Publishers
280 James Street North
Hamilton, ON L8R2L3
www.wolsakandwynn.ca

Editor: Noelle Allen | Copy editor: Anthony Nijssen
Cover and interior design: Jennifer Rawlinson
Author photograph: Lorraine Sommerfeld
Typeset in Adobe Caslon Pro and Neulis Neue
Printed by Brant Service Press Ltd., Brantford, Canada

The publisher gratefully acknowledges the support of the Canada Council for the Arts and the Ontario Arts Council. We also acknowledge the financial support of the Government of Canada through the Canada Book Fund and the Government of Ontario through the Ontario Book Publishing Tax Credit and Ontario Creates.

Library and Archives Canada Cataloguing in Publication

Title: Billy Crawford's double play / Brad Smith.
Other titles: Double play
Names: Smith, Brad (Brad J.), author
Identifiers: Canadiana 20250270110 | ISBN 9781998408306 (softcover)
Classification: LCC PS8587.M52354 B55 2025 | DDC C813/.54—dc23

ONE

The moon is nearly full as the boy and girl drive along Riverside Drive. It's late, nearing two in the morning, and they are heading for an after-prom party at somebody's place on the river. They're in the boy's father's car, a newer model Nissan SUV. The boy had wanted to drive his own vehicle, but the girl had nixed the idea, saying she didn't spend three hundred dollars on a dress and another hundred on hair and makeup to show up in a GMC four-wheel drive pickup with blatting mufflers and a decal of a half-naked cowgirl in the rear window.

The boy had reluctantly agreed. He'd been reluctantly agreeing to a lot of stuff since he'd (reluctantly) agreed to escort the girl to the prom. He hadn't wanted to borrow his father's Nissan and he hadn't wanted to rent the too-tight-in-the-crotch tuxedo he is now wearing. He'd gone along with the whole miserable enterprise in the hope that the girl would offer a little payback after the dance and agree to go "parking" in the woods by Turtle Creek.

"If you think I spent the last two days getting ready for tonight just to go out to dirty old Turtle Creek, you'd better think again. This dress cost three hundred dollars."

The boy is well aware of the cost of the dress. The cost of the dress has been mentioned roughly twenty times since the evening began. Even the cashier at the convenience store where they had stopped for Tic Tacs earlier had heard about the cost of the dress.

"Besides, everybody's going to Melissa's," the girl is saying now. "Everybody's going swimming. Her parents are away in Europe or one of those countries. I bought a brand-new bikini from Couture's. It cost seventy-eight dollars plus tax."

"You could model your new bathing suit for me in Turtle Creek," the boy suggests.

"If you think I paid seventy-eight dollars to swim in a –"

The boy doesn't hear the rest of the prattle. They are approaching a curve in the narrow road, and as the headlights sweep through the turn, he sees a car in the ditch on the outer arc of the curve.

The car is on its roof.

"Holy shit," the boy says. He hits the high beams and coasts to a stop thirty feet short of the wreck. The lights from the overturned car shine across the field to the south, illuminating an expanse of ripening wheat. "You think somebody's still in there?"

He gets out and slowly approaches the car, extremely nervous of what he might find. It's a red Camaro, fairly new. The odour of spilled gasoline and oil hangs in the air. When the boy gets close, he can feel the heat from the engine. The wreck obviously happened very recently. Ducking down, he sees a man sprawled in the driver's seat. The airbag has inflated and then deflated, and now half-covers the man. The girl comes up behind him and has a look.

"Oh my God! Is he dead? We need to call 911."

She turns and hurries back to the Nissan for her phone, but the ground is rough and she isn't used to walking in high heels. She catches her foot on a root and falls, dirtying the front of her three-hundred-dollar gown.

"Sonofabitch!"

When she returns, the boy is kneeling in the grass, his head cocked toward the driver's window of the Camaro. The glass is lowered maybe two inches. The girl crouches beside him as she punches in the number. She's not pleased about her tumble in the dirt.

"Well, where the fuck are we?" she asks. "They'll want to know where we are."

"Shh!" the boy says. "Listen."

"What?"

"He's snoring." The boy turns and smiles at the girl. "Fucking guy is sound asleep in there."

The girl hesitates, phone in hand. "Do I still call 911?"

"To report a guy snoring?" The boy hammers on the window. "Hey, buddy, wake up in there!"

After a bit, the pounding wakes Billy Crawford from his nap inside the Camaro. It takes several moments for him to realize he's still in his car and another moment or two to figure out that the car is on its roof. Twisting his head toward the sound of the rapping on the window, he sees in the bright moonlight a youth dressed in a tuxedo, looking in at him.

"The goddamn door locks won't work," he yells through the gap in the window.

"I know!" the kid replies. "I been trying them."

Billy rubs his head and finds a knot above his right eye. No blood, just a lump the size of a walnut. "You got a crowbar?" he asks the kid.

The boy grins. He's relieved that the man is alive. "I left my crowbar in my other suit."

Fucking wiseass, Billy thinks. He sees that there's a girl behind the boy, dressed in a fancy pink dress. She's looking at Billy as if he has landed in the ditch from outer space. Billy looks back at the boy.

"You must have a tire iron in your trunk," he says. He has a better look. "Hey – you wearing a tuxedo?"

"I am."

"What are you, a maître d'?"

"Nope," the boy says. "You want me to call the cops?"

"I'd rather you didn't," Billy tells him. "I been drinking a bit."

"We have to call the police!" the girl hisses.

The boy waves her off. He reaches in through the gap in the window and pulls on the glass, to no avail. He sees there's a guitar on the floor in front of the passenger seat.

"Look out of the way," Billy says. He manoeuvres himself around, so his back is to the passenger door. "I'm going to try to push the window out with my boot."

"Watch out for your guitar," the boy tells him. "What are you anyway, a musician?"

"Hell no," Billy says. "I'm a ballplayer."

The ball comes off the tee low and screaming, hit thin off the titanium club face. It starts out dead straight and then the spin takes over, the face of the driver having cut across the ball, causing it to careen crazily to the right as it rises into the wind. The classic slice, bane of many a duffer. Carroll Miller stands on the tee box and watches as the ball heads for the line of trees – and the area marked out of bounds – down the right side of the fairway. When it finally lands, the ball takes one huge bounce, projecting it even farther to the right, then disappears into the long grass.

"Should be all right," Carroll says to the others, his eyes fixed on the spot where the ball vanished.

None of the three offer any comment on this. Not one of them is convinced that the ball didn't bounce out of bounds, yet none is willing to suggest as much. They've played enough golf with Carroll Miller to know better.

Carroll is the alpha male in the group, or at least he regards himself as such. In fact, he regards himself as the big dog of any group. He takes his golf game seriously. Today's foursome is his regular game; they usually play three or four times a week, except for the frequent times when he is out of town. Carroll's partner in the matches is always Dale Gosling, who runs CM Enterprises, the development company that has built over a thousand new residences in Rose City over the past two decades. Dale is a lousy golfer, maybe even a terrible one, which means that the other two players in the foursome – Tony Vortman and Stan Chandler – are required to give Dale strokes, to offset his handicap and make the matches, on paper at least, more even-handed.

Carroll Miller needs no such crutch. He considers himself a scratch golfer and is the best player of the group by a large margin. It's Carroll's nature that he won't play with anyone better than himself. He'd started playing the game with his grandfather when he was five years old and had taken lessons off and on in the fifty-odd years since then. He drives the ball far off the tee, the odd banana slice notwithstanding, hits his long and short irons extremely well and possesses a fair touch around the greens. However, he is a barely average putter on his best day, a fact that aggravates him to no end and one that has led him to buy and discard dozens of putters over the decades, seeking one that would somehow overcome his failings. As with many a golfer, he is not willing to accept that the problem lies not in the club but in the hands of the man holding it. Most of the "failed" putters end up in a garbage can, or in a pond alongside a green, quite often with the shaft bent into a horseshoe. That concern aside, his other strengths in the game mean that he is a tough player to beat out on the course.

The fact that he cheats regularly makes beating him even tougher.

The game of choice for the foursome is Nassau, a two-man team game also known as high/low. A lone low score on a hole secures a point while a lone high number relinquishes one. So, if a player and his partner both make par and their opponents make bogey, the first team gets two points. Four pars – or bogeys or others – is a push, no points awarded. They play for twenty dollars a man for every nine holes. There are also "presses." A press can be called at any time during the match, effectively starting a brand-new twenty-dollar game, while the previous game is ongoing. By the end of a round, there are often six or seven or eight wagers at once. Golfing with Carroll Miller can be an expensive proposition.

The cheating, of course, makes it even more expensive.

Dale and Stan are up next, and both manage to hit the fairway, although neither ball travels very far. Tony steps up and hits a low hook off the tee, the ball heading for a deep elongated pond, down the left edge of the fairway. There's a slight rise before the pond, making it difficult to tell if the ball rolls into the water or not. While the others go to look for it, Carroll gets into his cart and drives off in pursuit of his own errant shot. A golf cart is usually shared by two players, but Carroll insists on driving solo, the better to get away with any nefarious actions he might feel inclined to pull.

Carroll never cheats on his scorecard. For instance, he doesn't make a five on a par four and claim otherwise. That kind of cheating is for pikers and people with little imagination. Not only that, but it is nearly impossible to get away with, unless your opponent happens to be a dyed-in-the-wool idiot who can't tell the difference between a five and a four, or a three and a two. Most players are quite aware of how many strokes their opponent takes on a hole. No, scorecard cheating is not Carroll's style. Instead, he is a master at never losing a ball, and rarely ending up in a bad lie. He is also quite skilled in the sleight of hand – or more specifically sleight of foot – required to keep his ball in play.

On this day, Carroll leaves the others to scour the pond for Tony's lost Top-Flite and drives over to the opposite edge of the course, where he'd last seen his Bridgestone bounding into the long grass. He finds four balls within a minute and a half; none are his. When he finally spots the Bridgestone with bright red CM logo, it's in the ditch alongside the paved road running outside the course. The ball is well out of bounds, but there happens to be an identical Bridgestone, marked the same, in the left front pocket of Carroll's Dockers. Glancing over at the three men alongside the pond, Carroll drops the ball in the intermediate rough at the edge of the fairway, a good three feet short of where his original shot was last seen. The ball hits the ground and hops forward a few inches, coming to rest in a slight impression. Not a good lie. A nudge from Carroll's toe solves that problem, then he pulls a fairway wood and hammers the ball directly down the middle of the fairway, leaving a third shot of about eighty yards on the par five. He poses with his finish, hands high, until the ball rolls to a stop, then gets into the cart and drives over to where the others have given up on finding the ball that is presumably at the bottom of the pond. Tony drops another ball just short of the water and knocks it down the fairway. Not being a beneficiary of a "miracle find" like Carroll's, he's obliged to take a one-shot penalty for his troubles.

In spite of Carroll's strategic manoeuvrings, the match ends up squared on the day, due in part to Dale's atrocious play. Whenever Carroll makes a birdie to gain a point, Dale ends up with a double or triple bogey, sawing off the hole.

In the clubhouse afterward, over drinks, Carroll adds up the scores while Dale apologizes at length for his performance. Stan swipes through his phone, checking his messages. Tony has gone to the gents.

"Seventy-three," Carroll says, referring to his own score. "Stan, you were seventy-eight. Tony was eighty-one." Carroll reaches for his Glenfiddich. "Dale, I think we'll need to send your card to IBM to get a total."

Stan smiles dutifully at the joke while Dale begins to apologize all over again.

"Oh, stop it," Carroll says. "We broke even so who cares." He picks up his drink and rattles the ice in the glass. "I mean, I did shoot one over par, which means I should have made a few bucks. Maybe I just need a new partner. Does anyone have Stevie Wonder's phone number? Ray Charles?"

"Ray Charles is dead," Stan says, still looking at his phone.

Carroll has a drink. "He could still beat Dale by about ten strokes."

"All right, all right," Dale says.

When Tony returns, he's carrying the sports section from the *Standard*, which someone left in the locker room.

"Holy shit, Carroll," he says, sitting down and reaching for his beer. "The Rounders have lost *eleven* in a row. What the fuck is going on over there?"

Dale smiles, happy to be off the subject of his pathetic golf game. "I'll tell you what's going on: They can't hit, they can't pitch and they can't catch. Otherwise, they're a great ball team."

"Says the man who couldn't beat a three-year-old at golf," Carroll says.

"Keep beating that drum," Dale sighs. "The Rounders are a mess. I think Mac wants to get fired. Rumour is that Ron Erskine has been making out the lineup every day. That's not the assistant manager's job. Mac sits in the dugout with his pants pulled up to his armpits, drinking whatever he has in that Styrofoam cup and telling anybody who'll listen about the time he struck out Reggie Jackson."

Stan scoffs. "As if that really happened."

"Oh, it happened," Dale interjects. "I googled it. Spring training game back in the 1980s. Keep in mind that striking out Reggie Jackson wasn't exactly the rarest feat in baseball back then."

"Long way from Mr. October to the Rose City Rounders," Tony says.

Carroll has fallen uncharacteristically quiet. He doesn't want to talk about the Rounders. He owns the team, and he doesn't like being associated with anything that isn't a winner.

Tony reads from the paper. "Jesus, you see how last night's game ended? Billy Crawford got thrown out trying to steal third base. They were down one run at the time. Why the fuck would he do that?"

"Because he still thinks he's twenty-five, that's why," Dale says. Dale is a baseball nut, a stats guy, a trivia buff. "He'll be forty next spring."

Tony shakes his head. "Then he should know better than to get thrown out at third base when he's the tying run, shouldn't he?"

"He's a fucking baseball player," Carroll says, finally addressing the subject. "That's pretty much synonymous with *moron*. I just might shitcan him. Maybe Mac too."

Dale has a drink. "The fans still love Crawford. Shit, the guy played for the Orioles. He's got history."

"He was in Baltimore for a cup of coffee," Stan says.

"Half a cup is more like it," Carroll adds.

Dale shrugs. "Hey – he was a hell of a ballplayer in his day. Keep in mind that the worst player in the major leagues is probably ten times better than anybody you've ever known to play the game. And he put some asses in the seats these past five years."

"Female asses especially," Stan says. "Women love the guy."

"And he loves them right back, if you believe the stories about him," Dale said. "The man is a serious hound dog."

Carroll rolls his Bridgestone back and forth on the tabletop. "Billy Crawford is about as deep as the dimples on this ball. Good-looking guy, dumb as a rock. Of course women flock to him. He's a play toy."

Walking through the clubhouse parking lot later, Carroll pulls a cigar from his pocket and lights it. He's no longer permitted to smoke in the clubhouse. He puffs away on the Cohiba for a few moments, stoking it, and watches as Dale opens the back hatch of his SUV and puts his clubs inside. Carroll indicates his Mercedes, parked a couple of spots over.

"Come on."

"Where we going?"

"Brownsville," Carroll tells him.

"What's in Brownsville?"

"Not a whole hell of a lot right now," Carroll says. "And that's the problem. We're meeting Rob Filsinger."

Brownsville is a few kilometres north of Rose City, along River Road. It's little more than a hamlet. In the nineteenth century, when the area was first being settled, the village was a going concern – with several tanneries, grist mills, distilleries and harness makers – and was being considered for county seat. In those days of corduroy and mud roads, it was determined that the county seat, to remain accessible year-round, should be on the railroad line. But when the railway came, it was decided that it would bypass Brownsville and run farther south, through Pumpkin Corners instead. The powers that be at the time decided that Pumpkin Corners wasn't a proper name for a seat of local government and decided to change it to Rose City. It is widely believed that the name came from the huge proliferation of roses around City Hall and the courthouse, but that isn't remotely true; the flowers came later. The city was actually named for Rose, the wife of the first mayor, Charles Danson. In fact, it was Danson's gift to Rose, delivered shortly after she discovered him and his second cousin Ethel half-naked in the stables behind their house, engaging in robust non-equestrian activities. Charles was a known skinflint; presumably renaming a city for one's wife was a cheaper form of spousal contrition than the traditional diamonds and furs.

Rejected by the railway, the bustling little village of Brownsville was left behind. A few years ago, it was amalgamated into Rose City but still maintains its own identity, even though it is now governed by Rose City council.

Rob Filsinger is the councillor for Brownsville and its rural environs, and today he's leaning against his car, sipping a Tims, as Carroll and Dale pull up and park. They're on a rise on the outskirts of the village, overlooking several farms that stretch along the river valley.

"Councillor," Carroll says, extending his hand. "You know Dale?"

"Of course," Filsinger says as he shakes hands with both men.

"Been waiting long?" Carroll asks. "We were involved in a high-stakes golf game."

Filsinger smiles. "I suspected as much."

"Dale shot his age," Carroll says. "Well, if his age was a hundred and fifty."

"Ouch," Filsinger says.

"You know, I never tire of this," Dale says.

Filsinger gestures to the scenery below them. "So what are we talking about here?"

Carroll makes a pistol with his right hand and points the imaginary barrel at the three nearest farms, ticking them off one by one. "This, this and this. A total of three hundred and fifty acres."

The farms he indicates are adjacent to each other, well-kept, with painted wood barns and modern steel outbuildings. The farmhouses are all from a hundred years ago or more, red brick buildings with wide porches and second-story dormers. The surrounding fields are planted mostly in soybeans.

"You've already bought these three?" Filsinger asks.

"Not exactly," Carroll says. "I'm not spending a nickel until I get some assurance from you guys on development. But I have made offers, contingent upon that, and the offers have been accepted. I also have NDAs with the owners, just so you know."

Filsinger nods, ignoring the thinly veiled warning. He stands looking at the farms. East of the properties, there is a greying old farmhouse, squatting between the last of the farms and the Chalk River.

"What's with that place?"

"I'm still working on it," Carroll says. "The owner just died and the grandson has power of attorney over the estate. He's out in Vancouver or somewhere, playing hard to get." He pulls on the cigar. "But I'll get him."

Filsinger shifts his attention back to the other properties.

"How do you propose to get this little three-hundred-acre project greenlit?"

"Three hundred and fifty," Carroll corrects him. "And isn't that the question I'm supposed to be asking you? Isn't that why we're meeting here? You do have a vote coming up, right?"

"I don't see that anything's changed since the last time we spoke, Carroll," Filsinger says. "People out here don't want this. They keep referencing Fairbrook, over and over. You know the history. Ten years ago, it was a hamlet of about two hundred people and now it's over nine thousand. And it's not what you'd call a traditional small town with park space and markets and all that. It's just a bedroom community. They built those new houses so tight together people have to take their lawn mowers through their houses to get from their front yards to the back."

"We didn't build those houses," Dale reminds him.

"I know you didn't," Filsinger says. "But you see my point."

"Not really," Carroll says. "The land is here for the taking. The real estate market is hot."

"There is virtually no vacant land left in the city proper," Dale adds.

"I know," Filsinger agrees. "I know all about it."

The three stand there for a bit in awkward silence. Carroll expects a little more from Rob Filsinger than "I know." Carroll has contributed to the Filsinger campaign for the past four elections, in ways both legal and not.

"Let's talk about Fairbrook then," Carroll says, tired of waiting. "What was the tax revenue for that little intersection ten years ago?"

Filsinger shrugs. "Off the top of my head, I wouldn't know."

"Okay," Carroll says. "I can see why an insignificant number like that wouldn't lodge itself in your memory. Next question: What was the tax revenue for Fairbrook last year?"

"Well, I could ballpark it maybe," Filsinger says.

"So could I," Carroll tells him. "Roughly three thousand new homes, average of say, four or five grand a year in taxes, we're talking somewhere between twelve and fifteen million dollars, Rob. Up from about a nickel a decade ago. From the viewpoint of a *progressive* and fiscally astute councillor like yourself, what's the downside to that?"

"I'm not claiming one," Filsinger tells him. "You're preaching to the choir here, Carroll. When have I voted against a single one of your applications? The problem here is Uncle Joe and you know it."

"Uncle Joe thinks he's the mayor of Bedford Falls," Dale says.

"Where the hell is Bedford Falls?" Carroll asks.

"The town in *It's a Wonderful Life*," Dale replies.

Carroll shakes his head. "You've got some fucked-up cultural references, Dale."

"My point is," Dale explains, "Joe Simmons still thinks of Rose City as the small town where he was born back in the horse-and-buggy days. He doesn't get that it's a metropolis now. We all know where he stands on the greenbelt issue. And he still has enough dinosaurs on council to back him." Dale pauses and nods toward Filsinger. "Present company excepted."

"Keep in mind that every election we lose another dinosaur or two," Filsinger says. "Eventually we'll be able to hold sway over these development issues. But it will take some patience."

"Patience," Carroll repeats. "So you're telling me to shell out millions to these farmers here and then just twiddle my thumbs while we wait for Uncle Joe and his gang of geezers to die off one by one?"

Filsinger is quiet for a long time, trying to decide what to say and how to say it. He has always been nervous around Carroll Miller. A lot of people are. "I guess I'm just telling you how it is. I have to head back, guys."

Carroll and Dale watch as he drives off. Carroll relights his cigar.

"What do we do about these properties?" Dale wants to know.

Carroll thinks on it for a time. "Buy them eventually," he says finally. "First, I'd like some assurances with regards to zoning. But there are few sure things in this world and this is one of them – nobody ever went broke buying land."

"What about Uncle Joe?"

"You let me worry about Uncle Joe," Carroll says.

TWO

Kate finds her father in his den, sitting by the bay window that overlooks the backyard and the river beyond. It has taken her over five hours to drive from Toronto, a trip that used to take less than three. The thruway has been expanded to six lanes, but the effort has been futile, as it is bottlenecked at both ends. Kate had idled along the road at a glacial pace, listening to a podcast about the Galapagos Islands that didn't hold her interest. She had no doubt that the story was engaging, but her attention span has been practically non-existent of late.

Joe Simmons is dozing in the chair, his head back. Kate stands inside the French doors and watches him for a bit. His chest rises slightly with each breath; his mouth is partly open. She doesn't want to wake him.

She goes into the kitchen and puts on water for tea. While she waits for it to boil, she sits at the island and flips through the morning *Standard*. There's not much there to hold her interest either. She doesn't know much about the city anymore, even if her father is the mayor and has been the mayor for over three decades; she's been gone for twenty years. After law school, she'd accepted a job with a firm in Toronto and has been there ever since.

Well, up until last Friday anyway.

The kettle whistles and apparently the shrill is enough to wake her father. He calls from the den, asking who's there.

"It's just me, Dad," she calls. "Do you want tea?"

"Tea?" he repeats and then mumbles something she doesn't catch.

"Is that a yes?"

When there's no further reply, she makes her own cup and goes to join him. "I asked if you want tea."

"I don't want any tea."

He has roused himself in the leather chair. His wiry grey hair is mussed and his reading glasses hang on a chain around his neck. He's wearing a plaid shirt and tan cotton pants with worn leather slippers. Kate sits on the couch across from him.

"How was the drive?" he asks.

"I had snails passing me," she tells him.

He nods. "My grandfather used to tell how he would take the old lake road to Toronto, in a wagon with horses. Gravel road, barely two lanes. It would take him, he'd say, all goddamn day to get there. In this modern age, it only takes . . . well, all goddamn day to get there."

Kate smiles. She's heard that story before, multiple times. In fact, her father often uses it on the stump while decrying the province's mishandling of the highway systems leading in and out of Rose City. Of course, over the years she's heard all her father's stories. She has noticed of late though that he has been repeating himself more frequently.

"Maybe I'll take a cue from Great-Grandfather and buy a team of horses," she tells him. "I have to believe that hay is cheaper than gas."

He laughs at that and coughs as his does. As he puts his hand over his mouth, she notices the shaking. It seems worse than the last time she'd been here, two months earlier. She wonders if that's why he refused a cup of tea – he didn't want her to see the tremors.

"Are you here on business or just playing hooky?" he asks.

"Personal business," she replies. She takes a moment to sip her tea, not sure that she wants to get into it right away. *What the hell.* "I came to ask about the availability of my old room."

He gives her a long look but says nothing. She's being cryptic and her father isn't a fan of cryptic.

"Jeremy and I are calling it quits," she says. "There have been problems for some time now."

"I sensed that," he says after a bit. "What about the firm?"

"I can stay if I want to," she tells him. "I don't want to. There are some new . . . personal . . . developments in the office that I don't need to witness on a daily basis."

"He's been stepping out on you," Joe assumes.

Stepping out on me, Kate repeats to herself. Typical of her father to utilize a phrase from the days of yore. It is his way and has over the years become a part of his persona, landing him the nickname Uncle Joe. As a figure of speech, *stepping out* works, although Kate is inclined to be somewhat less circumspect when mentioning that her husband of fourteen years has been fucking an intern at the firm. Potato, potahto.

"I gave notice Friday," she says, then drinks more tea. "This wasn't a snap decision. It's been coming for months and so I've had time to consider what I want to do next. I've been thinking I'd like to open a law office here in the city, Dad. Full circle and all that."

"I think that's a good idea," Joe tells her. "Of course, I've been in favour of that notion ever since you wrote the bar exam." He looks out the window a moment. "If I was a few years younger, I might find Jeremy and knock him on his ass a couple times."

She shakes her head. "That wouldn't change anything."

"Change wouldn't be my motivation."

She sets her cup aside, then stands and crosses over to kiss him on his forehead. Resting her hand on his shoulder, she straightens and looks outside.

"Oh, look at the blossoms on Mom's tulip tree," she says. "They're amazing this year. She would be so pleased."

"I'm sure she is pleased." Joe coughs again and reaches for a pack of lozenges on the table beside him. "Have you found office space?"

"Dad, I quit my job last Friday."

"I heard you," he says. "I thought maybe you were looking before that. There's space for lease in the Lester Block, across from City Hall. The rent might be on the dear side though."

Dear means expensive. *Stepping out* is cheating. Joe Simmons is a treasure trove of archaic terms. Kate knows it isn't an affectation, although some presume it to be. It's the way he has always talked, how his parents and grandparents had talked. Kate's sure her great-grandpa, he of the horse-and-wagon story, had used the same language.

"I have time to look around," she says. "I don't need to be downtown if there's something more suitable elsewhere. I'm not in a hurry. I'm getting a buyout from the firm."

"If you're in no hurry, I have an election coming up in the fall. You could work for me. Darby tells me he doesn't have another campaign in him. You could take over his job."

She laughs. "That's nepotism, Dad. The mean kids would call me Ivanka."

"Since when have you ever cared about the mean kids?"

Since one of them started stepping out with my husband, Kate thinks. "Why don't we drive into Brownsville for dinner? Is the Canfield still open?"

There's one restaurant in Brownsville, located in the Canfield Hotel, a fieldstone monstrosity built in 1882, high above the river gorge. The hotel has served food and beverages, in one capacity or another, ever since it opened. What had originally been a fancy dining room became more of a beer parlour in the middle of the last century, with both a men's and "ladies and escorts" side. That quaint arrangement went the way of the dodo fifty years ago. After a few stops and starts, the space had more recently adopted the name "The Brownsville Tavern" and began to offer what was referred to as pub fare. Some of the newcomers to the area, addicted to short forms and an innate need for cool-sounding phrases, call the place The Tav.

They take Kate's Lexus to the village and park in the hotel lot. Inside, they find a table by the front windows. They are early for dinner and the place isn't busy. Joe orders a vodka martini to start and Kate has a gin and tonic. After looking at the menu, she orders the special, broiled Atlantic salmon, while her father asks for liver and onions. Her father always asks for liver and onions.

"So, who's running against you this time?" she asks as they wait for their food. "Has anyone declared yet?"

"Zeb Zabrisky."

"Jesus," Kate says. "When was the last time that Zeb Zabrisky *didn't* run against you?"

"I'm going to miss that old hippie when he's gone," Joe says. "Other than him, nobody yet. But they're out there, lurking. A couple of young councillors are making noises. Whatshername from Central, the one with the monorail proposal. And Josh Henderson wants the job too. He's made no bones about that."

"Henderson," Kate repeats, searching her memory. "The climate change denier?"

"That's him."

"Sad to think somebody like that could get elected."

"He's not going to get elected," Joe says. "So far, he's been running off at the mouth like a soup sandwich, looking for financing, I suspect. He's a fart in a windstorm." He has a drink from the rock glass. "There are a couple of others who want the job but they're waiting on me to step down. I don't know if that's because they don't think they have the support to beat me yet, or they're sitting back, hoping to get my endorsement when I finally do hang 'em up. Probably both."

Kate notices her father's hand shaking as he places the glass on the table. When their meals arrive, she keeps an eye on him, how he trembles when he tries to cut the liver and when he lifts the fork to his mouth. She wants to ask if he's taking his pills but she knows he gets upset when she does. In truth, she's reasonably sure that he is. Around Rose City he may be the poster boy for old school, but he does believe in medical science. Which means that, even with the meds, the Parkinson's is advancing rather quickly.

"Wait a minute," she says, realizing something. "Zeb Zabrisky has been running on a platform to legalize marijuana for thirty years. Well, marijuana is now legal."

"Now he wants to get rid of cars," Joe says.

"Now that would solve my aforementioned thruway problems," Kate says. "Maybe I'll vote for the old communist."

"You're paying for your own dinner," Joe tells her.

THREE

Billy gets up early and calls ABC Towing to see about bringing his car in. Billy has had reason to use ABC a few times over the years. Today he rides with the driver in the flatbed to the scene of the accident. The cops are already there. Billy had sort of been expecting that; he'd hoped otherwise, of course. Maybe the kid in the tuxedo reported it, or his snotty girlfriend in the muddied dress. But it could have been anyone. The car had been upside down in the ditch for a few hours.

"Deer ran out in front of me, and I had to swerve to miss it," he tells the one officer. There's two of them there, a square-jawed guy of about forty and a woman, maybe mid-twenties, with blond hair tied back beneath her hat and the no-nonsense attitude of an eager rookie.

"You didn't think to report it?" the square jaw asks.

"Report a deer running around loose?"

"Report the accident," the cop says.

"I wouldn't bother you guys about something this minor," Billy says. "Shit, there's hardly any damage that I can see."

"Your car is on its roof!" the younger cop says.

Billy turns to look at the Camaro, as if noticing this fact for the first time.

The square jaw is walking around the wreck. He stops and looks at Billy over the undercarriage. "Were you drinking last night, Mr. Crawford?"

Billy isn't sure how the cop came up with his name. Maybe he recognized him from the Rounders. Or he could have run the licence plate number from the car. Didn't matter either way.

"No, sir, I was not."

"You sure about that? I mean, if I had gotten thrown out at third base to end the game, I might have cracked a cold one or two."

Jesus, Billy thinks. *Is there no such thing as anonymity anymore?* The square jaw smiles at Billy's blank expression and moves over to his partner. She drops her voice, but Billy can still hear.

"We won't get him on impaired, but this is careless driving at the very least. *And* leaving the scene of an accident to boot. This guy thinks he's smart, taking off like that to avoid a drinking charge and then showing up the next day."

The square jaw gives it some thought, then shakes his head at her. He turns to Billy.

"All right, Mr. Crawford, we're going to buy your deer-ran-out-in-front-of-me story. *This* time."

The rookie's eyes widen in disbelief.

"A big buck," Billy says. "Twelve point I'd say."

"Don't push it," the square jaw says. "I just said we'll buy it."

Billy can hear the woman protesting as the two get into the cruiser and drive off. She's a beginner, Billy decides. Square jaw will set her straight on the ways of the world. Flipping a car on its roof is not exactly a capital offence.

Back in town, the flatbed drops the Camaro off at a body shop on 23rd Street for an estimate. The shop, like the towing business, has also been used by Billy over the years he's been in Rose City. Billy gets a lift home from the flatbed driver. He showers, then walks over to Peg's Diner for breakfast. The diner is only two blocks from the house Billy has been renting for the past five years.

There is nobody named Peg associated with the operation of the diner anymore. In fact, there never really was, other than by a couple of degrees of separation. The original owner – a man named Fred – had named the place after his grandmother. He always maintained that the old girl was a master "homestyle" cook who had inspired in him an appreciation for good food at a reasonable price. The truth is that Grandma Peg was a chain-smoking casino regular who had never so much as fried an egg for Fred – but she had loaned him ten grand to get the place up and running.

Fred himself is gone now, having sold out a few years ago to Damon Montcalm. Damon had played in the CFL before ending up in Rose City, having married a woman who grew up there. Damon was a big man when he played, but is lighter now, down to around two forty. He almost always works the morning shift himself and is at the grill when Billy walks in today. He smiles slightly and watches as Billy takes a table by the front window, then brings over a coffee without any prompting. He holds the grin while shaking his head in great and feigned astonishment.

"What the hell were you thinking?" he asks.

"Here we go," Billy says.

"Yes, sir," Damon tells him. "What – did you think nobody noticed?"

"So I'm now three for my last thirty-one. Even Mickey Mantle had slumps."

"Nice pivot," Damon says. "I wasn't talking about the oh-for-five. What happened in the ninth?"

Billy shakes his head and takes a sip of the black coffee. "All right – here's the deal. That fucker McDuff never gave me a look, not one. He's a lefty, so he has to make a big turn to check on me, right? So I'm getting a bigger lead, and bigger and bigger, every pitch. I got a great jump, Damon. If McDuff had thrown something off-speed, I'd have been there easy. But he goes high heat and the catcher fired a pill. I tip my hat to the man."

"That's your story?" Damon asks.

"All I got for now," Billy says. "I'll have the usual, Damon."

The usual is known as Peg's Big Country Breakfast – three eggs, bacon and sausage, home fries, toast and jam, with bottomless coffee. As a rule, Billy has the Big Country Breakfast five or six days a week. He knows he should opt for oatmeal or cereal now and again, but that rarely happens. Oatmeal is boring; he'd eaten enough of it growing up on the farm. But his weight has been climbing the past couple of years, after holding steady at one ninety most of his career. He blames the extra pounds on the fact that he's a full-time designated hitter now and doesn't get the exercise he once did playing centre field. There is some truth to that, but there is also the fact that he leads a pretty languorous life. His physical activities off the ball field are limited to shooting pool, playing poker, riding in a golf cart and having sex. Only the latter manages to raise his heartbeat enough for it to be considered a workout, and he hasn't had sex in nearly two weeks; just last night he was turned down by Suzanne, the bartender at Shaky's.

"What – just because I got thrown out at third base?" Billy had asked.

"Yeah, that's it," she'd replied, rolling her eyes.

Her gesture led Billy to suspect that wasn't it. He and Suzanne have had an off-and-on relationship for a couple of years, mostly of a physical nature. She is no more interested in anything long term than he is. She didn't even like to sleep over at his place. But lately she'd been keeping Billy at arm's length, more so than usual, and he suspected that she either wanted more from him, or less. Maybe she'd found somebody else. Maybe she'd found somebody she actually did want to spend the entire night with. If so, that was okay with Billy. On the subject of women, he adheres to a piece of advice given to him by an old timer who coached him when he was starting out, a scout for the Bearcats who went by the name of Oshkosh, probably because he hailed from Wisconsin.

"Women are like streetcars," he'd say. "Miss one and another will come by right shortly."

As adages go, it was as good as any and better than most.

After breakfast, he calls a cab and rides to Rounders Field, the old ballpark along the river. There is no game tonight; the next morning the team is heading by bus to Buffalo for a three-game series on the weekend. None of the players or coaches would be at the field today, Billy suspects, but he's hoping to find somebody willing to throw to him for some batting practice. He doesn't care who does the throwing, whether it be the guy who cleans the bathrooms or one of the maintenance crew. Three for the last thirty-one will lead a man to desperate measures.

He's surprised to find Mac in the clubhouse, sitting in his office off the locker room, drinking from a Styrofoam cup and puffing on a cigarette, even though smoking has been banned at the park for years. At first Billy thinks that maybe Mac is there to go over the lineup for the weekend series, but he knows that Mac hasn't done any kind of homework like that in ages. Not only that, but when Billy walks in, Mac isn't "going over" anything. He is leaning back in his chair, his gaze on the ceiling as he pulls contentedly on the cigarette like it's his mother's breast. Mac is seventy-seven years old but looks even older. His face is lined and weather-beaten, and he's carrying an extra fifty pounds or so. He wears his pants hitched high over his big belly. He takes snuff when smoking is truly not allowed, and he drinks vodka and ginger ale whether it's allowed or not.

"Hey, Skip," Billy says.

Mac, intent on his blissful smoking, hadn't heard Billy come in. He starts in the chair and comes forward, the front legs hitting the floor. He stares at Billy a moment, as if he doesn't recognize him.

"Crawford," he says finally. "What're you doing here?"

"Come on out and throw me some BP, Skip," Billy says in reply.

"Me, throw BP?" Skip says. "That ain't happening. Shit, I can't lift nothing heavier than my pecker these days." He laughs and drinks from the cup. "Of course, it's quite a size."

Billy doesn't care to discuss Mac's pecker size, in jest or otherwise. "I need some work," he says. "I keep hearing how I'm mired in a horrible slump. Not that I'm buying that. Even Willie Mays had slumps. Come on out; you pitched your whole damn life. All I need is somebody to get it over the plate."

"Use the machine," Mac suggests.

"The machine's been down for near a month. Parts are on a slow boat from China."

Mac reaches for a scorecard on the desk, then picks up a pen and makes a show of contemplating a future lineup. That's enough for Billy. If Mac is going to go so far as the pretend to be doing his job, Billy will take the hint.

He grabs a shag bag full of balls and a bat and goes up the tunnel to the field. The groundskeeper is mowing the outfield on the big Kubota tractor, cutting the grass in diagonal passes. There is nobody else in sight. Billy sits in the dugout and watches for a while, the bat draped over his shoulder. The woman operating the mower is named Jessie. She'd been given the role of head groundskeeper a year ago and the media had made a big deal over the fact that a woman had gotten the job. Apparently cutting grass had been considered a man's game in the past. Billy thought at the time that everybody was making a mountain of a mole hill, and he was pretty sure that Jessie thought the same. He'd been there the day the *Standard* sent a photographer over to take various "action" pictures of the woman – sitting on the mower, wielding a rake, chalking the foul lines. Her bored expression at the time suggested that it was all a lot of hyperbolic shit, but she was going along with it as a team player.

Billy sits watching while she finishes the job, doing one last turn around the perimeter of the field before running the mower into an enclosure off the bullpen. A few moments later, she makes her way on foot toward the clubhouse. She spots Billy and nods as she passes.

"Hey – can you throw a ball?" he asks.

She stops. "Can I throw a ball?"

Billy stands up and gestures with the bat toward the cage down the right-field foul line. "I need somebody to throw BP."

Jessie gives him a long look, as if deciding whether or not the request is serious. She removes her sweat-stained Rounders ball cap and pushes her hair back before putting it on again. She's in her early thirties, Billy guesses, with shoulder-length dark hair and an athlete's body. Long legs, toned arms, tanned from her hours at the park. She has a small tattoo of a feather on the back of her right hand.

"I don't recall there being anything in my contract that obligates me to throw batting practice for random dudes lounging in the dugout on off-days."

Now it's Billy's turn to hesitate. Random dude? "Do you know who I am?" he asks after a moment.

"Let's see," Jessie replies. "Might you be Billy Crawford? The Billy Crawford who played for the Orioles back in the day and two years ago hit thirty-three home runs here for the Rounders? Might that be you? And right now, are you about one for your last fifty at the plate and last night did you try to steal third base with two out in the ninth inning and the team down a run? Or have I got you mixed up with somebody else?"

"Jesus Christ," Billy mutters. "You'd think I'd burned down a damn orphanage or something." When she makes no reply, he adds, "And for your information, I'm three for my last thirty-one."

"Well now," she laughs. "Cooperstown, here we come."

"Everybody in the cheap seats is an expert these days," Billy says. "I don't see you out there on the field."

"I'd have stayed at second if I was."

"Hindsight," Billy says. "Too bad a know-it-all like you can't actually throw a baseball."

"I can throw a baseball," Jessie replies. "I played on the national softball team that went to the Worlds."

"Wow," Billy says. "Cooperstown, here we come."

She stares at him at moment, then gestures. "Bring the fucking shag bag."

Jessie the groundskeeper isn't the second coming of Nolan Ryan but she can throw a baseball, as she claims. She lobs a few to warm up and then brings a little heat. Billy is lost at the plate, either popping pitches up or pulling weak grounders to the left. His frustration grows.

"Give me some giddy-up," he says after a few more ground balls.

She throws harder and the results are pretty much the same.

"You're out front," she tells him. "Stay on your back foot."

"I know how to hit."

"There is evidence to the contrary."

"Shut up and throw the damn ball," he barks. "Even Wade Boggs had slumps."

With that, she throws the next one at Billy's head. He spins away and hits the dirt. He gets up slowly, eyeballing her.

"Enough giddy-up?" she asks.

"Watch it," he warns.

"What are you going to do – have me fired from my job as batting practice pitcher?"

Billy digs in and takes a couple of practice swings. "You got an awful mouth on you for somebody who's a glorified gardener."

Jessie fires a strike and he pops it up.

"Shit!"

"You got a lot of lip for somebody who couldn't hit a bull in the ass with a shovel," she tells him. "You're still out front."

Shut the fuck up and throw the ball, Billy thinks, but he doesn't say it. Instead, he digs his right cleat into the dirt and tells himself to keep his weight back until the ball reaches him. She throws another pitch, and he lines it sharply to right field.

"Wow, the blind squirrel finds an acorn," she yells. She reaches into the bag for another ball. "You kept your weight back."

"Nah, just lifted my elbow a bit," he insists.

"You're full of shit," she replies and throws the ball.

He stays back again and hits a long fly ball to centre field. Now he makes a show of hoisting his left elbow before swinging, as if to convince Jessie of it. She throws twenty more pitches, and he squares up most of them, line drives, hard ground balls and a few long flies, with two going over the left-field fence. Finally, he signals to her he's had enough.

"I was dropping my elbow." No way is he going to give her any credit.

"Right, it was the elbow all along," Jessie replies. "You got any swampland you want to sell me?"

Billy shakes his head at her sass but decides not to respond. She's getting on his nerves. The part that bothers him isn't that she's doing it on purpose, although she clearly is. The part that bothers him is that she's right. He walks over and picks up the empty ball bag.

"You going to give me a hand picking up the balls?"

"Gosh, that would be an honour," she says and then turns and walks into the clubhouse without another word.

"What the hell is wrong with people nowadays?" Billy asks aloud. But he's somewhat happy, or at least happier than he was an hour ago. She was right; he wasn't keeping his weight back. Of course, he knew to do it but when a man is in a slump, his fundamentals tend to get forgotten. Sometimes all he needs is a fresh pair of eyes on the problem. Not that he would ever tell the sarcastic groundskeeper that.

When he leaves the ballpark, he cabs it back to his place. His cell rings on the way. It's the manager from the body shop, telling Billy that the Camaro is a write-off. Billy isn't surprised. Nowadays it costs a couple grand to fix a scratch on a fender. When he gets home, he calls his insurance company and tells the story about the deer running him off the road. The agent doesn't believe the story any more than the two cops had, but it seems as if he doesn't really care. He tells Billy to rent a car until he finds something to buy, and that was that. Around noon, he has a nap.

FOUR

Kate drives her father downtown Monday afternoon. He'd gone to City Hall that morning for some zoning meetings but was home by lunch time. He'd had a driver pick him up and bring him back. That was unlike him. He'd always favoured large North American cars – Lincolns or Cadillacs for the most part – and had always taken pride in driving himself wherever he had to go. Why waste the taxpayers' money on a driver he didn't need?

"Would you hire a man to paint your barn and then stand there watching him do it?" he'd ask.

Kate suspects that nowadays a large segment of the population would hire someone to paint their barn and then stand back to watch them at their work. Of course, not that many people had barns anymore. But Joe knows of what he speaks; he was raised on a farm down near the shores of Lake Erie.

After being home for a day and a half, she suspects that her father is using a driver now because he no longer trusts himself behind the wheel. All the acting in the world can't disguise the unsteadiness he is experiencing – the shaking, the shuffling, the odd dropped word. But giving up the wheel would have been a tough thing to concede, even to himself. He'd started driving when he was twelve years old, back on the farm. Kate knows the story well. His first time behind a wheel of any kind had been on a Ford 8N tractor. During haying season, young Joe would drive the tractor pulling the wagon while his father and brother loaded the bales. Some sixty years on, he still recalls the grown-up feeling, aiming the Ford across the rough fields, the steering wheel jerking in his small hands.

Kate has decided she would honour her father's wishes and run his campaign for him. This in spite of the fact that she has no real experience in politics, even though she'd grown up smack in the midst of it. Her father assures her that her job would be, for the most part, delegating authority and helping set up his schedule. He's mentioned more than once that this is going to be his last campaign.

There are other, more selfish, reasons behind her decision to sign on to the campaign. She finds that she's in no particular hurry to hang out her shingle and start practising law. She doesn't even know what kind of law she wants to practise. She could make a good living handling real estate and wills but she's pretty sure she'd get bored with that in a hurry. Criminal law has always interested her, but only if she could defend noble fictional outlaws like Robin Hood and avoid the Harvey Weinsteins of the world. Not exactly a pragmatic approach, she admits.

Her father's upcoming campaign, at the very least, makes it okay for her not to think about the little matter of what to do with the rest of her life, and so she begins to welcome it. It is a world far removed from the corporate landscape she's been navigating for the past decade or more. Because of her upbringing, she'd always had an outsider's fascination of the muddled world of politics, even though she'd watched it from a distance until now. Beyond that, working with her father every day means she can keep an eye on him and his diminishing skills. She doesn't like to admit that it is happening, but if she's learned anything over the past couple of years, it's that acting like an ostrich won't get her anywhere.

They take her car downtown. It is a cool summer's day, uncommon for the middle of July. It has been warm all week, and very humid, the kind of weather that has you perspiring just walking to the mailbox and back. Last night a thunderstorm hit, with whipping winds and a hard rain slanting in from the southwest. By daybreak, the storm had passed and the temperature dropped.

They hit a red light at the intersection near the entrance to Garrison Park and while they sit waiting, Kate takes in the scene in the park, where in recent months as many as a thousand people have taken up residence in tents and lean-tos and shacks made of cardboard and plywood.

"What's going on here?" she asks.

"You didn't know about the encampments?" Joe asks.

"I vaguely recall reading something about a homeless issue here," Kate says. "I guess I blocked it out. Too focused on my own shit, apparently."

"It's bad and getting worse," Joe says. "There are a lot of so-called solutions being floated, but at the end of the day, it's the same old thing. When all is said and done, more is said than done."

"Who are these people?" Kate asks. "More importantly, why don't they have a place to live?"

"They've fallen through the cracks," Joe tells her. "Some can't find work, some aren't looking. Many have drug problems. And most are not receiving the mental healthcare they need. You can thank Premier Dodge for that. But the housing is crucial. We're trying to come up with low-cost solutions."

"Wouldn't opening up the greenbelt help?"

"Now you sound like our illustrious premier," Joe says. "No – building million-dollar homes in new subdivisions out in the country isn't going to help this situation one bit. These people are desperate, and they have no finances to speak of."

The light changes and Kate has one last look into the park before idling through the intersection.

"This is sad."

"It is that," Joe agrees.

They drive on. Kate falls silent, thinking about what she has just witnessed, and chastising herself for being so oblivious to what was happening in her hometown. It's true she hasn't lived here for years but she has always considered herself to be in the loop at least to a certain extent when it came to Rose City. Apparently, that is no longer true.

"Stop at the farmers' market on the way," Joe says as they drive along Front Street. "See if Ron and Lucy have tomatoes yet."

Kate glances at the clock on the dash.

"We have time," Joe tells her.

The farmers' market is located on a plot of land along the river, where the loading docks had stood in the past century, back when many goods arrived by water. The market sprawls across two acres, in the shadow of Rounders Field. Kate parks in the lot between the ballpark and the market, and she and her father walk over to the rows of stalls. Many of the vendors – most in fact – know Joe personally and call out to him. Ted Belson, who raises goats and sheep a few kilometres south of the city, is of Joe's vintage. The two men have known each other since grade school. Ted is a lifelong farmer; he's built like a fireplug and has the voice of an auctioneer. He calls Joe over and offers him a thin slice of goat cheese.

"You need to try this," he says.

Joe tastes the cheese and it's only then that Ted recognizes Kate. "Well, stranger," he says. "It has been a while. The old man got you chauffeuring him around, does he?"

"Something like that," she replies. "Is he supposed to be accepting bribes of cheese?"

Joe snorts. "If somebody wants to impeach me for eating fifty cents worth of cheese, tell them to bring it on."

"Dairygate," Ted laughs and cuts another slice for Kate. The cheese is sharp, with the taste of apples. Ted turns back to Joe and points his chin toward the baseball stadium a couple hundred yards away.

"I guess you saw Crawford trying to steal third last night."

"I read about it," Joe says.

Kate hangs back and listens. Ever since she can remember, baseball has been a topic of conversation for her father and his friends. It was a topic that reached across party lines and the real and imagined social levels of the city.

"What the hell was he thinking?" Ted asks.

Joe shrugs. "I'm guessing he was thinking he could steal third."

"Rumour is that Mac's on his way out," Ted says. "Same old story. The players aren't doing their job, so fire the manager."

"That's usually how it goes. Then eventually the players come around and the new manager gets the credit."

Ted removes his John Deere cap and gives his scalp a vigorous scratching. "Problem is, Carroll Miller don't know squat about running a ball team. He's one of these guys, just likes to own shit. Sorry, Kate."

She laughs. "I'm shocked."

Joe nods and winks at Kate. "I've been telling people for years, Ted; they ought to hire you to run things over there."

"I'll stick to my goats."

With that, Joe and Kate move on. The Lynches have a stall close to the river, which is running high after last night's storm. They have fresh produce of all kinds that they grow themselves on thirty acres north of Brownsville.

"Any tomatoes yet?" Joe asks. "And not the hothouse variety."

"Would I sell Joe Simmons a hothouse tomato?" Ken asks. "You'd have me tarred and feathered."

"And justifiably so."

Lucy laughs. "You guys have known each other too long," she says. "We have some Glamours here, Joe. First of the season. Not as pretty as some, but tasty."

"When it comes to vegetables, pretty is overrated," Joe tells her.

Kate watches as her father inspects the tomatoes, one by one, like an assayer scrutinizing a pile of gold nuggets. She shifts her attention to the river. There are a few boats in sight, fishermen mostly, either anchored by the Walden Bridge or trolling along the far shore, where bass have been known to lurk in the weed beds.

The water is roiled from the rain; Kate doubts the fishing would be all that good. When she was a little girl, she and her father and mother and brother Andrew would fish from the shore under the ancient railway trestle. Kate recalls catching bullheads, a few bass and the occasional carp. Her mother would catch a catfish no more than five inches long and squeal like she'd just landed a marlin.

Joe eventually decides upon six plump but somewhat misshapen Glamours and pays for them with cash. Nearly all the vendors take plastic these days but in this, Joe is once again old school. He doesn't even own a debit card. Ken counts out his change.

"You see that bonehead stunt by Crawford last night?" he asks.

"Been hearing about it," Joe says.

"Never mind Crawford," Lucy says. "He's my favourite. They need to fire that damn hitting coach."

"They were hitting the ball last month," Ken reminds her. "Same coach."

"I'd take a bat to the lot of them," Lucy says. "They're all spoiled these days."

"They weren't spoiled last month, when they were hitting."

"Oh, you don't know."

Kate and Joe leave before finding out precisely what it is that Ken doesn't know. When they get to City Hall, Ben Craig is in the outer office, talking to Joe's secretary, Maria. The four of them go into Joe's office. He had informed them just that morning by email that Kate would be his campaign manager.

They settle in around the large oak table that has been in the mayor's office for over a hundred years. The table is scarred and blemished with cigar burns and rings from coffee cups (and other beverages) and gouges from staplers and inkwells and ancient fountain pens. It has been suggested many times over Joe's tenure that the piece be sent out, sanded and refinished, but he'd always nixed the idea.

"That slab of red oak is a piece of Rose City history," he'd say.

"Can you imagine the stories it would have, if it could talk? You can't sand that away."

Joe's desk is across the room by a bay window overlooking Main Street. There's a flat-screen TV on the wall opposite, above a leather couch. The set is on, the sound muted, showing RCTV, the city's all-news station.

"So, I know that my father told you guys that I'll be running the campaign," Kate says. "Did he happen to mention the fact that I have no idea how to actually do that?"

"Minor detail," Ben tells her.

Ben Craig is an unflappable presence. Kate has known him virtually her entire life and has never seen him agitated. He's six feet four inches tall, lean as a sapling. In his early sixties now, he was a councillor for nearly twenty years before taking the deputy mayor's job. He has no designs on the mayoralty, which makes him an exception to most of the other present and former councillors in Rose City.

"We've been doing this a while now," he continues. "At this juncture, it's mostly just paperwork anyway. We need to file this week, but that's an email. We'll set up a presser for, I don't know – is Thursday or Friday good, Maria?"

"Let's do it Friday," she replies. "That way, we get the six and eleven o'clock news that night and some repeats on Saturday."

"We have to pick up the fundraising," Ben says. "We have money but not enough. How much are we going to need this time around?"

"Depends who is running against us," Maria replies. "We don't need a large war chest to take on Zeb Zabrisky."

"There will be others," Joe says.

Kate has been watching her father. At first glance he seems as he always has. But under scrutiny, she's noticing a lot of little things. He's slow to join a conversation, always seeming half a beat behind everything, and he again refused water or coffee. She is convinced he doesn't want anyone to see his hands shaking.

"Tell me what you need me to do now," she says. "Gotta get my feet wet."

"Let's do a press release right away," Maria says. "The city needs to know that you're joining the team." She thinks a moment. "You know what – why not do both on Friday? Announce that Joe has filed and that he's hired you to manage the campaign. You can say a few words."

Kate nods. "Something along the lines of – 'I don't know what I'm doing'?"

"We might want to finesse that a bit," Maria says. "Maybe we can make it the return of the prodigal."

Kate thinks a moment. "Wait a minute. Didn't the prodigal blow all his money and end up a swineherd in the parable?"

"Give me a choice and these days I'd vote for a swineherd in a heartbeat," Joe says.

Kate smiles. The old man hasn't lost his fastball yet.

FIVE

Buffalo is a disaster. The Rounders lose all three games, scoring a total of four runs in the process. The feeling in the clubhouse after Sunday's 12–2 loss is one of extreme frustration. Nobody has any answers for the sportswriters mingling in the locker room. It's Triple A ball, not the major leagues, but there is still a media presence, and it is an insistent presence. As usual, the most insistent – and persistent and annoying – of the scribes is Scoop Sutherland from the Rose City *Standard.* Scoop isn't particularly interested in reporting on the games. Taking a cue from guys like Don Cherry, Scoop is of a type – flamboyant in his attire and his language, opinionated to a fault. His real name is Arnold and he bestowed his nickname on himself, after some hard-boiled newspaperman he saw in a Gary Cooper movie from the 1930s. On his best days, Scoop is little more than a navel-gazer; he doesn't want to report on the show, he wants to be a part of it. Actually, he wants to be bigger than it.

Billy's weekend is, if not worse than that of the team, every bit as bad. He goes one for sixteen at the plate, the lone hit being a seeing-eye single up the middle during the eighth inning of Saturday's rout. Billy is left stranded at first base after the lucky swing. He might just as well have remained back in Rose City for the weekend. Whatever "progress" he'd made while swinging the bat against Jessie the groundskeeper a few days earlier disappears in Buffalo. He's back to his old, bad habits, jumping at the ball instead of staying back. He knows what to do but – for some reason – can't force himself to do it.

It doesn't help that Scoop Sutherland decides that Billy should be the spokesperson for the team after Sunday's massacre. Billy is sitting in front of his locker in his shorts, drinking a Gatorade, when the diminutive peacock of a sportswriter approaches. Scoop is, as usual, decked out in a loud suit, this one a red-and-yellow plaid, with a bow tie the size of a catcher's mitt. Scoop also owns a couple dozen fedoras and is never seen without one. The hats are either another gesture to the ink-stained scribe in the Cooper movie, or a cover for Scoop's retreating hairline. Maybe a bit of both.

Billy watches the approach. "Nice suit, Scoop," he says. "Somewhere a clown is filing a theft report."

Scoop is used to the comments; in fact, he cultivates them. "Billy, Billy," he says as he pulls a folding chair up and sits down a couple of feet away. "We are now looking at a catastrophic situation. What is going on here?"

Scoop is so close that Billy can smell his cologne, or aftershave, or whatever he's doused himself in. Billy makes a point of moving his chair back. He needs a beer instead of a Gatorade, and he needs anything instead of Scoop Sutherland. "Where is here?" he asks.

"This ball club," Scoop says. "This *here* ball club."

"And you think it's a catastrophe?"

"That's what I said."

"The Hindenburg was a catastrophe," Billy tells him. "This is a ball club in a bit of a slump."

"A bit?"

"Bit of a rough patch," Billy says. "We'll be all right. We still have time to turn this thing around."

"Ah, from the big bag of sports clichés," Scoop mutters as he fiddles with the recording app on his phone. "What about this theory that the players have quit on Mac? That they're losing games on purpose, trying to get him canned?"

"That's a bunch of nonsense, Scoop." Billy takes a moment, regarding the phone. "You want a sound bite? You want a quote as to whether or not the players have bailed on the manager?" Billy leans into the cellphone. "That's a load of horseshit, Scoop. Okay?

That's a colossal load of fucking horseshit. I look forward to seeing that in tomorrow's paper."

Scoop doesn't faze easily, mainly because he doesn't listen very closely to the answers he elicits. He's always moving on to his next question.

"I now have you at four for your last fifty," he says. "Is it time to face facts, Billy? Is your bat slowing down?"

"My bat is as quick as it ever was," Billy says. "And it's four for my last forty-three, thank you. Everybody slumps. Babe Ruth once went two for twenty-two in the World Series."

"With all due respect, you're not Babe Ruth."

"And you ain't Studs Terkel," Billy says. "Let's call it even."

Scoop smiles at that but just slightly. He has no idea who Studs Terkel is or was. His frame of reference only goes back so far, Depression-era films notwithstanding.

"The fact is," he says now, "you're going to be forty next April. Everybody slows down. Even the Babe."

"You keep writing that I'm about to turn forty," Billy says. "Why do you keep writing that when it's June now and my birthday isn't until next spring? Why not just tell people that I'm thirty-nine? You know: the truth."

"It's true that you're going to be forty next spring," Scoop points out.

"It's also true that I'm going to be ninety in fifty more springs," Billy says. "Stop by around then and I'll update you on whether or not my bat is slowing down."

Scoop ignores the jibe. "This team is in a free fall. What's Carroll Miller going to do about this situation? Is he about to fire Mac?"

"Isn't that a question for Carroll Miller?"

"Carroll Miller has been a winner all his life. He can't be happy. Do you want him to fire Mac?"

"No."

"Why not?"

"Because he's my skipper," Billy says.

"Loyalty is an admirable trait," Scoop tells him. "But it rarely shows up in the win column."

Billy stares the sportswriter down, thinking, *What would you know about loyalty, you little shit?* He keeps it to himself though. Scoop mistakes his silence for resignation or – worse yet – acquiescence.

"The consensus is that you and Mac are both over the hill," he says. "It happens to everybody. You brought up Babe Ruth. He was done by age thirty-five. And like I said, you're no Babe Ruth."

Billy stands up. "Nope, I am not. But there is still one thing I can do every bit as good as the Babe – and that is take a shower. Why don't you tag along?" He reaches over and takes Scoop forcefully by the ear, leading him squirming across the room.

"Let me go, you fucking asshole!" Scoop yells.

Billy has no such intention. He leads the writer into the showers and turns on the cold water, holding him under the nozzle for a full minute. The man's protests are louder than his suit.

"Never tell a man who's four for his last forty-three that he's over the hill, Scoop," he says. "Gee, I hope those colours don't run."

Scoop doesn't mention the impromptu shower when he meets with Carroll Miller the next morning back in Rose City. He'd actually considered pressing assault charges against Billy Crawford after the incident but decided against it. He really didn't care for the entire city to learn about the matter, embarrassing as it was, and he wasn't sure that a forced dunking in a shower stall could be interpreted as a crime anyway.

"The team's a laughingstock," he tells Carroll. They're drinking coffee in Carroll's office on the top floor of CM Enterprises in the city's west end. Scoop has been running reports to Carroll since the season began, when he'd approached Carroll and volunteered to be his "man behind the scenes," as he had phrased it. For a price, of course.

Carroll stands and retrieves a putter leaning against the wall and begins to hit balls across the plush carpet into a machine that returns the ball with a spring release whenever a putt is made. He hits a dozen balls while half-listening to Scoop. Carroll isn't much of a baseball fan, has never played the game in fact. He claims that the notion of owning a professional team, even a Triple A team, was the culmination of a lifelong dream, even declaring far and wide that he would quickly turn it into a winner, but the real reason he bought the franchise was that in the process he acquired ownership of the stadium itself. The location was on the river downtown, prime real estate. The transaction had seemed to be failsafe. Either the team succeeded, or Carroll could shut it down, tear down the stadium and develop the property. That plan had backfired. He found out after taking ownership that Rounders Field and the surrounding block was designated as historical. In other words, there would be no development there. Carroll's interest in the team, never all that intense, fell off the table at that point.

He hits one last putt now, missing the ball return completely. "I don't give a shit about the ball team, but I don't like being laughed at," he says as he gathers the balls for another round. "And I really don't like being associated with a loser. I've never been identified as such and I refuse to be so now."

Scoop has a drink of coffee and lifts his stubby legs to plant his feet on Carroll's desk. He's wearing a lime-green track suit, with Nike runners. Today's fedora is straw. "I didn't think so," he says. "On either count."

"So what do you suggest?" Carroll asks, turning back to Scoop. "Hey, get your fucking feet off my desk."

Scoop does as he's told, his feet hitting the floor with a thud as he leans forward. "First order of business, you have to get rid of Lloyd MacDonald," he says. "The players don't listen to him. Not that he says anything anyway."

Carroll drops the putter head on the carpet and practises his stroke. Scoop waits for a comment that doesn't come.

"Besides," he continues. "The guy's a hundred years old. You have kids out there in their early twenties. How are they going to relate to Mac? Pro sports these days is all about image, and the Rounders have a manager who played with fucking Moses."

Carroll takes another stroke. "So who do I replace Moses with?"

"Ron Erskine has been making out the lineup every day, or so I'm told," Scoop says. "Make him manager, at least for the rest of the season. That sends a message to the players. Come fall, you can poach somebody from some other club. Somebody young, with a little panache."

"Which one is Erskine?"

"The assistant manager," Scoop says. He should be surprised that Carroll Miller doesn't know the names of the people working for him, but he's not. "You hired him last year. He played ball in Japan before that."

Carroll shrugs, still not recalling Erskine. "I hire a lot of people."

"Black guy with the shaved head. Big as a fucking bus."

"Right," Carroll says. He sits down at the desk. "You think he can turn things around? How would he do that? Same players, different manager. How does that work?"

"Like I said, they've quit on Mac," Scoop tells him. "They make fun of him behind his back. How he wears his pants, how he tells the same stories over and over. He drinks vodka all day long from a coffee cup. The man's a joke."

Carroll considers the suggestion. "Well, it's an easy move to make."

"There's one more I'd recommend."

"What's that?"

"Billy Crawford has to go," Scoop says. "He's poison in that clubhouse. And he's even worse now that he can't hit anymore. He's in a foul mood and he infects everybody around him with it. He doesn't listen to Mac. He doesn't listen to anybody."

"You just said that Mac isn't doing any managing," Carroll reminds him. "Why would Crawford listen to somebody who's not saying anything?"

"I'm telling you he's bad news," Scoop said. "He's an arrogant bastard too. Hitting .190 on the season and he still struts around that clubhouse like he's the second coming. What's that about?"

"I thought he was a draw."

Scoop waves away the notion. "Maybe at one time. He's an albatross now. And keep in mind he's signed for another year. You're not getting much return on your dollar, Carroll."

"Do I have to pay him anyway?"

"Not for next year. You can buy him out. It's a team option. More specifically, it's *your* option."

Carroll is quiet for a time. "All right, I'll take this under advisement. We can't keep losing games. I can't keep losing games. It's not who I am. Attendance is spotty at the best of times."

"The attendance will take care of itself if the team starts winning."

Carroll nods. The baseball team is not important to him, other than his concern about his name being linked with a loser. But now he's already thinking of something else. "Thanks for the update," he says.

Scoop takes the hint. He's walking out the door just as Dale is coming in. The two men eye each other distastefully. They speak, a couple of words each, and then Scoop is gone.

"Why would a man want to dress like a popsicle?" Carroll asks.

Dale shrugs. "Compensating for something, I suspect."

"Compensating for the fact that he's three feet tall or that he has no personality?"

"I'd say that's a pick 'em," Dale replies.

He is fresh from his appearance that morning before the planning board at City Hall, a meeting he wasn't in the least bit optimistic about, going in. He'd been hoping that Carroll would appear with him, but the boss had nixed the idea. They were going to get turned down and Carroll doesn't like being rejected, especially in person. He's okay with it happening to Dale though.

The matter at hand was once again the issue of the greenbelt and future city planning. Dale wasn't sure that there even was a matter at hand though. How could there be a question when everybody involved already knew the answer?

In this, he was correct. There were no surprises. Dale made his case, citing the obvious tax benefits, new housing for young families, new commerce due to the increase of population. He never specifically mentioned the company plans for the Brownsville area. He didn't have to. Everyone in the room knew what (and where) was at the heart of the proposal. That is, if the proposal was actually considered to the point that it would move forward.

Of course, it was not. Rob Filsinger and four other councillors voted in favour of the plan. The remaining five councillors voted nay. Mayor Joe Simmons was the tiebreaker and the man known as Uncle Joe was, predictably, a thumbs down.

After the vote, Dale headed directly to the CM offices, but bad news travels faster than any car. By the time he walks into Carroll's office, just as Scoop is taking his leave, the boss already knows. He knows and doesn't seem particularly upset about it, presumably because he didn't expect anything different. Still, he is oddly upbeat when Dale gives him the report.

"The good news is we're just a vote away," he points out.

"We've been one vote away for years," Dale reminds him.

"Yeah, but in the past we never knew where that swing vote might come from."

"We still don't."

"I'm not so sure about that." Carroll stands and returns to his putting practice. "How's John-Boy making out at the Maple Creek subdivision?"

"He's doing fine," Dale says.

"Is he ready to take over?"

"Take over?" Dale repeats. "You mean, as in take over *my* job? Gee – I have one bad round of golf, and you can me?" He smiles half-heartedly at his own joke.

"If you think you've only had one bad round, I *should* can you," Carroll says. "But no, I've created a new position for you."

"A new position," Dale says. He's not certain he should ask. "And what is that?"

"Campaign manager," Carroll says.

Dale makes a futile attempt to put it together. "Okay, I'll bite. Campaign manager for who?"

"For me."

"For you," Dale says, finally getting it. "Wait – you're going to run for council? You're going to be the swing vote?"

"You're getting closer," Carroll says. "But I have no desire to be a fucking councillor. I don't need a bunch of whiny constituents calling me night and day, bitching about garbage collection and snowplows and 'where's my welfare check?'"

Carroll cocks an eyebrow at Dale, inviting him to follow his path a little further. Spreading cryptic breadcrumbs is Carroll's style. Dale takes maybe ten seconds then nods.

"You're running for mayor."

"I'm running for mayor."

"Well, now," Dale says. "That's out of left field. You really want to take on Uncle Joe?"

Carroll whacks a putt too hard and the ball bounces across the carpet and careens off the baseboard. Carroll tosses the PING putter onto the leather couch and goes to sit at his desk. "The time is ripe. And even riper if what I'm hearing is true. Were you aware that the man has Parkinson's?"

"No," Dale says. "I mean, I know he's had health issues over the years. The guy's in his seventies. But I never heard he had Parkinson's."

"I'm hearing it from a very reliable source," Carroll says. "Somebody with MD after his name. Tell me – what did you see him do today?"

"What did he *do*?" Dale asks. "There was nothing for him *to* do. I mean, he chaired the hearing."

"Yes, but did you see him *do* anything? Of a physical nature – sign papers, take a drink of water, walk and chew gum. Anything like that?"

"I suppose not," Dale replies. "I didn't pay that much attention to the man. I mean, he's basically part of the furniture over there."

"He's failing," Carroll says. "Pretty quickly if what I'm hearing is accurate. And like I said, I'm hearing it from someone in the know. Uncle Joe's a popular enough guy – lord knows why – but if I can plant the seed that's he's no longer competent, I can take him out."

Dale sits down across from the desk. "Bigger question – do you *want* to be mayor?"

Carroll shrugs. "Why not? It's not exactly a taxing job. Cut some ribbons, make a few speeches. Pretty sure I can handle it."

"There's more to it than that," Dale persists. "You have to run City Hall. What makes you think you can do that?"

"The fact that I'm smarter than all the rest of those fucking wafflers put together?"

It's a typical Carroll Miller statement and Dale lets it pass. "This is about the greenbelt obviously. You do realize you'd have to recuse yourself if a proposal involved CM Homes in any way?"

"Not if I put everything in a blind trust when I take office."

"Is that even legal?"

"Everything is legal – if you can get away with it."

SIX

It's Monday, the day after the Rounders' lost weekend in Buffalo, and Jessie the sassy groundskeeper is once again telling Billy what to do.

"You need to slow down," she says. "What – you got someplace you have to be?"

Billy slows his motion, but soon picks up the pace, in spite of himself and her somewhat urgent instructions. After a few moments, she pushes him off her, over onto his back. She mounts him then, her right hand flat on his chest, her left cupped under her breast.

"Slow . . . the . . . fuck . . . down," she says. "This isn't a sprint."

Billy laughs and lets her take control. He'd been back in the batting cage that morning, and once again enlisted Jessie to pitch to him. She'd been greasing one of the mowers when he arrived. Afterward, Billy offered to buy her lunch and she agreed. They had pizza and beer at a place on Queen Street and one thing led to another – and then to Billy's bed. That part had been Jessie's idea, after a fashion. Over a few beers, Billy had asked about her personal life, and she'd told him she'd broken up with her deadbeat boyfriend the previous winter.

"I was with him two years and he never had a job the entire time," she'd said. "He claimed nobody was willing to pay him a wage commensurate to his skill set. Yeah, that's exactly how he talked. Problem was – talking was his only skill set."

It was shortly after that when she had mentioned to Billy that she hadn't been laid in six months. There was a certain glint to her eye when she said it. Billy took the glint as a hint; forty minutes later they were naked in his bed. Jessie wasn't shy. Billy should have figured that out the other day, when she'd thrown the ball at his head.

They spend a couple hours in bed, making out and screwing at Jessie's tempo. Billy has no problem with that. At one point he goes into the kitchen for a couple more beers. When he comes back, she's outside on the back deck, dressed in Billy's Steve Earle T-shirt and smoking a joint. Billy pulls on a pair of shorts and joins her.

"You smoking that shit?" he asks, handing her a Budweiser.

Jessie has a long drink. "You got something against pot? What is with you old dudes? You don't want to stop lunging at the ball, you fuck like you left your car running, and now you're giving me grief for smoking a little ganja. What's next – you going to take away my right to vote?"

Billy sits down across from her and has a drink of Bud. "I'm not all that old, you know. Maybe I'm trying to keep you on the straight and narrow."

"From what I've heard, you couldn't find the straight and narrow with a fucking road map, Crawford," she says. "Everybody says you've drunk an ocean of beer since you got here and slept with half the single women in Rose City. And about a quarter of the married ones."

"*Everybody says*," Billy repeats. "You do realize that *everybody says* is not a credible source of information. It's right up there with *everybody knows* and *it's common knowledge*. You want to know what everybody knows? Everybody knows nothing."

She smiles as she exhales smoke. Billy reaches over for the joint and takes a hit off it.

"Oh, so you were faking," she says. "You're not so pure after all."

"Who is?" he asks.

"Nobody worth knowing." She tilts back the beer. "I saw a guitar in your living room. You play?"

"Just learning," Billy replies. "I can play the theme from the old

Batman show."

"How long you been playing?"

Billy shrugs. "Twenty years."

She laughs at that and they sit quietly in the afternoon sun for a time. Billy sips his beer and looks at her in profile – the slight crook in her nose and her sexy, sassy mouth. She's aggressive in a good way and a great kisser – possibly the best Billy has ever known. She looks good in Billy's shirt, just as she looks very good out of it. She watches him watching her.

"You see today's paper?" she asks after a while.

Billy shakes his head. He usually skims the sports section every morning, but he didn't need to read about the Rounders' nightmare weekend in Buffalo. He'd lived it, every horrific detail as if in slow motion.

"What did you do to Scoop Sutherland – shit in his hat?" she asks.

"No, but I'll put that on my list of things I might do to him."

"Whatever it was, he must have taken it kinda personal," she says. "Do you want me to tell you what he wrote?"

Billy has a drink. "Nope."

"I don't blame you."

Billy leans his head back and closes his eyes for a few moments. He exhales heavily. "All right – what did he write?"

She laughs. "You didn't hold out very long. What did I tell you about slowing down?"

"You've been telling me so many things; I can't hardly recall."

"I think you can," she says. "Anyway, he beats around the bush like he always does, but he's basically suggesting that the players have quit on Mac, and that you're the one leading the mutiny. He suggests that you're slumping at the plate on purpose, looking to get Mac canned."

"For Chrissakes."

She takes another toke, then butts the joint on the decking. "If you want, as head groundskeeper I can release a statement saying that he's full of shit. I mean – I've been watching you and you really do suck at the plate. Nobody could fake that."

"Hard to believe you can't hold on to a boyfriend," Billy says.

"Kicking a loafer out of my house and not holding on to a boyfriend are two different things."

From inside the bedroom, a cellphone pings. Billy looks at her. "Yours?"

Jessie shrugs it off and has a drink. "Do you think the team has quit on Mac?"

"No," Billy replies. "I've been in this game a long time and I can tell you the team isn't playing up to its potential. It happens to every team, just as sometimes a team plays above its potential. It ain't rocket science. Right now, we're not hitting, our pitching is so-so and most of all – we can't catch a break. First inning yesterday, two men on, Saunders hits that ball a ton to right field. The wind happens to be blowing in, fifty kilometres an hour, and the ball's caught. Any other day that's a three-run homer. In that case, we go up three zip in the first inning and maybe, just maybe, that changes everything. It's the nature of the game, always has been. Some days you're the windshield, some days you're the bug."

Jessie's cellphone pings again.

"Popular girl," Billy says.

Then there's another ping, but a different tone. Billy glances into the bedroom, where his phone is on the nightstand.

"Popular boy," Jessie says.

Billy laughs.

"So what's the answer for the team?" she asks. "What's the secret for pulling out of a slump?"

"There's no secret," Billy says. "It'll happen when it happens. Nobody ever went into a slump and didn't come out again. We have the horses. Every team goes through a bad patch. Even the 1927 Yankees had slumps."

"You sure about that? The '27 Yankees?"

"I might be speculating a bit on that one."

Jessie's cell sounds again and then Billy's phone pings three times in quick succession.

"Jesus," Jessie jokes. "Is that your wife?"

"Nah, she's at work."

Jessie sits up straight, stares at him. "You're married, you asshole?"

Billy smiles. "Now that got your attention. I don't have a wife."

"Didn't think so, not with that messy bathroom," Jessie says and her phone pings again. "All right, all right," she says and goes inside to fetch it.

Billy turns in his chair and watches through the open doors as she sits on the edge of the bed to read her messages. His T-shirt does little to cover her up. She really does have great legs. Billy's cell sounds off again, then again.

When she stands up, she grabs Billy's phone from the table and carries it outside. "I think you need to check in."

He takes it from her but doesn't look at it. "What's going on?"

"Let's just say that Sutherland's piece worked," she says. "They just fired Mac."

"Sonofabitch."

"There's more," she says. "You're gone too. Outright release, according to Sutherland's X account."

Now Billy goes into his phone. There's a message from a reporter from the *Standard*, and several from other players on the team. The texts ranged from "did you hear this shit?" to "what the fuck is going on here?"

"Well, there it is," Billy says, and he doesn't say anything else.

Jessie watches him. She's pretty high and now wishes she wasn't. "That damn wind in Buffalo," she says after a moment.

Billy smiles slightly.

Jessie stands up. "Fuck it," she tells him. "Come on inside."

She walks inside, peeling Billy's shirt off as she does. She gets into bed, pulls the sheet loosely over herself and smiles at him. Billy watches her for a full minute, thinking about his lot in life, then drains his beer and goes inside.

Some days you're the windshield, some days you're the bug.

SEVEN

The campaign team meets again late Monday afternoon in Joe's office, this time to go over platform details and scheduling. Arriving earlier, Kate discovered she now has her own office, a few yards down the hall from her father's. The space is small, and she suspects it may have been some sort of storage room at one time, but she's okay with that. There's a desk and chairs from IKEA and a new laptop, programmed to a bunch of city websites she's never heard of. Some hastily arranged plants line the windowsill. The view outside is of the towering building next door, an unsightly block of grey concrete, a recent addition to the downtown core. It is massive and plain and blocks the morning sun.

When everyone is settled, Ben leads things off. "It's not as if we're going to come out with some earth-shattering new policy proposals," he says. "Joe's hallmark has been steady as it goes. Well, if it ain't broke, don't fix it, people."

He's standing in the centre of the room. Joe is at his desk, with Maria across from him, recording the conversation for later. Kate sits on a leather couch along the wall. She is dressed casually in jeans and Blundstones and a cotton shirt. There's a large flat-screen TV mounted on the wall, tuned to RCTV, the news station. The sound is muted.

"People already know where Joe stands," Ben continues. "In favour of the LRT, better wages for nurses, PSWs and other health care workers, especially after Covid, against expanding the greenbelt. Pretty simple stuff. We're not reinventing the wheel here. We've won eight elections by keeping it simple."

"The LRT?" Kate asks. "Remind me."

"The light rail transit proposal," Maria says.

"I'm in favour of it in theory," Joe says. "But not if it's going to bankrupt the city. The province has to come up with at least half the financing."

"The province might be more inclined to commit to that now," Ben says. "Keep in mind that our foot-dragging premier also is up for re-election and he needs votes from Rose City. The timing couldn't be better for this."

"And what about the situation at Garrison Park?" Kate asks.

"You mean the homeless," Maria says. "Tent city."

Kate nods.

"First of all, it's not just Garrison Park," Ben says, "Encampments are widespread across the city. It's becoming epidemic."

"And?"

"There are viable solutions," Joe says, "at least in the short term. Have you heard of tiny houses?"

"I haven't," Kate admits.

"Just as it sounds," Ben says. "Small, inexpensive houses, designed for one specific reason. And we have space here in the city. The old hospital grounds, for instance, or the defunct railyards."

"What we don't have currently is the funding," Joe says. "Council is split on the issue. There seems to be a consensus among certain people that the homeless don't deserve help. I'd go so far as to say that certain people would like to truck these unfortunates out of the city altogether."

"Which would just make them someone else's problem," Kate says. "How is that a solution?"

"Exactly," Maria says.

"This sounds like something that should be an election issue," Kate suggests then.

"It's a critical damn issue, election or not," Joe says.

"But once again, it comes down to money," Ben says.

"Doesn't everything?" Maria asks. "But I agree – it's something that needs to be addressed."

"So how does this work?" Kate asks. "How do we begin?"

"Joe continues his weekly pressers from the chamber here," Ben says. "And we start to do the usual interviews. Again, this is pretty much a template. There's a tried-and-true pattern and the only time we have to veer away from it is when something new comes up. Or somebody new. Even old Zabrisky hasn't announced yet."

Kate smiles at her father. "Maybe you'll run unopposed. Does that mean I'm out of a job?"

Joe laughs. "You can retire undefeated, like Marciano."

"Who is Marciano?" Maria asks.

"You're a Philistine," Joe says.

"Hey – check this out," Ben says, pointing his chin to the TV on the wall.

Carroll Miller is standing in brilliant sunlight in front of Rounders Field. A makeshift podium, scrounged from somewhere in the stadium, has been set up and there are cameras and reporters galore gathered around, some standing in the flower beds along the walkways leading into the ballpark.

Ben reaches for the remote to unmute the set. "Looks like Miller is about to tell us why he cleaned house earlier today. I don't recall ever even seeing him at the stadium before. I'm surprised he could find the place."

"It's my contention that we've been living in the past long enough," Carroll is saying. "How do we attract progressive businesses to a city whose reputation is that of a backwater? We are now a quarter of the way through the twenty-first century. Isn't it time for Rose City to enter that century? Well, that's not going to happen under the current administration. Now, some might say I'm stepping out of my comfort zone here. The fact is, the whole world is my comfort zone." With that, Carroll flashes his smile, thousands of dollars' worth of veneers on display, to show that he has a sense of humour about himself. "Somebody has to do this, so why not me? I've been pretty darned successful in my career as a builder and developer. I know how to get things done. I know how to multi-task. I know how to appoint competent people to positions of power. Most of all, I know how to put Rose City on a progressive track."

With that, Carroll pauses dramatically as he produces a bright red baseball cap and pulls it on. The logo across the front reads:

MILLER FOR MAYOR
THE PROGRESSIVE CHOICE

"I'll be goddamned," Ben says. "We have a contender."

Joe, settled back in his chair, smiles as he looks from the TV to Kate. "Better hit the gym, Marciano."

After Jessie leaves on Monday, Billy sits around stewing for a bit, then walks down the street to The Crooked Shamrock and gets mildly drunk on Guinness. The next morning, he gets up around mid-morning and drives over to the stadium. After wrecking the Camaro, he'd gone to a used car dealer downtown and bought a three-year-old Ford pickup truck. He almost bought a Mustang convertible of the same vintage but decided against it at the last minute, figuring that in the (altogether possible) event that he roll another vehicle over, he'd stand a better chance of survival in the truck than in a convertible.

The Pirates are due in that evening for a three-game set. The clubhouse is still closed when Billy arrives so he can't pack up his stuff even if he wanted to. He doesn't want to.

The day before, Jessie had gone home after they'd received the deluge of text messages, people anxious to share the bad news. When she was gone, Billy had realized he didn't know where she lives. He'd asked once and she was vague about it, saying she had a place out of the city. Billy doesn't know if she lives in a house or apartment, a motor home or a pup tent. It isn't a big deal to him. He'd only been alone with the woman twice. The first time she'd thrown a baseball at his head and the second she'd pushed him onto his bed and ridden him like a bronco. Both activities had managed to elevate his pulse rate significantly, which is not a bad thing, he reasons.

But today he has other things on his mind, like the news that his baseball career has apparently arrived at a sudden and screeching halt. He isn't happy about that, and he definitely isn't happy to have heard about it by text.

The Rounders general manager is a guy named Tom Plunkett. He is known as a Carroll Miller man, and rarely interacts with the players. He has no background in the game and – as far as Billy can tell – knows nothing about it. He's a cohort of Miller's from years ago, involved on some level with developing commercial properties in and around the city. He claims to have a law degree but has never actually practised. The rumour around town is that Miller gave him the job of GM as payment for some favour or favours rendered. Billy has spoken to the man maybe six times in the five years he's been with the team, but he's determined to speak to him today.

Plunkett is actually at the ballpark this morning, in his office above the infield bleachers. Billy thought he might be hiding out somewhere. His secretary gives Billy a wary look as he walks through the door of the outer office. Billy points his chin at the door behind her.

"He in there?"

"What's this about?" she asks.

"Seriously?" Billy asks. "You know what it's about."

She gives him a long look. She's sixty or so, with a helmet of stiff blond hair and blue-framed glasses. She has shoulders like a fullback and the permanent expression of someone who has caught a whiff of something unpleasant.

"Is he expecting you?" she asks.

"If he isn't, he should be," Billy says and opens the door to Plunkett's office.

"Hold on," she protests, but too late.

Tom Plunkett is a large man, maybe two hundred and fifty pounds, and he has a coif of silver hair that's he inordinately proud of. Billy finds him at this moment sitting behind a desk, with his back to the door. He's looking out a huge plate-glass window, down at the diamond, or maybe past the field to the river beyond. The office overlooks the entire ballpark. Plunkett can watch the games from there, although he seldom does.

When he hears Billy enter, he swivels around in his chair. If he's surprised to see Billy showing up unannounced, he doesn't show it.

"Mr. Crawford." He pauses, making a show of checking a calendar on the desk. "I wasn't aware we had a meeting scheduled."

Billy walks over and sits down across from Plunkett. "Geez . . . I didn't blindside you, did I? Welcome to my world."

Plunkett shows his hands. "Come on, Billy. These things happen. You've been around long enough to know that. It's just part of the game."

"Since when is it part of the game that I hear by *text* that I've been released? And not even texts from anyone within the organization. What if I didn't own a cellphone? Was I going to show up tonight and find my locker cleaned out?"

"I wasn't aware of that dynamic," Plunkett says. "I assumed that Mac would have told you."

"Maybe Mac is preoccupied with the fact that he's just been shitcanned himself."

Plunkett shrugs. There's a bowl of almonds on his desk; he takes a handful and shovels them into his mouth. He isn't good at even faking interest. It seems that he intends to gnaw away at the nuts, biding his time until Billy leaves, so he can get back to the important business of gazing out his window.

"I'm going to pull out of this," Billy tells him. "I've been in slumps before."

"You're about to turn forty."

"I'm thirty-nine."

"Which is almost forty," Plunkett replies. "It's not just the batting. You've lost a step too. More than a step."

Not just the batting. The fucking guy is a GM and he doesn't even know how to talk baseball, Billy thinks. *It's hitting – not batting, dipshit.*

"Hell, I've always been slow," Billy tells him. "When I was a kid, old people could outrun me."

"You're making a hell of a case for yourself, Crawford."

"My point is – I've always hit the ball, my whole career. I'm not about to stop now. Shit, I might go four for four tomorrow night and then it's Katie-bar-the-door."

Plunkett attempts a joke. "If you figure on going four for four tomorrow night, you'd better find a team to play for in a hurry."

Billy is taken aback by the attitude. Who the hell is he to talk to Billy like that? He's quiet for a moment as Plunkett reaches for more almonds.

"You know I'm signed through next season, right?"

Plunkett nods. "It's a team option. We'll have to buy you out. Unfortunately."

Unfortunately. *Fuck you*, Billy thinks.

"Then why not let me run out the string this season?" Billy asks. "You're paying me anyway. If you pass on next year's option, I'll have to be okay with that. But if I finish the year, the way I know I can, you'll either pick up my option or another team will sign me. This way, I look like damaged goods."

Plunkett starts shaking his head when Billy is still halfway through his plea.

"There are other issues here."

"What other issues?" Billy demands.

"Come on," Plunkett says. "You going to tell me you don't read about yourself in the newspaper?"

"Not when it's Scoop Sutherland spreading his crap," Billy says. "That little prick has a problem with me."

"Why would a sportswriter have a problem with you?"

"Because I baptized him the other day. I think he may have taken it the wrong way."

Plunkett looks at his calendar again. "I have no idea what you're talking about. Besides, I see here I have a ten o'clock." He glances up at Billy. "And it's two minutes of."

Billy hesitates before turning toward the door. His hand on the knob, he looks back. "You're saying this is it? What if I talk to Carroll Miller?" He hates the tone in his own voice. Begging. "Chrissakes, all I want is to play out the year."

"This came from Carroll," Plunkett tells him. "He owns the team."

Billy has nothing else to say. He opens the door.

"What did you think?" Plunkett asks then. "That you'd play forever?"

Billy looks back. "Yeah, I did."

EIGHT

The announcement creates the desired effect. Within twenty-four hours, every newspaper, radio and TV outlet in the city wants to talk to Carroll Miller about his bid for the mayor's office. Carroll, of course, has no problem with it. He likes to talk, and he particularly likes to talk about himself. Now he finds himself in a position to pick and choose just who he's willing to have a conversation with. He has no problem with that either.

"The *Standard* keeps calling," Dale tells him.

It's Tuesday morning. The two men are in Carroll's office, working on a game plan. Neither man has been involved in an election campaign before and they're feeling their way in the dark, but that isn't a problem. Carroll Miller isn't one to play by the rules anyway.

"Who are they offering?"

"The Watson girl still," Dale says.

"She's a neophyte," Carroll says. "I checked her out – she doesn't even have her own byline."

"I suggested Sutherland," Dale tells him.

Carroll shakes his head. "One, he's a sportswriter. Two, I need him to be my man on the inside over there. That's not going to work if he's doing a profile on me. Why not Billings?"

"I asked for Billings but all I got back is that he's the editor. He doesn't write stories about politics or anything else. It's not in his job description."

"He's my age," Carroll says. "Which means he can relate to me, better than that twinkie Watson. And we're pretty sure he's a progressive."

"Maybe that's the problem. He doesn't want to be seen as partial to your platform." Saying it, Dale decides not to mention the fact that as of the present moment Caroll Miller doesn't have a platform. Pointing out the obvious to Carroll Miller rarely works out well.

Carroll gets up and crosses the room, to where his putter and spring-loaded ball return are. He places the return on the carpet and hits a couple of putts. "That's the problem with the world today. Everybody's walking around on fucking eggshells. Whatever happened to having an opinion and voicing it?" He flushes a ball into the return and it boomerangs back to him. He stops it with the toe of his loafer.

"Keep in mind the *Standard* in general likes Uncle Joe," Dale says. "They've been endorsing him pretty consistently over the years."

"That's because there's been nothing but a bunch of flakes and communists running against him." Carroll has a thought as he centres another putt. "Is Billings a golfer?"

Dale shrugs. "No idea."

"Find out," Carroll says. "We can suggest a casual round of golf, meet-the-candidate type thing. He might go for that. If nothing else, he might like a free round of golf at my club."

"I can ask."

"If he's worried about any supposed bias, he can offer to play a round with Uncle Joe too."

"Joe doesn't golf."

"Neither do you, but you keep trying," Carroll says.

Dale starts to respond but thinks better of it. He's been Carroll's whipping boy on the matter of golf for years. It comes with the territory. Sometimes Dale wishes there was something he could do better than Carroll, if only so he could chuck shit back at him. But Carroll only does things that he excels at. He wouldn't play checkers with Dale if he thought for a moment that he might lose.

The landline on the desk rings and Carroll steps over to answer it.

"Who?" he says impatiently. "Hell, no." He hangs up.

"What's that?" Dale asks.

"Billy Crawford is down in the foyer," Carroll says. "Wants to talk to me. Why would I talk to a washed-up ballplayer? Or anybody from that team for that matter. Fucking losers."

"I hear he paid Plunkett a visit. Pretty much begged not to be released."

"Done and done," Carroll says. "Now what's going on over at RCTV? You get anywhere with the producer whatshername?"

"Well, they'll be handling the debate," Dale says. "Or debates, if there's more than one."

"I'm talking now," Carroll says. "I want airtime now. What about a one-on-one with somebody over there? I've been thinking about it. We suggest a one-on-one with me, and then – in the interest of fairness – the same for Uncle Joe. We need to plunk him under a spotlight any way we can. Show the people who he is these days. And who he isn't."

"I can ask," Dale says. "John Comstock over there might go for that. He's not a big fan of Uncle Joe, I've heard. But it could backfire. He won't want to look as if he's playing favourites."

"It's his fucking job to cover my campaign," Carroll says. "Politics these days is all about sound bites. People are ADD. They don't want to hear an hour-long speech. They want to hear me say a few choice words they'll remember."

"And what are those words?"

"I don't know yet," Carroll laughs. "I suppose 'Make Rose City Great Again' isn't terribly original."

Dale grimaces, as if experiencing a stomachache.

Carroll nods. "But that's the idea. That's the message we need to convey. People love the idea of change, even if most of them would rather eat a bucket of maggots than change anything in their own lives."

"I'll work on a catchphrase," Dale says. "For the present, we don't turn anything down. We need to saturate the media with your name and face. So, if that little cable station at the university wants to sit down with you and talk about the ash borer, or plastic versus paper, you probably should do it. No such thing as bad press, right?"

"There is definitely such a thing as bad press," Carroll contradicts him. "The trick is to avoid it."

Kate cooks a chicken for dinner that night, along with dumplings and corn and a garden salad. She likes to cook but hasn't done much of it in recent years. Jeremy fancied himself a chef and so he took on most of the kitchen duties, especially early in their marriage, when they entertained a lot at home. The past two or three years, there hadn't been much of that. Breakfast was toast and coffee, lunch anything they could grab at the office and dinner often takeout. And then, gradually, there were more and more dinners alone, when Jeremy was "working late."

She and Joe eat in the dining room. Kate opens a bottle of Chilean red. Joe is enthused about the dumplings and says so.

"Well, they're Mother's," Kate says.

"I know they're Mother's," Joe says. "This is the first I've had them since she passed. She taught you well, daughter."

"Well, these don't hold a candle to hers." Kate has a sip of wine. "But I'm hell on wheels with a corkscrew."

"How did it go with Ben Craig today?" Joe asks.

"All right, I guess," Kate says. "He keeps saying we're going to have to come up with a brand-new game plan to take on Miller. But he doesn't say what it is."

"That's why they called him Vague Craig when he was on the council. He can be big on notions and soft on ideas. I don't know that I agree with the idea that we need a brand-new plan. At this point, it's a bit of a waiting game anyway."

Kate watches without being too obvious about it as Joe manoeuvres a forkful of dumpling to his mouth. His hand shakes badly and she fears the food will fall off, but it doesn't.

"What are we waiting for?" she asks.

Joe sets his fork aside, as if needing a break from the effort of eating. "To see what Carroll Miller is up to. Why does he want to be mayor all of a sudden? He's been a big-time developer in Rose City for years but has never shown one iota of interest in politics before."

"Didn't you just answer your own question?" Kate asks. "He's running out of places to build his ugly subdivisions."

"Is that reason enough to run for office?"

"Apparently he has decided it is," Kate says. "More importantly – does the electorate believe it is? He's already promoting himself as the progressive candidate."

"Of course, he is," Joe says. "He's twenty years younger than me. He can't exactly tell people he's for the status quo when I'm the status quo." He has a drink of wine, taking the glass in both hands.

"It's pretty clear he's going to make the greenbelt his signature issue," Kate says.

"It is."

"How will you respond to that?"

"The same as I always have," Joe says. "I'm against bulldozing farms to put up condos. There's lots of land in this country. We don't need to be ruining our best farmland. Once a farm is gone, it's gone for good."

Kate has a mouthful of chicken. It really is pretty good. She's managed to surprise herself. "Maybe we should get the rights to Joni Mitchell's 'Big Yellow Taxi.'"

It takes Joe a moment. "Something about paving paradise?"

Kate smiles. "How do you know that song?"

Joe laughs. "How old am I, daughter?"

"Seventy-four."

"And how old is Joni Mitchell?"

Kate shrugs. "Are you going to tell me seventy-four?"

"Older, I suspect," Joe says. "So why wouldn't I know her songs? Now, you might just stump me with one of these newcomers, like Taylor Swift or the Gaga woman. But not Joni."

Kate smiles. "Not sure that Gaga or Swift would consider themselves rookies anymore, but point taken."

She goes back to her dinner, one eye on her own plate and the other on her father's shaky efforts to feed himself while trying to hide his tremors from his daughter.

NINE

The Rounders lose two out of three to the Bucs. Billy tells himself not to check the scores every morning but then does it anyway. He's torn between wanting the team to win and hoping it doesn't. If the team was to go on a winning streak immediately after letting both Billy and Mac go, it would appear that they were part of the problem after all, and maybe more than just part of it. If they keep losing, then the opposite view would be true; Billy wants them to lose for that reason. However, the players that remain are his friends, most of them anyway, and he wants them to succeed. He'd heard that a number of the players had signed a letter written to Plunkett, asking that he reconsider letting Billy go. Billy also heard that Plunkett didn't respond at all to the petition. Odds are he never he even read it.

The team drops the first two games to the Bucs by scores of 8–1 and 5–0, with the hitting woes obviously continuing. But then the Rounders win by a count of 12–4 in the Thursday afternoon tilt. The bats finally break out. Billy's absence has nothing to do with it, one way or the other. Streaks are finite, whether they be good or bad.

Billy spends the week drinking beer, shooting pool and trying to find a new job. He hasn't had an agent for a few years. He didn't feel as if he needed one upon signing with the Rounders. He's been around the block enough times that he can negotiate his own contracts. Now that lack is coming back to bite him on the ass. He calls his old agent – Lenny Drinkwater – about repping him now, in hopes of landing a spot on another team. In fact, he calls Lenny three times, leaving a message each time. As of Friday, there's been no response. Lenny has quite a client list these days, mostly major league players. Billy isn't going to pretend to be shocked that the agent isn't all that interested in repping a thirty-nine-year-old who's just been released by a Triple A team. Even if Lenny was interested, the commission he'd receive from whatever contract he could negotiate would be the very definition of small change.

Fans of the team are making their feelings known. Billy has been a crowd favourite since he arrived in Rose City, and they do their best to tell management that they're not happy with the release. The new manager, Erskine, has to face the music over it, even though releasing Billy wasn't his call. But he's been around long enough to know which cliché to apply when asked by the media.

"The decision was to move in another direction."

"It was decided that the team needs a change."

"We need to focus on the future."

To take Billy's place in the lineup, the team signs Danny Tarantino. Tarantino has been looking for a job since getting cut by the Cubs in spring training. He'd been given a tryout, with no contract, by the team and hadn't measured up. He has a checkered past. He is known as a long ball hitter who doesn't hit for average. He has also been suspected of using steroids, but has never been caught. One year, he hit forty-two home runs for the Royals. The season prior to that, he'd hit twelve, with the same number of at-bats. Still, he never tested positive and that was all that mattered.

Tarantino is thirty-seven now. Billy wonders if Scoop Sutherland will insist that the slugger is "about to turn thirty-eight." Whatever the case, Tarantino is the designated hitter for all three games against the Bucs. In fourteen at-bats, he manages two walks and a bloop single that ticks off the second baseman's glove. He looks lost at the plate, but Billy can't hold that against him, after he himself spent the past month flailing away like a man caught in a hornet's nest.

Tarantino has a reputation for being an obnoxious shithead and one bloop single in fourteen plate appearances does nothing to change that. Billy catches some of his act on the six o'clock sportscast.

"Hard to get my timing down against this weak-ass pitching," he tells the beat reporters. This is in the clubhouse, after the third game.

"What do you mean?"

"I'm used to heat," Tarantino says. "Don't throw me that cheese. Throw me a hundred plus and I'll turn that sucker around in a hurry."

"You're saying that bad pitching is harder to hit than good?" comes the next question. This from a new reporter for the *Gazette*, a young woman.

"That's what I'm saying. What would you know about it?"

Billy misses the response because he turns the TV off. He doesn't need to hear Tarantino talking shit to a reporter who just happens to be a woman. He sends a text to Jessie, asking if she is up for some pool at Shaky's. When she doesn't respond he decides to head there anyway. He drives the truck to the roadhouse and parks out back. The place is fairly busy with the dinner crowd, but he finds an empty stool at the bar. Suzanne is working, looking very nice in a short skirt and Shaky's tee. They haven't spoken since she turned him down the previous week. She brings over a Moosehead without being asked.

"How's it going?" she asks.

"All good," he tells her.

"I heard the news. Sorry about that."

He shrugs to show her an indifference he doesn't feel. "Hey, nature of the game. You get hired to be fired."

"Right," she says doubtfully. "So what's next?"

Billy takes a long drink of the cold beer. "Just waiting on my agent to get back to me. See what kind of offers are out there."

"Thought you said you don't have an agent."

"Okay, ex-agent."

Suzanne looks at him a moment. "Does the notion of retirement enter into it at all?"

"I'm a ballplayer," Billy says. "Why would I retire?"

"Because that's what pro athletes do at a certain age."

"When I get to a certain age, I'll let you know." Billy drinks from the bottle. He's getting agitated. "Why do people always say that about ballplayers and nobody else? Do you ask your doctor or your plumber or your hairdresser when they're going to retire?"

"My hairdresser is about sixty years old and still on top of his game," she replies. "I don't see any sixty-year-old ballplayers out there."

"Satchel Paige," Billy says.

"Who's that?"

"You don't know who Satchel Paige is?" Billy asks. His expression suggests that Suzanne has just revealed she'd never heard of Abraham Lincoln or Jesus Christ. "He was maybe the greatest pitcher ever. Played in both the Negro Leagues and the majors. He only pitched until he was about a hundred."

Suzanne raises her eyebrows. "Sure he did."

Billy has another drink. "Okay then, what about you – you ready to hang 'em up?"

"I'd love to retire," Suzanne says. "But I'm thirty-six years old. What am I going to live on?"

"I thought maybe your new boyfriend might support you."

"I don't have a new boyfriend," Suzanne says. "I never even had an old boyfriend."

"Oh, come on," Billy says. "I thought I was your old boyfriend."

She gives him a long, strange look. "Billy, you have a certain charm, you're easy to look at and you have a sense of humour. But I swear, you are the most oblivious fucker I've ever known."

*

They're in the back of the Lincoln town car, heading for the RCTV studios in the west end. It's late morning and Carroll is wearing a dark-blue suit with a red tie. He rarely wears a suit or a tie but today he's reluctantly playing the game – at Dale's insistence.

"You're a developer rumoured to be worth upward of a billion dollars," Dale had told him. "You need to dress the part."

Carroll is well aware of the rumour regarding his worth and just as aware that the number is hugely inflated. He should be aware; he's the one who did the inflating.

"Maybe I should go the other way," he'd argued. "I'm a builder. Why not wear jeans and work boots every day? Put a pencil behind my ear and a pair of work gloves in my hip pocket."

"First of all, you don't own any jeans or a pair of work boots," Dale had replied. "Brand new would look phony as a three-dollar bill. What are you going to do – shop at Sally Ann's proletariat department? Besides, we're not looking to present yourself as everyman. Uncle Joe's got that sewn up. You're the progressive guy. The guy who gets things done. You're a huge success in your field and you should look like it."

Now, crossing town, Carroll looks out the window to the pedestrian traffic on King Street. Dale is on his phone, texting the reporter from the weekly paper out in Brownsville. The woman isn't keen, for some reason, to interview Carroll. Dale is pretty sure he knows why. People in Brownsville in general take a dim view of Carroll Miller. The small town wants to remain just that. The good thing is that there are not enough votes out there to worry about.

"Did you read the budget stuff I sent over?" he asks as he shuts his phone down.

Carroll waves the question away with the back of his hand. "I'm not reading that shit, so you can quit sending it. Five hundred pages of numbers. I got no time for that."

"It was more like forty pages," Dale says. "And you'll be asked about the budget. A lot."

"I told you," Carroll says. "Politics today is about sound bites. All I need to do is say something like – I don't know – 'I promise to trim the fat and balance the budget within my first year.' People will hear that and then turn to *Wheel of Fortune*. They'll figure ol' Carroll has it covered."

"I'd like to believe that people are a little more intuitive than that," Dale suggests.

"People are fucking stupid," Carroll tells him.

"We going to put that on a baseball cap?" Dale asks. He shakes his head. He's been wondering how serious Carroll is about running for mayor. It seems like little more than a lark sometimes, and now is one of those times.

"So what's this interview going to do for me?" Carroll asks. "What is it again?"

"*Rose City Review*, the nightly show," Dale replies. "It's John Comstock, the main guy over there. We can assume he's going to ask about all the usual stuff. Keep in mind whatever you say stays out there forever. We don't need any flip-flopping. If there's a topic you're not sure of, pivot to your strengths. Keep in mind that the word progressive is your go-to."

Carroll nods, only half-listening. Dale is more than accustomed to that.

"Another thing," Dale says. "He might ask you about the tent cities."

"What the hell is that?"

"You know what it is," Dale tells him. "The homeless people in Garrison Park and a half-dozen smaller parks around town."

"You're talking about a bunch of fucking bums," Carroll says. "What's that got to do with me running for mayor?"

"First of all, you can't call them bums," Dale says. "They're homeless and you have the greatest sympathy for their plight."

Carroll laughs at that. "Sure I do. Fucking losers."

"You have the greatest sympathy for them," Dale repeats. "Okay?"

"Whatever."

"You actually might be able to use the issue to your advantage," Dale says, giving the matter some thought. "These people need housing, and you are the candidate in favour of more housing. The argument doesn't stand up well under scrutiny because the homeless can't afford the types of homes you're talking about, but on the surface, it might make a good sound bite. If nothing else, it shows that you're aware of the situation and have nothing but empathy for these people. Nothing but empathy. Got it?"

"Yeah, I got it." Carroll looks out the window a moment before turning back to Dale. "Can I slide into the conversation that Joe Simmons is a doddering old fuck?"

"I wouldn't suggest that, no."

"I mean in a subtle way," Carroll insists. "Is there some sort of code for that? I'd really like to hit the age thing hard."

"It's a tricky path to trod," Dale tells him. "It could work against you. You have to remember that Uncle Joe's base loves him because he's Uncle Joe, and his age has become part of that. People are reassured by the tried and true. I suppose you could try to work a passive-aggressive angle. Something like – 'well, that worked fine in the *old* days but not in modern times.'"

"I suppose I can't bring up the Parkinson's either."

"You absolutely cannot," Dale says. "You don't even know if it's true."

"It's true."

Dale shakes his head. "Doesn't matter. That's off limits. The only person who should talk about Joe's health is Joe."

Carroll nods. Dale knows that he heard, but he doesn't know if he actually *heard*.

TEN

As it turned out, it wouldn't have mattered if Carroll Miller gave in to his base instincts and talked about Joe's health or not. By month's end, everybody is discussing it. Before then, though, things went pretty much according to everyone's expectations. Joe ran his new campaign just as he'd run the previous one – and the seven prior to that. The man called Uncle Joe was known to take the high road while on the stump. Over the course of his tenure as mayor, he had never once resorted to badmouthing an opponent. On the other hand, he was a politician, maybe the most successful in the city's history, and as such he was a master at the subliminal approach. So, when Carroll Miller went on TV and touted his intention to open up the greenbelt for housing, Joe's campaign in quick order filmed and released an ad showing Joe on a tractor, reaching down to shake the hand of a farmer standing alongside it, while the farmer's wife stood holding a fat red hen in her arms like it was her first-born child. Other than VOTE FOR JOE, there were no other words. None were required.

The Norman Rockwell–esque ad, as corny and even outdated as it was, had been Kate's idea. It had become clear from the onset that Carroll Miller was not a details guy. In fact, he had one arrow in his quiver, and he seemed content to let it fly day after day. He never did much actual campaigning, at least not in the traditional sense. Like certain other modern politicians, he had discovered the world of social media and used it extensively to deliver his message, or what was in his mind perceived to be a message. His X handle was New Deal Miller, and he tweeted several times a day, a stream-of-consciousness that always circled back to one word: *progressive.*

Carroll had obviously been aware of X but never paid it any mind until recently. He'd thought it was for kids and layabouts, not for serious men. Once he got into it, he became somewhat obsessed with the app. He'd always considered himself a man of great wit, and now he had a stage to display that wit to the world at large. Both his spelling and grammar were atrocious, so he had Dale type the actual tweets. At first Dale found himself balking at some of the more obnoxious posts, but after seeing Carroll refer to himself several times as "the next mayer of Rose City," he gave in.

"The sad thing is, it's working for him," Kate says.

It's the first Monday of August. Ben and Kate are in Joe's office, working on the schedule for the month. Maria sits on the couch with her laptop. Council is in session, so Joe is in the chamber downstairs.

"If you're suggesting that your father open an X account, that's not going to happen," Ben says.

"Oh, I'm aware of that," Kate replies. "But the polls are up a tick for Carroll."

Ben shrugs. "That could just be that people are getting around to noticing there's an election coming up in two months. And just noticing that Carroll Miller is even in the race. We have to admit he's a known entity around the city. He plasters his name on everything he has any connection to. People see that and assume he's this great success. They can't be bothered to look a little closer. If they did, they'd see he's basically a blowhard who got lucky when he bought the old Westinghouse building for a song and then snuck in a zoning change, from commercial to residential, before the city – and Joe – put an end to such things. That was over twenty years ago now. He made a fortune on those condos."

"My Aunt Lucy bought one," Maria says. "Place is falling apart now. The roof leaks, the windowsills are rotting, the cheap flooring buckles. A couple years ago, she got together with the other owners and went after Carroll Miller. Apparently he built the condos, slapped his name on the place and then sold the building to some Russians. In other words, it's no longer his concern. Or his problem."

"Is that something we can make public?" Kate asks.

"Probably not in any official way," Ben says. "Going after a man about the conditions in a building he *used* to own won't really fly. If he was still the owner, be a different story. But now, he'll just pull a Pontius Pilate. Tried and true."

"The man is made of Teflon," Maria says.

"It will take more than a shady reputation and a snotty X account to beat Joe Simmons," Ben says.

Kate is quiet for a time, sipping her coffee. "I'm still worried about the debate coming up. The Parkinson's. I know you guys are seeing what I'm seeing. There are times when I don't know if he can make it through the day, with his schedule. What if something happens during the debate?"

Ben and Maria look at each other. They've been having conversations on the same topic. They've been having conversations on that topic for nearly a year now. Kate waits for a comment from either, and when it appears that each is waiting for the other to speak, she presses on.

"I hate to say it, but there are times I find myself wishing that he'd never decided to run again. But then I think that if he wasn't running, Carroll Miller would have a clear path. So I'm feeling very conflicted."

"Your old man is a bull," Ben says. "He can handle Carroll Miller."

"But he's a bull with Parkinson's," Kate reminds him. "Keep in mind, we're not just talking about an election. We're talking about the next four years, assuming he wins. What will things look like a year from now? Or two years?"

Nobody says anything for a while. Finally, Ben speaks.

"Nobody knows the answer to that, Kate, but for the here and now, we have an election to win. On his best day, Carroll Miller couldn't lay a glove on Joe. I have no doubt he'll show that in the debate."

In that, Ben is wrong. Joe never makes it to the debate. A week before, he suffers a stroke. Even worse, he suffers a stroke in the council chamber, in full view of pretty much the entire administration.

The stroke isn't a bad one, but there's no such thing as a good one. The paramedics arrive at City Hall within fifteen minutes and administer clot busters. By the time they get Joe to St. Bartholomew's Hospital, he is already feeling better. In the days that follow, though, he continues to show signs of debilitation, his situation made worse by the complications brought on by the Parkinson's. A week after falling ill, the neurologist from St. Bart's tells Kate what she has known for days: "No way in hell can this man serve another term."

Back at City Hall, Ben and Maria have already come to the same conclusion, but they've been keeping it to themselves. When Kate arrives to tell them what the doctor said, they are almost relieved.

"This could add years to his life, Kate," Ben tells her.

"You know he's not going to look at it that way," she replies.

"He might eventually," Maria says. "He wasn't going to be mayor forever."

Kate crosses the room and sits down. "I'm not so sure he would have acknowledged that either. You know how much he's going to hate turning this race over to Carroll Miller?"

"About as much as we do," Maria says.

"We have some thoughts on that," Ben adds.

*

Carroll Miller is, predictably, on the golf course when he gets the call about Joe's stroke. He is playing in a scramble with a couple of brothers from London, owners of a roofing company, who are angling for some of Carroll's business. The fourth player is a friend of the two. Carroll never does find out what the guy does for a living; he's there because he's a scratch golfer who hits it three hundred yards off the tee. Never a bad thing in a best-ball format.

Carroll hears about Uncle Joe's collapse by text from Dale. He resists the urge to do a cartwheel (not that he could) and – not knowing anything of the brothers' political views (and not caring, since they were from out of town) – he keeps the news to himself. He does take a moment to text Dale back.

I just became mayor.

The scramble is a fundraiser for something or other and, as is usually the case, there are a lot of non-golfers in the field, which means the pace of play is glacial. Carroll doesn't enjoy himself in particular. He's not a fan of the format and he doesn't like the fact that the roofing brothers brought along a player who is much better than him. Halfway through the front nine, he invents a chronic knee injury and plays it up for the rest of the round, blaming the faux ailment every time he makes a substandard shot.

Afterward, there's a fish fry and trophy presentation under a large marquee by the clubhouse. Carroll is eager to take his fake limp and get out of Dodge. He declines the meal, buys a couple of rounds of drinks for his foursome, then begs off, just as people start approaching him, asking if he'd heard the news from City Hall. Carroll feigns ignorance and makes a beeline for the parking lot. Once he's out of sight of the clubhouse, he leaves his limp behind.

Back at the office, Dale is waiting.

"What do we know?" Carroll asks.

"Not a lot," Dale says. "But it certainly sounds like a stroke.

I talked to Rob Filsinger, who was there. He was actually in the middle of proposing something when he said he suddenly realized nobody was paying attention. There was something about Joe's head dropping, like he'd fallen asleep, and then he fell off his chair. Ambulance came and took him to St. Bart's. Nothing since, but a stroke is most likely."

"Along with Parkinson's," Carroll says. "Game, set, match."

He crosses the room to an armoire and produces a bottle of Glenfiddich and two glasses. He pours and hands one to Dale. "Here's to lame duck Mayor Simmons. Thanks for making my job easier, Joe."

Dale takes the glass but doesn't drink. "We don't know how serious this is. It could be something minor. Maybe he just fainted. Dehydration or something. Let's not get ahead of ourselves."

"I don't care if it's just a head cold," Carroll says. "When a man his age collapses in front of the whole world, it's time to back another horse. We don't even have to say it. I just won the election. Unless you think that old hippie Zabrisky is going to give me a run for my money. Him and his French fry oil-eating car."

"First of all, Joe's still in the race until he says otherwise," Dale says. "Secondly, if he does drop out, I can just about guarantee you that one of these old-school councillors will take up the cause, claiming they're continuing Joe's legacy."

"I don't care," Carroll says. "They're all in the same mode as Uncle Joe. And if he's yesterday's news, so are they." He has a drink of the liquor. "If Joe's finished, we can put this thing on cruise control."

Dale wants to remind Carroll that the campaign has been on cruise control from the start, at least as far as Carroll's involvement is concerned, but he holds his tongue. It's just one more thing he'd never say out loud.

ELEVEN

Kate tells them she needs the weekend to decide. Neither Ben nor Maria press her on it. She senses that they might be every bit as uncertain about the idea as she is. Well, maybe not quite, but uncertain enough. Maybe the whole idea is unreasonable and the fact that they approached her with it is merely evidence that they don't currently have a better idea. Leading Kate to wonder – is a bad idea better than none at all?

"I'll let you know Monday," she says. "But I can say right now I'm leaning heavily against. You're talking about tossing me in the deep end when I'm currently treading water in the kiddie pool."

Saturday night she goes out to dinner in Toronto with Todd Melton, a guy she's known for ten years or more. He's been flirting with her harmlessly for most of those years, even though he knew she was married. Todd does something in finance; Kate isn't exactly sure what. He talks in vague terms about big money deals and throws words around that Kate really doesn't recognize. Money in general doesn't interest Kate all that much and, frankly, high finance is a mystery to her. She agrees to go out with Todd partly because he's been calling since he'd heard about her marriage dissolving, but mainly because she needs a diversion from the situation in Rose City. Joe is back home now, doing fairly well, but not at all comfortable about the doctor's emphatic recommendation that he quit the race. No announcement has been made as yet with regards to that, but only because Joe hasn't quite come to grips with the finality of it.

Todd is a good-looking guy, tall and athletic, one of those men who plays squash and softball and downhill skis. He has good hair and pays a lot of money, Kate suspects, to keep it looking that way. He could pass for a male model. Maybe that's another reason Kate agrees to go out with him. Just the other day, she'd been told by Laura, one of her friends from law school, that she needs to get laid.

"For fun, for one thing," Laura had said. "And to get that shit with Jeremy out of your head."

Kate didn't take the advice too seriously. Laura's solutions to most of her friends' troubles is that they go out and get laid. But Laura herself is a bit of a mess, recently divorced for the third time, and currently head-over-heels in love with a guy slated to be husband number four. If getting laid was the miracle cure for all woes, Laura would be the most problem-free person in the world.

Kate has no idea if she is going to go to bed with Todd or not, tonight or any other night, but dinner seems like a good idea. They meet at seven-thirty at a fusion place on Bloor Street. Todd had suggested meeting at his condo and driving together to the restaurant, but that meant ending back up at his place afterward and Kate was still undecided about that.

Having known Todd for a decade or more, Kate is surprised to figure out, about halfway through dinner, that if he isn't the most boring man on the planet, he's certainly in the running. In conversation he sticks mainly to one subject – himself – and only detours from that to talk about his car, his boat and his many romantic conquests. It's the last of these sub-topics Kate finds rather intriguing. Did this guy think he could get Kate into bed by bragging about all the women he's fucked? At least the food is good.

By dessert, Todd has somehow run out of all things Todd to talk about, and actually shifts the conversation to Kate. Two hours in, she has basically lost any desire to say much.

"So – still hiding out in Hooterville, eh?" he asks. "You must be stagnating there."

Hooterville, Kate thinks. "I wouldn't say I'm hiding out. And you realize that Rose City has a population of over half a million."

"Yeah, but it's – well, Rose City," he replies. "It's always had this stigma about it."

"What is that?"

"I don't know," Todd says. "Blue-collar, down and dirty. It's not the most sophisticated place in the world."

Kate has ordered a raspberry torte for dessert and now she takes a mouthful, rather than respond. Todd decides against anything for himself but asks for a cognac, after tutoring the waiter for several minutes on the subtle differences between the brandies from northern France and those in the south, along the Mediterranean coast. The waiter is every bit as unimpressed as Kate but doesn't show it, perhaps in the hope that the self-absorbed know-it-all would turn out to be a good tipper.

"I think Rose City is sophisticated enough," she says eventually.

"But you have to say that," he jokes. "Your father is the fucking mayor, for Chrissakes."

It's the first he's mentioned Joe all evening and Kate is quite certain he doesn't know about the stroke, or really anything else that's happening in Rose City. She might have been surprised at that a few hours ago, but now she is not. It's obvious to her now that Todd is not the type to watch the news or read a paper, unless it's the financial section. If he turned on a TV, it would be to watch sports, or porn.

She decides not to tell him about her father. For all she knows, in Todd's eyes, having a stroke might be a very unsophisticated thing to do.

"So," he presses, "when are you coming back home?"

"Home," Kate repeats slowly. "First I need to figure out where that is."

She offers to split the bill, but Todd insists on paying. He tells her that he always tips 20 percent and to prove it shows her the amount on the debit machine, displaying it long enough that she wonders if she's supposed to take a picture.

Walking out into the rainy night, he suggests they go to his place.

"I'd love to show you the videos of my trip to Aspen this winter," he says. "Have you been? The powder there is second to none. And I have some great footage of myself in a chalet with Kurt and Goldie. Now, they know how to party."

Kate can't think of anything she'd like less at this moment than to watch phone videos of Todd with his perfect hair schussing down a mountain. She thinks for a moment to invent a migraine coming on but realizes that it's just such an obvious lie that he might very well be offended by it. In fact, he might get so pissed that he will never call her again.

"I have a migraine coming on," she says.

It's late as she drives west along the QEW. The traffic, for once, is only moderately busy. She's halfway home when she calls Ben's number, hoping not to rouse him. He answers on the first ring, sounding wide awake.

"Let's do it," she says.

TWELVE

They're in Carroll's office. He's behind the ugly chrome desk, his feet up. He's slightly hungover, working on his third coffee of the day and waiting for the Tylenol to do its job. Dale had called earlier and asked for a nine o'clock meeting. Carroll had shown up at quarter to eleven.

"Did you see this coming?" Carroll asks.

"It occurred to me," Dale replies. "More in the abstract."

"I don't even know what the fuck that means," Carroll snaps.

Dales hesitates before elaborating. It's just like Carroll to show up two hours late and then get pissed off about his own lack of insight. "It occurred to me that they might come up with some sort of surrogate. But I was thinking maybe Ben Craig, or one of Joe's other cronies. Somebody from the inner circle."

"Instead, it's the daughter," Carroll says. "I never even knew that Joe had a daughter, for fucksakes."

That's because you're oblivious to most things, Dale thinks. *And even more so on mornings like this.* Kate Simmons has been her father's campaign manager for a month or more, but Carroll never noticed? Dale thinks it, but of course doesn't say it. "She's a lawyer," he says. "Been with a Toronto firm the past fifteen years or so. Story is her marriage went kaput and she moved back home."

Carroll sips from his Starbucks. The pain behind his eyes is a dull throb. "So she's what, forty-something, and living with Daddy?" he asks. "Is that something we can use?"

"I don't know if we want to criticize someone for taking care of her father who's just had a stroke," Dale says.

Carroll glowers at this. "Well, she has no experience," he says after a bit. "Are we allowed to say that, or will that make her sympathetic too?"

"We can absolutely say that," Dale agrees. "But I suspect they just might make mention of the fact that you have no experience either."

Carroll whips the half-empty coffee cup against the far wall. "I have no fucking experience? I've built over two thousand housing units in this city over the past twenty years! And you're going to sit there and tell me that some bimbo who's been a law clerk in Toronto is a match for me?"

Dale sits quietly on the red leather couch, watching the coffee running in rivulets down the wall, gathering on the baseboards before seeping into the carpet. He's not going to respond to Carroll's tantrum. What would be the point?

So he waits. Under the pain of his hangover, Carroll is even surlier than usual this morning. Dale can see that he's already regretting throwing the coffee. Worse yet, there's nobody but himself to blame it on. That rarely occurs; Carroll is a master at appointing blame.

"I asked you a fucking question," he says now.

"She's a lawyer, not a clerk," Dale says. "And that doesn't really matter. She could be a tinker or tailor. What matters is that you've insisted on basing your entire campaign – such as it is – on this whole concept of new versus old. Uncle Joe is an out-of-touch dinosaur and you're the future. And now all of a sudden Joe's gone and your new opponent is ten years younger than you. Where are you now? That's what happens when you put all your eggs in one basket. Along comes somebody with a better basket."

"Fuck you and your baskets," Carroll says. "How do you know the daughter won't toe the old man's line? Isn't that why she's taking his place?"

"She's taking his place because of name recognition," Dale says. "There are people who have voted for a Simmons for mayor for thirty plus years, and they're going to keep voting for a Simmons, doesn't matter what the first name happens to be. That's what you're up against."

Carroll pinches the bridge of his nose, trying to curb the pain, then glances at his watch. He has a golf game scheduled for noon with Rob Filsinger. He isn't worried about the match, even if it is for money. For some reason he can't explain, he plays well when hungover. He suspects that the alcohol in his system slows him down; not a bad thing when playing the game of golf. He squints across the room to Dale.

"Okay – what about this?" he says. "This woman has been gone for twenty years and all of a sudden she conveniently lands back here, just in time to run for mayor. I'd call that opportunistic."

"When you phrase it like that, it sounds as if Joe's stroke was planned," Dale says. "That's not going to fly. But we might be able to make something of the whole parachute issue. Kate Simmons has been gone for a good many years, while you've been here the entire time. You've been building things, improving neighbourhoods, making Rose City a better place to live."

"Fucking right," Carroll agrees. Carroll is always in favour of ideas that paint him in a glowing light. "And she's been AWOL all this time. Right?"

Dale nods carefully. "Might be something there. Let's see what she comes up with, policy-wise." He pauses. "Meanwhile, we need to up your public exposure. I don't mean showing up and making speeches necessarily. I just mean showing up. Visit a Tims once or twice a day, for instance, shake some hands, tell some jokes. Make it blue-collar. And play to your strengths. What would you say is the key issue facing the city these days?"

"I don't know," Carroll says. "Probably that rail thing."

Dale sighs. *That rail thing.* "It's housing," he says. "We have people living in tents and cardboard boxes in parks and backstreets. The visuals alone are alarming, straight out of the Great Depression.

You need to talk about that. Stop in at a lumberyard or a hardware store. You're a builder, so you can relate to these people. Talk about the price of plywood or drywall. Talk about the ridiculous rent increases in those basement apartments downtown. Talk housing, housing, housing."

Carroll finds himself nodding. Showing up at a coffee shop appeals to him; it requires no preparation, for one thing. He can even bring Dale along and make fun of him. People seem to enjoy that. Some people anyway.

"I was also thinking you could start going to some Rounders games," Dale says. "Your owner's box sits there empty. When was the last time you actually attended a game?"

"I don't know about that," Carroll says. "The team's a loser. Do I want to be associated with a loser?"

"The public won't look at it that way," Dale replies. "They'll see you as an ordinary guy, having a beer and a dog at a ball game. You could maybe invite your kids along to sit with you."

"That's a long shot."

Dale knows it's a long shot. Carroll never had much time for his kids when they were growing up and now the kids are repaying the favour. Carroll Jr. is in school in Toronto and Rachel lives with a boyfriend on a horse farm out near Lake Erie. She works as a nurse. Dale has met them no more than three or four times each in all the years he's worked for Carroll Miller.

"Either way, we need to work on appearances," he says. "And the ballpark is a good place to start."

"Too bad we couldn't pick a game where we knew the Rounders were going to win," Carroll says. "Check the schedule, see if they have a weak opponent coming up. I mean, if there's anybody out there weaker than them."

Dale nods. "We need to start thinking about the debate too, now that Kate Simmons is in the race. I have some notes –"

Carroll stands. "Save 'em. I have to go. Got a game at Dundurn

Valley with Filsinger. I love taking that little fucker's money."

Dale shakes his head. Filsinger is a couple inches taller than Carroll Miller and twenty pounds heavier, but in Carroll Miller's eyes, he's a little fucker. Sometimes it seems that everybody not named Carroll Miller is a little fucker, at least to Carroll Miller.

"Be interesting to get his take on Kate Simmons. Pick his brain, see what the other councillors think about her entering the race. They might resent the nepotism. Wouldn't hurt to get a couple of them dissing her on record. Even the slightest criticism could come off as an endorsement of you."

Carroll nods absently, but his mind is already on the golf game, not the election. He's thinking of the first hole at Dundurn, a par four, slight dogleg left. Driver or three-wood off the tee?

Dale can see that he's lost the boss. He sighs again to himself. It's like trying to corral a toddler. "You hear me? I said pick his brain on this."

"I'll pick his pocket first," Carroll says." As he stands, he gestures to the wall where the coffee has splashed. "Call janitorial and have them clean up that mess."

The pocket of Rob Filsinger is easy enough to pick. He's a very good golfer, having played on the university team at Western. On his worst day, he's equal to or better than Carroll Miller. But Filsinger has his heart set on becoming deputy mayor when Carroll wins the election and he knows that there's no upside to thrashing Carroll on the golf course. Carroll's fragile ego is the worst-kept secret in the club.

They play eighteen holes, straight up for fifty dollars, and Carroll wins by two strokes. They are all even after fourteen holes. Filsinger three-putts the fifteenth on purpose to lose the hole, then drops another stroke when Carroll chips in from the rough for birdie on the final hole. Carroll actually skulled the chip; if it hadn't hit the pin and dropped, the ball would have ended up in the sand trap across the green. Filsinger was feeling anxious before the chip-in. He had a six-footer for par that he thought he would have to deliberately miss in order to lose the game.

They go into the clubhouse for drinks and a late lunch. The only good thing about throwing a match to Carroll Miller is that he insists on picking up the tab afterward, not out of any sense of benevolence, but because he loves to play the part of the big spender in front of the wait staff.

The subject of the mayor's race hadn't come up during their match. When playing golf, Carroll doesn't like to talk about anything other than the game. More to the point, he doesn't talk about anything other than his game. Filsinger has played with Carroll a dozen or more times and has never once heard him compliment an opponent's shot. Such courtesies aren't in Carroll Miller's repertoire.

"So," Filsinger says, once they are settled with their drinks. "Kate Simmons, eh?"

Carroll scoffs and has a drink from his glass, Kentucky bourbon on the rocks. "Fucking twinkie."

"You guys must have seen it coming," Filsinger says.

"I saw it coming," Carroll lies. "The minute Uncle Joe hit the floor at City Hall, I said you watch, they'll be coming up with a surrogate, and it's probably going to be the daughter. Well, bring it on."

Filsinger has a drink of beer. "I don't know anything about the woman. I mean, she's obviously playing off the name, but that's only going to carry her so far. But I assume it means a change in your game plan?"

"My game plan is to get elected mayor," Carroll replies. "How has that changed?"

"The goal line hasn't moved," Filsinger agrees. "But the daughter kind of throws a monkey wrench into your whole 'out with the old, in with the new' approach, wouldn't you say?"

"As far as I'm concerned, she's Uncle Joe in a dress," Carroll assures him. "She has to run on his record, right? I'm still the progressive and *they* are still the past. I'm not worried."

"What about the debate?" Filsinger asks.

"What about it?"

"Have you heard from them? Is it still on?'

"I assume it's on," Carroll says. "Unless she bails. I can see her not wanting to go mano a mano with me. This isn't some boardroom of sheltered corporate types in Toronto. This is the real world."

Filsinger starts to respond but then reaches for the menu and makes a point of studying it. Carroll has already decided against eating. The beer he drank on the course and the bourbon now in his glass are curing him of his hangover, but he has no appetite. He watches Filsinger carefully over the rim of the glass.

"What is it?" he asks. "Something you're not saying."

Filsinger puts the menu aside. "Don't underestimate her."

"You know her?" Carroll asks.

"Nope," Filsinger admits. "I never even knew what the woman looked like until I saw her on the news. But if she's Uncle Joe's daughter, I wouldn't assume she's a lightweight."

Carroll drains the whiskey and signals to the waitress for more. "Somebody needs to tell her she'd better not underestimate *me*."

THIRTEEN

After the announcement at City Hall Monday afternoon, there's no shortage of interview requests for Kate. The team spends the next few days fielding them and sorting them in order of prominence. Ben Craig buys several whiteboards from a local stationary store and aligns them along the wall of the office space he'd hurriedly rented on King Street. It's suggested at first that Kate might run her campaign out of City Hall, from her father's office, but the notion is shot down early on by both Ben and Kate. Moving into her father's space at this point would have been too presumptuous, Kate said, and very bad optics to boot.

"They're already hitting the nepotism angle," she said. "The daughter climbing into Daddy's chair will not help."

Ben had agreed and had, in fact, gone looking for a campaign office even before Kate made the decision to run. He reasoned that if she declined, he could pay the penalty and give the place up. But he had a premonition that Kate would say yes, and this way they could hit the ground running.

The place he'd found was a thousand square feet above a Vietnamese restaurant. Maria had managed to move Joe Simmons's campaign funds to a new account, backing Kate. Joe had to approve of the transaction, and he did so reluctantly, having yet to really come to grips that his time in office was about to end.

"He knows it, but there's part of him that doesn't," Ben tells them, standing in the disarray of the new office.

"As a result of the stroke?" Maria asks.

"As a result of being human," Ben says.

Sitting in the half-furnished space, drinking takeout coffee, they get down to what Ben calls the nuts and bolts of the campaign.

"We're going to keep you hopping," he says to Kate. "If this is going to work, you can't say no to anybody. And I'm not talking about just the media now. I'm talking about grassroots groups, Legion lunches, church socials, car shows, bingo nights, gator rasslin'. They ask and you show up."

"Gator rasslin'?" Kate asks.

"Okay, we'll draw the line at reptile combat," Ben says. "But just about everything else goes. You're going to be busier than a one-armed switchboard operator."

"That's a Joe-ism," Maria says.

Kate smiles. "I'm well aware of that." She has a drink of coffee and makes a face. "Just how big is our budget anyway? Any chance we could get a Keurig in here?"

It is decided that Kate will give her first interview to Lisbeth Seville at RCTV, in the six o'clock hour. Seville is looked upon as the city's senior political bellwether, in spite of the fact that she's just a year or two over fifty. She'd garnered a reputation as a hard-nosed reporter for twenty years at the CBC in Halifax before returning home to Rose City and taking the job at RCTV. She has always been a bit of a maverick and is sometimes chastised for a lack of decorum that is in no way unintentional. She was suspended during the last municipal election for suggesting on-air that a bottom-dealing candidate for Ward 3 was, in fact, a bottom-dealing candidate for Ward 3. The suspension served only to bolster her reputation – and her ratings – when she returned to the air. The fact that the failed candidate lost his bid and was later indicted for embezzling funds from his ex-wife's family business only helped.

Kate assures the team that she is not at all apprehensive about talking to Lisbeth, as she's known around the city. As for speaking in public, she's done plenty of that over her career in litigation.

"But this is different," she admits.

"How is it different?" Maria asks.

"All those other times I knew what I was talking about."

Lisbeth Seville leans slightly to the left politically, although as a journalist she is required to conceal the fact, something she does with varying degrees of success. She's been the face of Rose City TV, at least the political arm, for several years; an interview on *The Lisbeth Hour* is considered the widest exposure – for good or bad – in the city.

The show is taped in a studio downstairs from the main news division. Kate sits across a glass table from the host, who is in a navy-blue dress, short enough to show her legs when the camera is pulled back. Lisbeth is known to have good legs and just as well-known for showing them off on-air. It was her former producer's theory regarding her job. He was of a certain age and not overly concerned with political correctness.

"At the end of the day, TV is still a visual medium," he would say. "Draw them in with the legs, and then give them the dope. Simple as that."

Kate arrives in a red summer dress, after Maria had nixed the brown suit she chose first.

"Show some colour," Maria had advised. "I'm sick of all these politicians in their browns and blacks."

While the technicians tweak the lighting and the sound, Kate and Lisbeth Seville sit and chat. They talk about everything except the matter at hand. They touch on the weather, of course, which has been remarkably boring of late. They talk briefly of the national political scene, which has been anything but boring recently, then the conversation segues to the Rounders. The team is still losing, but over at the stadium there's been drama to spare with the recent firings.

"I don't follow it like I used to when I still lived here," Kate admits. "But I know my father is a big fan of Lloyd Mac, so he wasn't happy when he got the boot. My father never blames the manager." She imitates Joe's raspy baritone and does it fairly well.

"You got nine players out on the field but you're gonna blame the guy sitting in the dugout?"

Lisbeth smiles. "Pretty good impersonation."

"I've been practising it since I was about five," Kate admits. "Fathers and daughters, right? But that's my dad when it comes to the Rounders."

"The front office always has to blame somebody," Lisbeth says. "They need a scapegoat so they can keep their own jobs. So they tied the can to old Mac and threw Billy Crawford under the bus for good measure. Not that I pretend to know much about the sport. I'm a soccer fan."

"I don't know much about Crawford, other than he was apparently a fan favourite," Kate admits. "Like I said, I haven't been to a game in years."

"Oh – we'll be talking about that very fact," Lisbeth says.

They do talk about that, and a host of other things, when they begin a few minutes later.

"To start," Lisbeth asks. "Look where you are. Could you have foreseen this six months ago?"

"Not at all," Kate replies. "Six months ago, my father's health was fine. He would be sitting here with you today."

"But he's not," Lisbeth says. "Given the circumstances – and your surname, obviously – do you see yourself as merely a surrogate for the man known affectionately as Uncle Joe, or are you a brand-new political entity?"

"I have to say that I sort of chafe at any description of me that begins with the word *merely*," Kate says. "Wouldn't you?"

Lisbeth smiles. "Okay, you got me there. I respectfully remove that word from the question."

Kate shrugs. "I'm my own entity. Do I agree with my father's policies? I'd say I do, more often than not. I'm obviously biased but you can make a pretty good argument that he's the best mayor this city has known. He's certainly the longest tenured, by a wide margin. However, that doesn't mean I'm in lockstep with him on everything. For instance, he doesn't think we need the LRT. Specifically, he doesn't think the city can afford it. I think we need it, but I also think we need to persuade the provincial government to pay for at least some of it."

"Your opponent, Carroll Miller, agrees with you on that," Lisbeth says.

Kate nods. "I'm sure he and I have common ground on certain issues. However, Mr. Miller says that the city can pay for it. We're talking about somewhere in the neighbourhood of three to four billion dollars here. The way I see it, the only way to raise that kind of money is through higher taxes."

"Property taxes?"

"Yes."

"Carroll Miller says that's very doable, once we open up the greenbelt to more development."

Kate smiles. "That's where we differ."

Lisbeth presses her. "So you're taking your father's stance on the greenbelt issue?"

"I'd like to think I'm taking *my* stance on that issue."

"Okay," Lisbeth says. "We can press Carroll Miller on that, if he ever agrees to appear here." She pauses, enjoying her own barb. "Back to the housing issue, I'm sure you're aware of the homeless situation here. The lack of apartments, people living in tents and cardboard boxes in the parks. Don't you agree we need to build more homes?"

"I do," Kate says. "But affordable homes. And we don't need to gobble up farmland to do it. We have the old hospital grounds on the west end. There's thirty acres there, big enough to build homes for thousands. I'm talking about quality, low-cost homes and apartments. The same with the defunct railyards. But these developers are only interested in high-end subdivisions, outside the city. Houses worth a million dollars and up. Do you think a man like Carroll Miller, with his track record, is interested in building cheap housing?"

"I have no idea," Lisbeth replies.

Oh yes, you do, Kate thinks. *You just can't say as much on-air.* Lisbeth confirms this by switching gears.

"Now what about party affiliation? Are you a Liberal?"

"I'm not registered as anything."

"But you identify as a Liberal?"

"Why do you think that?" Kate asks. "And what does it matter? Municipal politics are usually detached from party. The only way I would declare myself as a Liberal or Conservative, or Green or blue or plaid, would be if such an association would somehow serve Rose City. I don't see it."

"Carroll Miller is a staunch Conservative," Lisbeth reminds her.

Kate shrugs. "Fine by me. I'm not familiar yet with all the viewpoints of my opponents."

"Opponents, plural," Lisbeth repeats. "Do you consider Zeb Zabrisky to be a viable candidate?"

"I'd better," Kate says, "if I expect him to consider the same of me."

Lisbeth nods, liking that reply. "One last thing we need to discuss. The so-called parachute issue. You're already taking heat about that. Carroll Miller's campaign manager, Dale Gosling, said in an interview yesterday, and I quote, 'The old guard must be getting nervous, if they feel they have to recruit a high-profile Toronto lawyer in an attempt to take down the rolling juggernaut that is the mayoral campaign of Mr. Miller.'" Lisbeth looks at Kate. "Your response?"

Kate smiles. "Wow. So much to unpack there. First of all, I defy you to find anyone, other than this Gosling gentleman, who considers me a high-profile Toronto lawyer. I doubt I even qualify as medium-profile. Secondly, I have lived over half my life in Rose City so it's not as though I can't find the art museum, or the farmers' market, or show you the creek beneath the railway trestle where I got my first soaker. The thing is, I really don't feel like a newcomer to the city. And I think I'm up to the challenge, even in the face of a – what was it – a rolling juggernaut."

"You did well," Lisbeth tells Kate afterward. They walk together to the elevator. "Listening to the pundits, I was half-expecting some arrogant entitled female."

"I'm saving that for the debate," Kate laughs.

"I'm serious though," Lisbeth says. "You have no idea how many people I interview who don't have the slightest idea what they're even talking about. They show up with a head full of sound bites and it turns out they don't know their ass from their elbow. But you – well, it's almost as if you're familiar with the world of Rose City politics." She smiles. "Gee, I wonder why?"

Kate shrugs. "When the mayor of the city has been pouring your corn flakes since you were about two years old, you're bound to have gained a bit of insight, through osmosis if nothing else."

They stop and wait by the elevator doors. "Tell me what you think of Carroll Miller," Lisbeth says. "We're off the record."

"I don't really know," Kate replies. "I suppose I was vaguely aware of his name before this. He likes to display it on buildings and other things. But I never had an opinion on him, one way or the other. I can tell you what my team thinks." She hesitates. "Is it weird for me to say I have a team?"

"No, because you do."

"Okay, then I'll tell you what my team thinks. And that is that Carroll Miller only wants to be mayor so he can open up the countryside for development."

The elevator doors slide open.

"Your team is right," Lisbeth says.

FOURTEEN

Billy has been a creature of habit his entire adult life, mainly because he's been a ballplayer the whole time. Sleep late, eat breakfast when most people are having lunch. Watch a little TV, sports or game shows for the most part, take it easy until game time, whether it be afternoon or evening. Play ball, have a good meal and a few drinks afterward. Go to bed in the wee hours.

Rinse and repeat.

Now that he's out of a job, his life hasn't changed as much as he might have thought. In fact, his time passes virtually the same as before, minus the part where he plays a baseball game every day. He still sleeps late and drives the two blocks to Peg's for breakfast. He still watches mindless TV but spends more time at Shaky's, drinking beer and shooting pool. He checks with Lenny Drinkwater every other day, asking if any teams have inquired about him. With his current roster, Lenny has no desire to take on a thirty-nine-year-old minor leaguer, but he has agreed to keep his ear to the ground for any openings, for old times' sake. Billy has no idea just how diligent Lenny is in this; usually when he checks in, he gets the man's voicemail. But Billy firmly believes he'll land a job, and soon. The dog days of summer are here, and the combination of oppressive heat and daily grind means more injuries, with more players going down with chronic complaints of bad knees, bad arms and plain old-fashioned fatigue.

Billy knows when the call finally comes, he'll have to move away from Rose City, but he can live with that. All he wants is to play ball, and he can come back when the season ends. He's lived here for only five years but he's come to view the city as home. And, for all he knows, the Rounders might decide next spring that they made a mistake signing that loudmouth shithead Danny Tarantino and realize they need a player like Billy after all.

That might be a stretch. After his unsuccessful appeal to Tom Plunkett, he's made three attempts to get an audience with Carroll Miller. Each time a snotty secretary or receptionist has turned him away. The third time a large doughy guy by the name of Dale something had advised him ominously that he would be making a phone call if Billy showed his face at CM Enterprises again. The doughy guy didn't specify exactly who he would be calling – the police or building security or his mommy. Billy had resisted the urge to punch the man in his doughy face and left.

At the bar, Suzanne is still keeping him at arm's length. Apparently, Billy is even less attractive now that he is no longer a shiftless ballplayer and is now merely shiftless. Suzanne isn't saying as much, but it occurs to Billy that she's trying to get her life together and that she's decided that sleeping with Billy off and on isn't part of that plan. She's probably thinking about having kids. At her age, most women are.

He gets together with Jessie occasionally, either to shoot a little pool or to go to his place to fuck. Sometimes she tells Billy what is going on at the stadium but it's really not what he wants to hear. It's too soon for that. It's human nature; nobody wants to hear about the great guy his ex-girlfriend is now seeing. Not that things are going all that well with the team. She does mention that there's a large contingent of fans in the bleachers every night, holding signs that say BRING BACK BILLY and other variations on that theme. Billy, of course, likes to hear that and in his more optimistic moments he wonders if Tom Plunkett or Carroll Miller are aware of the sentiments of the true fans; the fans who pay good money to get into the games, the fans who keep the team afloat, the fans who understand the nature of the game more than those two jerkoffs ever will.

He doubts it.

One day Jessie takes him fishing down along the river. He'd called her when she was still at the ballpark, working, and asked if she wanted to come over after she got off.

"I'm going to try for some bass in the upper river," she'd said. "Want to come along?"

"I don't fish."

"About time you started," she'd said. "You're kinda at loose ends, buster."

Billy packs a few cans of Bud and a bag of pistachios in a cooler and meets her in Munroe Park, a ten-acre clearing along the river about three kilometres south of the city. The glen slopes to the water's edge, surrounded by poplars and sugar maples. A path through the trees leads down to the riverbank.

There are a half-dozen other vehicles in the gravel lot. Billy parks his truck beside Jessie's Jeep and gets out. She's brought along tackle for the two of them.

"How is it that you've never fished, Crawford?" she asks. "I thought you were a country boy."

"I didn't say I never fished," he corrects her. "I said I don't fish."

"Cuts into your busy schedule, does it?"

"Don't start that," he tells her.

She takes the lead and they follow the winding path to the river, then continue upstream for a few hundred yards, following a well-trod trail. There are other anglers, both upstream and down. One man, dressed like a fly fisherman in a magazine ad, wades in a shallow part of the river along the far bank, casting with long lazy loops into the riffles there.

"Where we going?" Billy asks after a while. He's carrying the cooler and the tackle box and rod Jessie had handed him in the parking lot.

"Not far," she says over her shoulder.

"It's already far."

"Stop your whining."

They walk another seventy-five yards and then Jessie slows, watching across the water for something in particular. At one point, she stops completely, then begins to walk again.

"What are you looking for?" Billy asks.

"There's a mouse hole here somewhere."

"A what?"

She stops, watching the water. "A mouse hole. Deep spot in the river. I thought you were a country boy."

"Stop saying that," Billy tells her. "Where I came from a mouse hole was a hole made by a mouse. Which makes a whole lot more sense than a deep spot in a river."

She ignores him as she sets down her tackle box. "I think this is it."

Billy looks at the stream but sees nothing to suggest a deep spot. How could you see it? Jessie puts her rod together and begins to thread the line through the eyes.

"If you think I'm going to bait your hook, you're crazy," she says.

"I can bait my own hook," Billy says. "You want a beer?"

"Yup."

Jessie threads a worm onto a treble hook and casts out into the river. It takes her a few attempts to find the deep spot and when she does, she props the rod in the bank, with the tip extending over a log at a forty-five-degree angle. She opens the beer and has a drink, glancing over to see Billy squinting as he attempts to feed the line through the eye of the rod.

"Where's your reading glasses, Grandpa?" she asks.

"Never mind your sass."

She watches the end of her rod for any movement. "What's the latest from that agent of yours?"

"Never checked with him today," Billy says. "But I would have to say that in this case, no news is bad news." He tries to bait the hook, drops the worm and has to pick it up from the dirt. He brushes it off with his fingers. "Something will come up."

"What if it doesn't?"

With the worm haphazardly entwined on the hook, Billy tosses the bait out into the stream. "I'm not thinking about that, because I know something will come up."

The tip of Jessie's rod begins to dance, and she grabs it and gives it a yank. She pulls a fat yellow bullhead from the water. Luckily the fish didn't swallow the hook, as a catfish will often do. She unhooks it and tosses it into the shallows before baiting up again.

"We're not after catfish?" Billy asks.

"You can be after whatever you want," Jessie says. "I'm not cleaning any bullheads. I'm fishing for smallmouth."

"You can say whatever you want," Billy says. "You can say you're after marlin, but I doubt you'll catch one here."

"Is it possible you've become more aggravating since you lost your job?" she asks.

"I'd say it's damn likely."

Billy has a bite then but jerks the rod too soon and misses the chance. He reels in to check his bait, then casts again. He finds a two-pronged stick, left there by another angler no doubt, and jams it into the mud of the riverbank. He props his rod into the Y, then opens a beer and has a drink.

"Answer me this," Jessie says. "You say you know you're going to get picked up by a team. And maybe you are. But you must know that one of these days it's going to come to an end. And no offence, old man, but sooner than later. Just what do you see yourself doing, say, five years from now, or ten?"

Billy keeps a steady watch on the end of the rod, waiting for that next nibble. He drinks from the can, then sets it in the dirt without looking. His entire focus is on the fishing pole, as befitting a man who's been asked a question he'd rather not consider.

"Holy shit," Jessie says. "You've never actually thought about that, have you?"

Billy grabs the rod again and gives it a jerk. Nothing.

"You never had a bite," she tells him. "That's the current pulling your line."

"Is there something you're not an expert on?" Billy asks.

"Yeah, the thought process of the eternal adolescent."

"Well shit," Billy says. He takes the slack from his line, then has another drink of beer while he contemplates. "I expect when I'm finally done playing, I'll stay in baseball. Coach or manager, something like that. I know a little about the game after all these years. But that's down the road. Long ways off, I predict."

"You know, there's something kinda refreshing about how simple you are," Jessie tells him.

"That a compliment or an insult?" Billy asks.

"I'm not sure," she admits. "Little bit of both, I guess. But mostly I'd say it's a compliment. Your life isn't exactly complicated."

"And yours is?"

She shrugs. "A little more than yours, I'd say. Maybe it's as complicated as I let it be. Most days, I'd prefer simple."

"Why do I always feel as if there's something you're not telling me?" Billy asks.

Looking over the river, Jessie smiles, almost to herself. "Probably because there is."

"And what is that something?"

"I'm not telling you." She laughs as she grabs her rod, gives it one sharp pull and hooks a smallmouth. The fish comes out of the water several times, fighting the hook, as she reels it in and flops it on the bank. It's a nice bass, a good two pounds.

"Now that's what I'm talking about," she says.

FIFTEEN

Ben's line suggesting that Kate was about to become as busy as a one-armed switchboard operator may have been as dated as the hula hoop but that doesn't make it any less accurate. For the next couple of weeks, she is busier than she's been since studying for the bar twenty years ago. She had no idea how many radio programs there were in the city. She speaks to every one – or at least every one that requests her. Sometimes she talks to them by phone, but usually she goes into the various studios in person. The same with TV, although time restraints make it necessary to do some interviews by Skype or Zoom. She even has a few requests from some of the Toronto stations, where her candidacy – at least for the time being – is considered more of a human-interest story, about the daughter stepping in for her ailing father, who happens to be a local legend in politics.

There isn't much variety in the questions she's being asked. The fact is that there are only a few issues that voters want to hear about, so Kate finds herself on autopilot most of the time, giving the same answers to queries about the LRT or the greenbelt or the tent cities. She constantly reminds herself not to sound as bored as she sometimes is.

The venues she likes most are the non-media events. She meets with people in community centres and church basements and coffee shops. There's something organic and agenda-free about the interplay in these places, even if the questions are sometimes straight out of left field.

"How can you dictate to us about childcare when you have no kids of your own?" she's asked one day in a diner on Cannon Street.

"Do you have kids?" Kate replies.

The woman doing the asking is thirty-something, wearing a black track suit with pink piping. She has tattoos in Sanskrit on her arms and more piercings than Kate can count, at least without being too obvious about it.

"Three," the woman says.

"And you think I'm dictating to you?" Kate asks.

"Well, you got no kids," the woman says again. "How do you know what I'm up against, what with the price of childcare and all that?"

"What do you propose I do?" Kate asks then. "What if I was to go out in the community and talk to women who do have kids?"

"You should absolutely do that."

"That's kind of what I'm doing," Kate points out.

By the time she leaves the café, the inquisitive woman is calling her by her first name and wearing a KATE FOR MAYOR button.

Things settle down after the onslaught of requests early on. Ben tells her it's time to start thinking about the first debate. On a Wednesday night, Kate meets with him at the campaign office. The place has more furniture now, and there's a half-dozen volunteers roaming about, photocopying and making calls. They are for the most part young, in their twenties, and there's a bit of a party vibe in the room. Maria is in charge of the volunteers. She calls them Kate's Rangers. Kate doesn't know why but doesn't bother asking. She actually likes the sound of it.

Ben sits at the large table in the middle of the room, drinking from a bottle of water. Kate sips from her sixth cup of coffee of the day. Since campaigning, she's been having trouble shutting her brain off at night, so she's switched to decaf for the evening hours.

"To begin, what do you know about the fine art of debating?" Ben asks. "And don't tell me you debated some pimply faced kid in ninth grade about urban smog or something."

"I seem to recall dating a couple pimply faced boys, but I never debated any of them," Kate says.

"Good, because that would only screw you up for this," Ben tells her. "You're going to need an expert to coach you."

"And where do we find a debate expert?"

"You're living with one," Ben replies. "Your old man knows more about political discourse than anybody I've ever met. And when it comes to running a city, he's forgotten more than Carroll Miller will ever know."

While it seems to be not just convenient but advantageous for Kate to be living with this seasoned debater, in truth it is less than that. Since his return home from the hospital, Joe Simmons is feeling much better. Almost chipper. The stroke has restricted his motor ability but only slightly. He has trouble grasping anything with his left hand and there's a slight drooping in the muscles on the left side of his face. His speech has slowed somewhat but is not in any way unintelligible. In other words, Uncle Joe is feeling pretty good and, as such, having second thoughts about his decision not to run.

"Hell, it wasn't even my decision," he tells Kate the morning after her meeting with Ben. She'd broached the subject of the debate with him over breakfast.

"But we agreed that it was the best decision," Kate replies carefully. "This isn't about the mayor's office. This is your health we're talking about here."

"The day I couldn't handle a snot like Carroll Miller –"

"I'm talking about your health long term," Kate presses. "Forget about Carroll Miller and forget about the election. You have Parkinson's. You were basically ignoring that fact, so your body threw in a stroke to get your attention. It's time, Dad."

"I always thought that retiring would be up to *me*," Joe insists.

"And it pretty much was."

"Shit."

Joe doesn't have much else to say as he finishes his oatmeal. Kate has toast and jam, along with her first cup of coffee of the day.

They're sitting at the kitchen table, with the light coming in the big window facing the river.

"Don't over-answer," Joe says as he pushes the bowl away.

"What?"

"As adages go, it's as old as the hills, but KISS is still the best piece of advice anybody ever gave, or got," Joe says. "'Keep it simple, stupid.' Although I guess you're not allowed to say stupid anymore. Which is puzzling because I swear the world is getting dumber by the day."

"Good advice nonetheless."

"It is that," Joe says. "Make your point and let it lie. You don't want to muddy the response with a lot of numbers or data. The average person tunes out when faced with too much information. It wasn't always that way, but it is today." He pauses then chuckles softly. "There I go again, saying things were better way back when. Maybe people never did listen."

"No, I think you're on to something there."

Joe sits quietly for a bit, idly tapping his spoon against the empty bowl in front of him. "I've always considered Carroll Miller to be a lightweight when it comes to brains. Don't treat him that way. For one thing, he might surprise you, but more than that, if you talk down to him, it could make you come off as superior or arrogant. The same with Zabrisky. If the old pothead wants to ramble on about outlawing cars, you let him. Every four years he gets to climb on a stump and talk. Let him. What does it hurt?"

Kate pours more coffee. "What should I expect from Miller?"

Joe shrugs. "I haven't the slightest notion. He has no track record. He's never shown any interest in municipal politics in the past."

"You just described me, Dad."

Joe smiles. "Yeah, but I like you. There's the rub. Carroll Miller is as transparent as that window there. He's in this for himself. But that doesn't mean he can't convince voters that he's going to help them out. He's going to rely heavily on this image he has of being this great businessman who can get things done. There are a dozen developers in this city who have been more successful than him, but they don't run around tooting their own horns day and night. They don't plaster their name on everything they build. Miller's a very insecure man. But, as I said, don't take him lightly. He has a knack for self-aggrandizing and he also has a mean streak. The truth is, the man is a bully."

"You're saying he won't keep it simple?" Kate asks.

"He'll keep it any way that makes Carroll Miller look good," Joe says.

The debate is held at the convention centre downtown and is moderated by Lisbeth Seville. There's a decent crowd on hand but the place is hardly packed. Mayoral election campaigns aren't exactly hotbed events. Besides, the debate is being aired live on RCTV and several streaming platforms, so people can stay home and watch if they choose.

The night doesn't begin well for perennial fringe candidate Zeb Zabrisky and doesn't end particularly well for Carroll Miller. Zabrisky – running solely on his newly minted "outlaw all motor vehicles" platform – comes out on stage riding a vintage CCM bicycle. Problems arise immediately. The old hippie, as he calls himself, is pushing eighty and sporting a beard that reaches his belt buckle. The bicycle has an old-style bell mounted on the handlebars, operated by a small thumb-operated lever. Working the tinny device, Zabrisky somehow gets his whiskers tangled in the mechanism. The handlebars twist sideways and Zabrisky takes a header on the polished stage boards. He's unhurt but shaken and a little embarrassed that his symbolic bicycle proves to be more dangerous to him than the cars he's protesting against.

The old bohemian doesn't have much to say during the debate, although Lisbeth attempts to draw him out. After his fall, he seems determined to sit on the sidelines. It's revealed later than he fractured the radius in his right arm when he took the tumble, the pain of which might have hindered his performance. The fact that he's seventy-nine years old and higher than a Georgian pine tree may also have factored in.

There are no real sparks between Kate and Carroll Miller for most of the night. Kate adheres to her father's advice on simplicity while Carroll arrives seemingly with a single strategy – to insert the word *old* as often as possible into the conversation while describing Kate's platform.

"In the old days, the streetcars served us well," he says when pushed on the LRT. He smirks in Kate's direction. "But then so did rotary-dial telephones and poodle skirts."

When Lisbeth goes to Kate for a comment, she makes a show of sifting through her notes.

"Sorry," she finally responds. "I'm just looking to see where I stand on the contentious issue of poodle skirts."

The audience laughs. Carroll Miller does not.

The matter of expanding the greenbelt comes up at the end of the debate. Carroll Miller has made it his signature issue and in this – if little else – he's prepared.

"The city has two choices," he says. "It can expand or stagnate. Stagnation has been the political hallmark of my opponent's father for thirty years. It's a quaint philosophy, I suppose. I mean – what else can you expect from a man known around the city as Uncle Joe? That name sounds like somebody who should be sitting in a rocking chair, telling his grandkids how he used to walk five miles to school every day through four feet of snow, not the name of somebody leading a city into modern times. Now is the time for growth. Which means new leadership, helmed by someone who knows a little about growth and progress."

"My father's philosophy is stagnation?" Kate asks in response. "Gosh – I'm learning so much here tonight. Rotary-dial phones and all that." She pauses. "I'm here as my own candidate but if Mr. Miller wants to make this about my father, I'm happy to do that. In the early nineties my father spearheaded a complete overhaul of Rose City's sanitary system, which had been pumping sewage into the Chalk River since the days of Confederation. He also engineered a program that removed virtually all the asbestos from the ancient buildings in the downtown core. He fought for – and won – more money for nurses and PSWs. And on that note, my father was behind the construction of fourteen new assisted living centres in the city over the past ten years alone. And apparently he did all of this while promoting a policy of – what was it again – stagnation?"

Carroll is silent for a moment. He glances quickly over at Zeb Zabrisky, hoping that the old boy might wade in at this point. But Zabrisky is holding his right arm tight to his body, wishing only for the evening to be over.

"There you are, living in the past," Carroll finally says to Kate. "I don't care what happened in the nineties."

"You don't care that we now have a safe sewer system?" Kate asks. "That's interesting."

"Don't try that," Carroll says. "Typical lawyer, turning my words around. You don't want to talk about the obvious here. We need to open the greenbelt. Maybe you haven't noticed but Canada's a pretty big country. We have plenty of land to build on so why not use it?"

"You're right," Kate says. "We have plenty of land. So why destroy the best farmland in order to build rowhouses that jam families together two feet apart? You call them subdivisions; I call them ant farms. I've already mentioned the old hospital grounds and the railyards, perfect for urban renewal. I'm talking inexpensive, quality housing. We have tent cities that are growing in leaps and bounds. The encampments lack running water and power, and frankly they can be unsafe. These people need cheap housing."

"Those people need to get a job," Carroll snaps.

"Hold on," Lisbeth interjects. "Are you suggesting that the homeless in the city are homeless because they're lazy?"

Carroll knows he slipped up. "Not at all. I have nothing but empathy for those people. I would never suggest that."

"You sort of just did," Lisbeth tells him.

Carroll glares at her but decides to retreat. He turns to Kate. "You know those railroad properties will require extensive clean-up before you can build anything there. You'd have to haul out thousands of tons of contaminated soil."

"That's the cost of doing business," Kate tells him. "And that's why it's a logical place to build. It's not viable farmland to begin with." She wants to add that she heard through the grapevine that Carroll tried to buy the property in question but that the owners – a consortium from Germany – either refused to sell or declined his low-ball offer. She decides against it though; she doesn't know for certain that the story is true.

"Can you stay neutral on the greenbelt issue?" Lisbeth asks Carroll. "Given your record as a developer?"

"Of course," he replies. "When I'm elected, I'll put all my businesses, real estate–related and otherwise, in a blind trust for the duration of my time in office. Let's face it – I make so much money I can limp along on the mayor's salary for a few years if it means saving the city I love."

"It seems a bit of a paradox," Lisbeth continues. "You're running on your record as a successful housing developer but say you'll refrain from doing that as mayor. But it's been suggested all along that your only interest in running for mayor is because of your desire to open up prime farmland for housing."

"That's ridiculous."

"But there was a vote just last month in council regarding some properties south of the city," Lisbeth persists. "It was a vote that your company, CM Enterprises, initiated. Is that just a coincidence?"

"CM Enterprises is in the business of building quality homes," Carroll replies. "Of course, in general we want to see more land opened up for that. But my company has no interest in the land you're talking about."

"You're certain about that?" Lisbeth asked. "You've never spoken to the farmers who currently own the properties in question?"

Carroll grows flustered. "Absolutely not." He juts his chin in Kate's direction. "Why are you grilling me on this? Where are your questions for her? Or Methuselah over there?"

The audience groans at the statement, although the intended target, Zeb Zabrisky, barely seems to notice.

Kate raises her hand. "I welcome the question. I am not at this time looking into purchasing any farmland with the intent of turning it into an ant farm."

When the audience laughs, Carroll begins to pout. The debate ends a few moments later. Carroll doesn't bother shaking hands with Kate or Zabrisky but follows Lisbeth Seville into a corridor backstage.

"What the fuck was that?" he demands.

"I beg your pardon?"

"To hell with you and your biased bullshit," Carroll says. "I won't be participating in another one of these shit shows if you're involved. See how your ratings look when you're stuck with Uncle Joe's daughter and some old coot on a bicycle."

"What biased bullshit are you referring to?" Lisbeth asks. "You saying it's my fault you showed up unprepared?"

"What was that nonsense about the farmland? It's pretty obvious whose side you're on here. I didn't see you asking the woman any tough questions."

"The woman?" Lisbeth says, feigning confusion. "Oh, you mean Kate Simmons, your opponent. One of your opponents, that is. The other one you called 'Methuselah.'"

"Give me a fucking break."

"I did give you a break," Lisbeth said. "I could have mentioned that I've been talking to a Mr. Oscar Anderson, who owns one of the farms in question outside of Brownsville. And he tells me that you are very much interested in his property."

Carroll starts to speak, but then stops.

Lisbeth smiles. "You were going to mention the NDA but then you thought better of it, didn't you? It kind of flies in the face of the NDA if you start talking about it, right? Self-incrimination and all that. Or maybe you remembered that the non-disclosure only takes effect if and when you actually buy the man's farm." She pauses, enjoying the moment. "Don't you hate it?"

Carroll stands fuming. "Hate what?"

"When your own duplicity bites you on the ass."

SIXTEEN

"It wasn't good," Dale tells him. Again.

"I think I did all right," Carroll says. Again.

They're having breakfast at the Main Street Diner, a couple of blocks from the offices of CM Enterprises. Carroll had suggested they meet there, thinking he might press the flesh and eat an omelette. He was hoping for some positive reaction from the debate. There are a few handshakes, but nothing resembling feedback before the two men settle in a back booth, out of earshot of the thinning breakfast crowd. Dale has the morning *Standard* tucked under his arm. He places it on the empty chair beside him.

"Both the *Standard* and RCTV did overnight polls and they disagree with you," Dale says after they order. He had been toying with the idea of not telling Carroll about the polls but Carroll's denial – although typical – left him no choice.

"Fucking RCTV," Carroll says. "It's pretty obvious who they're backing. I might have a word with the boss man over there – whatshisname?" He pauses, his inherent paranoia kicking in. "You know . . . I wouldn't be surprised if the Seville woman is sleeping with Kate Simmons."

Dale ignores the ridiculous statement. He knows there's a bit of history between Carroll and Lisbeth. There are times when it's best to let things slide.

"Besides, I did a hell of a lot better than the old geezer who fell off his fucking bike," Carroll laughs.

"The geezer has no chance of getting elected," Dale says. "I was under the impression that that was our goal here. Both polls gave Kate Simmons a fifty-five percent approval rating. You're at thirty-five."

"That's only ninety."

"The rest are either undecided or for Zabrisky."

"Shit," Carroll says. "There's more potheads in this city than I ever imagined. That explains a lot of things."

Dale hesitates as the waitress arrives with their orders. He's having a stack of pancakes with bacon on the side. The waitress is young, early twenties at the most. Probably a college student working part time.

"What's your name?" Carroll asks.

"Vanessa."

"You watch the debate last night?"

"What debate?" Vanessa asks.

Carroll watches as she walks away. "Fucking kids. They have no clue what's going on around them."

The pot calling the kettle black, Dale thinks, but doesn't say as much as he tucks into his stack. Carroll eats his omelette while watching the rest of the diners there. He wonders how many of them watched the debate. If the polls are correct, he's hoping not many. It was a Friday night. Most people have stuff going on.

When Dale finishes eating, he orders more coffee. There's been an idea percolating in his mind since he saw the disappointing numbers earlier. At this point, it's only half-baked, but then half-baked is a pretty good description of Carroll Miller's campaign so far.

"Getting back to Zabrisky," he says now. "The old man showed up, fell down and then basically said nothing the rest of the night, yet he still registers at four percent in the polls. I think we can assume that people ticked that box either to be smartasses or to register a protest vote."

"Protest against what?" Carroll asks.

"The status quo."

"I thought I was the anti–status quo candidate. Isn't that our message?"

Dale nods in deference. Now isn't the time to admit that he has no idea what Carroll's message is. He's still trying to get his half-baked idea into focus.

"What I'm thinking is this – what if there was a *viable* third-party candidate running?" he asks. "Kate Simmons is obviously the real deal. She was going to be a problem on name recognition alone, but last night she showed that she's more than just her father's daughter."

"I wasn't all that impressed," Carroll says. He waves to the waitress across the room, signalling for more coffee.

Dale takes the newspaper from the chair and slaps it on the table to display the numbers again. "She polled twenty points higher than you, Carroll."

"So now you're suggesting that I need *more* competition?" Carroll asks. "Sounds like you're the one who fell off his fucking bike."

"Huey Long," Dale says.

"What's a Huey Long?" Carroll smiles at the waitress as she refills his cup.

"Who, not what," Dale replies. "He was the governor of Louisiana and then a US senator in the 1930s. He might have become president, but he was assassinated before he could run."

Carroll has a drink of coffee, watching the waitress's legs as she walks away. "You have a lot of useless information in that head of yours, don't you?"

Dale nods. He knows it's sometimes true. "The first time Huey Long ran for office, he was duped. The big-city status quo in Louisiana needed someone to split the rural vote, so they recruited him as a third-party candidate, and it worked. That's what we could use here. We need somebody legitimate to campaign on the same issues as Kate Simmons. We split that vote and you win going away."

Carroll thinks about it. The deceptive element of the plan appeals to his nature. "How would you convince somebody to do that? Would we have to pay them?"

Dale shakes his head. "Not in the sense you mean. We'd have to find somebody who could benefit from it. Quid pro quo."

"How would they benefit from deliberately losing an election?"

"Like I just said, we'd have to guarantee them something."

"Like what?"

Dale drains his cup. "That's the part I haven't figured out yet."

When Kate gets up the next morning, her father is still asleep. She looks in on him before going downstairs. He's on his back, his breathing somewhat ragged, his hands over his chest. Since her earliest memories, Joe Simmons has always risen at dawn, no matter how late he'd gone to bed the night before, or how many nightcaps he might have consumed while playing cards with his cronies or bridge with Kate's mother and their friends. Since the stroke, he's been sleeping in, another sign of the changes he's going through. Of that thing called old age.

She drinks a smoothie while sitting outside on the patio beneath a red rising sun, then laces up her runners and heads out along the river trail. She used to do fives kilometres a day when she first moved into the Leaside house with Doug, only stopping a year or so ago. She couldn't remember exactly when she stopped, nor could she recall any particular reason for it. She suspects now that it was something subliminal, stemming from the realization that her marriage was in trouble. If she was going to quit the marriage, she'd quit other things too. The time usually spent running was then spent fretting. It wasn't a particularly healthy trade-off.

It had rained overnight, and the morning is cool as a result. There are a number of others on the trail – joggers and walkers, cyclists and rollerbladers. A few people walking their dogs, with little plastic poop bags tied onto the leashes.

Kate has been using the trail frequently since she's returned home. Since before she'd decided to run for mayor, in fact. People have always been friendly, saying hello or waving, but today it seems to her that more people were making a point of it. It might be her imagination, but she has to wonder if it's true and, if so, is it because of last night's debate?

She's been rerunning the debate in her head since waking up. Ben and Maria and the volunteers back at the office had been thrilled with her performance and were pretty effusive with their congratulations over wine and beers afterward. Basking in their praise, Kate had allowed herself to be flattered, especially after a couple of glasses of Chardonnay. This morning, she isn't so sure. She has a nagging feeling that the main reason she did well is that Carroll Miller did not.

That conclusion only adds fuel to the general feeling of inadequacy she harbours over her decision to run for mayor. She's acutely aware that her name is on the ballot because of just that – her name. If she was Kate Jones or Kate McGillicuddy, some corporate lawyer recently arrived from Toronto, not only would she not be considered a viable candidate, she might not be in the conversation at all. What does she know about running a city?

As she runs across the pedestrian bridge that crosses the river, she reminds herself that – if nothing else – she is every bit as qualified to be mayor as Carroll Miller, as low as that bar happens to be. Perhaps even more so, since she can honestly say that – unlike him – she has no ulterior motive for running. But maybe that's not true either, she realizes. Who's to say that keeping a Simmons in the mayor's chair isn't a purely selfish motive?

Of course, that leads to the next question, one that's been on her mind more than she cares to admit. Does she really want to be mayor? The opportunity arrived in a very serendipitous manner, on a couple of levels. First off, if her father hadn't suffered a stroke, he'd still be in the race, in spite of his Parkinson's, which he was doing his best to ignore. Secondly, if Kate's husband hadn't been seduced by an intern with perfect breasts and 10 percent body fat, Kate would still be in Toronto, watching the upcoming Rose City election from a distance and assuming her father would win. After all, he always had in the past.

But serendipity did play a hand and here she is, running for an office she isn't sure she wants. In truth, since she'd agreed to run, she hasn't had time to even consider what she's doing – or maybe it's simply a case of her avoiding any such consideration. It's as if she's been thrown into deep water and she's been too busy dog-paddling to think about anything else. Now, as she heads for home, she wonders if her dog-paddle metaphor means she's in over her head?

Maybe so, but maybe not. Approaching the house, she seeks reassurance in the knowledge that last night she was the only one onstage who didn't fall off a bicycle or come across as a feckless baboon.

"Well, that's the first one under your belt," Joe says. He is up when Kate returns, and they have coffee and scones at the kitchen table. "How did it feel?"

"Well, I didn't fall off my bike or – never mind," she smiles. "It was okay. At least, it felt okay."

Joe indicates the *Standard* on the table. "You're up twenty points. That's good. Better than good, in fact. I'd be jealous if you didn't happen to be my favourite person on the planet."

"Your bias is much appreciated," Kate says, sipping her coffee. "I have to say though . . ." She hesitates.

"What?"

She takes a moment. "I really have my doubts as to whether I'm qualified for the job. I mean, I have zero experience in government in general. As for finance, I have trouble keeping my credit cards straight. I know nothing about tax structure. I know less than nothing about transit."

"Good bloody thing you didn't include all that in your opening statement last night," Joe laughs.

"I've been kind of keeping it under my hat."

Joe leans forward to pour more coffee, taking the carafe in both hands to steady it. "Let me tell you a story. There was a fellow who grew up on a little farm. Nothing fancy, just a rough patch of land, only good for subsistence farming. He wasn't exposed to any big-city ways or ideals. He spent long days cutting hay and splitting wood and plowing fields. He felt the back of his father's hand more than once. But there came a time when he decided he wanted to run for office. And as green as he was, he would not let anyone discourage him. He made a lot of mistakes, but he was nothing if not stubborn, and after a while he gradually got his feet under him. The mistakes became less frequent and, more importantly, he learned from them. He didn't know how things worked but he figured it out, by and by. And he became a damn good elected official." Joe takes a drink of coffee. "Do you know that fellow's name?"

Kate smiles. "Gosh – it wouldn't by any chance be Joe Simmons?"

Joe frowns. "Hell no. I was talking about Abraham Lincoln."

SEVENTEEN

Carroll isn't happy with the arrangement, but he allows Dale to talk him into going to the Rounders game Saturday night, the day after the debate. Carroll complains and balks until the last moment, before finally agreeing late that afternoon. The truth is, for a man who owns a professional baseball team, Carroll isn't much a fan of the game. He'd played a bit in his teens but wasn't very good at it. He prefers golf; he has a certain talent for the game, augmented by the fact that he is an accomplished cheater. In baseball, it's hard to get away with cheating; too many people are watching.

Dale suspects there are a couple of determining factors to Carroll's finally coming around; one is that Carroll realizes he needs something positive on his plate – and in his mind – after his shaky debate performance (although he's loath to admit to it), and two, the team actually won the night before, snapping a five-game losing streak, making the Rounders – at least for a day – winners.

The Redbirds are in town for a three-game series and it's looked upon as a battle of bottom feeders. The Redbirds are twelve games under five hundred on the season; the Rounders just ten after last night's win. Even then, Friday night wasn't pretty. The final score was 16–12, not exactly a classic pitching duel or a masterful display of defence. By the ninth inning, the Redbirds had their backup shortstop on the mound, tossing knuckleballs.

Dale intends for the night to be part campaign stop, part photo-op, and to that end he insists that Carroll wear a Rounders cap and windbreaker. They arrive an hour before game time. Carroll, his doubts about even showing up aside, is in an expansive mood as he shakes a few hands on his way to the owner's box over home plate. The box can accommodate a couple dozen people but is usually empty, except for the odd time Carroll gives tickets to someone or other in business who has done him a favour, or who might be inclined to do so. Tonight is the first time since the home opener that Carroll himself has been to a game.

Dale goes to the press box and instructs the PA announcer to announce Carroll's presence to the crowd, but not until after the third inning, to be sure that everybody who's going to arrive has found their seats. Dale has a printout of precisely what he wants said. The announcer, an old-time radio guy named Meadows who's been with the team since its inception twenty-eight years earlier, is reticent after reading the script.

"This part about him being the next mayor of Rose City," he says. "I don't know if we need to get into politics."

"He signs your paycheque," Dale reminds the man.

"Why don't I just say something like – 'Say hello to Rounders' owner Carroll Miller'? Why even mention the election?"

"Because . . . he signs your paycheque," Dale repeats more pointedly before walking away.

Meadows reluctantly goes along with it. It really doesn't matter; the crowd, which has remained sizable all season long in spite of the team's woes, pays little attention to the words or to the man in the cap and jacket who stands and waves to them.

In spite of last night's score, Carroll continues to be worried about being associated with a "loser," bringing it up with Dale several times during the day. His concerns are eased early on. The Rounders jump all over the ineffective pitcher for the Redbirds, scoring three runs in the first inning and four more in the third. The pitcher is gone by the end of that frame and the Birds are then stuck with using their bullpen, already overextended by last night's blowout.

Carroll, a glass of Glenfiddich ever at his elbow, settles in his comfortable lounge chair, suddenly content with his team. There are a dozen people in the box. Among others, Dale has invited team GM Tom Plunkett, Councillor Rob Filsinger, and their wives. It's the first time Plunkett has been in the box in a month. The two men are there at Dale's insistence.

"Either one of them just might make a suitable third-party candidate," he told Carroll. "You could promise Filsinger deputy mayor after you get elected, and Plunkett already owes you big time after you bailed him out of his money problems. He'll do whatever you tell him."

Carroll isn't too sure about either choice, but he agreed to ask them to join him at the game. By the end of the night, the notion that either man might run would be forgotten.

Carroll shows up with Missy Hemphill in tow. Dale is surprised. He knows that the two of them have dated off and on since Carroll's second marriage broke up a couple years ago, but since he hasn't seen Missy around for weeks now, he's been under the assumption that the bloom was off the rose. Missy manages the clubhouse at Black Briar Golf, which is where Carroll first met her. Missy is fifty, tall, and blond. She had done some modelling in her younger years and has kept her figure. Dale wonders if Carroll has recently decided that a would-be mayor needs an attractive woman on his arm. If so, he hasn't mentioned it. Dale further wonders if the notion of being the first lady of Rose City might appeal to Missy, who is known to be a bit of a social climber. In the past, she has dated, among others, a TV actor and a wide receiver for the Toronto Argonauts.

When the score reaches 9–1 after four innings, Carroll typically acts as if the Rounders' success can in some way be attributed to him. After all, he is the owner. Nobody present challenges him on this or mentions that the team has lost seventeen of its last twenty games.

The lone weak link in the Rounders lineup is Danny Tarantino. The pouting designated hitter strikes out his first two at-bats, flailing at breaking balls a foot wide of the strike zone. Approaching the plate for the third time, his average flashes on the big screen in centre field – .160. That number sinks even lower after he nubs a weak ground ball toward the third baseman and then jogs to first before being thrown out by thirty feet.

As Tarantino makes his way back to the dugout, the crowd begins to express their displeasure, more at his lack of hustle than his ineptitude, with the loudest boos coming from the right-field bleachers where a contingent of diehard fans can be found at virtually every home game, no matter what the team's record. The catcalling naturally sets Carroll off. He takes it personally, as he does most things.

"You sure missed your mark, signing this guy," he tells Plunkett. "He allegedly played for the Brewers? By that big belly, I think maybe he *worked* for some brewers."

Tom Plunkett dutifully laughs at Carroll's lame joke.

But Carroll is now in full-bore owner mode. The crowd is still booing, and that doesn't help. "You think that's funny? What am I paying that clown?"

Plunkett begins to stammer. He does that a lot when in Carroll's presence. "Well, his salary is pro-rated based on –"

"I don't give a shit," Carroll snaps. "I want him gone."

"Of course," Plunkett says. "First thing tomorrow it'll be done."

"Not tomorrow," Carroll says. "Now. I want him out of that dugout and out of that uniform."

Plunkett gets to his feet uneasily, unsure of what's expected of him. Carroll stares daggers at him, then offers up his palms, as if to say – well?

"Okay," Plunkett says dejectedly as he leaves, heading to the dugout on the unenviable – and unheard of – task of firing a player in the middle of a game.

As for Carroll, he really couldn't care less about Tarantino. He likes to watch Tom Plunkett scamper. He'd been obliged to hire Plunkett as manager a few years earlier, after Plunkett had provided some false testimony on Carroll's behalf in a civil lawsuit. Plunkett had, at the time, been floundering in his own construction business, and after he lied under oath, Carroll had rewarded him with the Rounders job. But the truth is that Carroll has never really cared for the man and has never made much of an attempt to hide the fact.

When Plunkett is gone, Carroll winks at Missy over the rim of his Scotch glass. "That's how you run a baseball team."

She smiles back. Missy is the sort who loves this kind of thing; an alpha male exerting his alpha-ness. "That's how *you* run a baseball team."

In the stands, the boos continue to rain down on the doomed Tarantino, the loudest still coming from the raucous, well-lubricated contingent in the right-field bleachers. As a group, they've been campaigning for Billy Crawford's return ever since the team let him go a few weeks earlier, and now – to further display their displeasure of Tarantino – they return to that refrain, holding up BRING BACK BILLY signs and chanting his name before breaking into song.

And we sang and we watched and we waited for our Billy Boy
He'll come a waltzing the Rounders again.

"What the hell is that?" Carroll asks.

"'Waltzing Matilda,'" Dale tells him. "They've taken some poetic licence with the lyrics."

"What's a Billy Boy?"

Dale is past being surprised by Carroll's general lack of awareness. "Billy Boy is Billy Crawford. You knew when you dumped him how popular he was. It doesn't help that the guy who replaced him owns a non-existent batting average and just showed everybody in the stadium that he can't be bothered to run out a ground ball."

"Didn't I just fix that?" Carroll points out. "Who is this Matilda?"

"It's from the old Aussie folk song," Dale says. "You've never heard it?"

"What kind of fucking moron listens to Aussie folk songs?" Carroll asks absently. He's already forgotten about Matilda though; he's watching the fans in the bleachers. There are at least a couple hundred of them, it appears, and they are loud.

"You say I shitcanned this Crawford?"

Dale knows damn well that Carroll is playing the part now, feigning ignorance, as if the comings and goings of the team are beneath his interest. Trying to impress Missy maybe. "When you let Mac go," Dale says, "you fired them both. Well, you had Tom Plunkett do it."

Carroll puts his hand on Missy's bare knee as he smiles at her. "I hire and fire people every day, Dale, my boy. You really think I remember every single one? Plus, you may have heard that I'm currently running for mayor of our fair city. I have a lot on my plate."

By this time Tom Plunkett has made his way to the dugout, his body language suggesting a young boy trudging home from school with a bad report card. From above the field, Carroll watches as he speaks briefly to the Ron Erskine, who seems to balk emphatically at whatever Plunkett is saying. Plunkett leans into Erskine, poking a forefinger in the manager's face and then gesturing to the owner's box. Erskine, looking up at Carroll Miller, hesitates a while longer before he seems to reluctantly concede. Plunkett turns and departs, eager to be gone, leaving Erskine to engage in an awkward and very short conversation with Danny Tarantino, who immediately flies into a tantrum and begins to toss bats and balls and a large cooler of Gatorade onto the field.

As the umpires attempt to restore some semblance of order to the game, the crowd in right field, realizing what they are seeing, becomes even more vociferous in their disapproval of Tarantino and their support of Billy Crawford. For his part, Tarantino will not go quietly into the night. He makes the most of his exit, strutting up and down along the first base line, giving the fans the middle finger before he finally leaves the field.

In the owner's box, Carroll watches it all with interest as he sips his Scotch, his hand still on Missy's knee but his eyes, and his calculations, on the Billy Crawford–loving crowd in right field.

The wheels are turning.

EIGHTEEN

When Billy gets up Monday morning around ten, he pulls on jeans and a T-shirt, then walks out front to gather the *Standard* from the stoop, checking his phone as he does. There are a couple of text messages and a voice message from a number he doesn't recognize. One of the texts is from Jessie, a picture she'd taken of Danny Tarantino flipping off the crowd Saturday night, his last act as a Rose City Rounder. Beneath the pic, Jessie wrote, "thought you'd like this."

Of course, Billy already knew about the shenanigans at the stadium that night. It had been all over the sports channels on Sunday. Most of the pundits, while unimpressed with Tarantino and his act, were critical of how he'd been dismissed. All of them placed the blame at the feet of GM Plunkett. The assumption is that he and he alone had made the decision to can Tarantino – and to do it mid-game. Plunkett wasn't available for comment Sunday, and even if he was, he wouldn't dare throw Carroll Miller to the wolves. Such was his tenuous hold on a job that he wasn't particularly suited for, but needed. He'd been a failure as a developer, constantly in debt while declaring bankruptcy three separate times, and he was too old to learn anything new.

Billy considers walking the two blocks to Peg's for breakfast, but decides against it and gets into his truck instead. Damon Montcalm brings him coffee while Billy looks at the sports section from the *Standard*. Danny Tarantino's picture is there, of course, the same shot of him giving the crowd the middle finger. Billy suspects this is the most press the big slugger has ever received, even though there's nothing remotely positive about it.

"You ever see a guy get cut in the middle of a game like that?" Damon asks.

"Never," Billy laughs. "But then I've never seen a guy run that slow to first base before either. I had a coach one time, back when I was in single-A ball in Iowa, who told me, 'I don't care if you're the best player in the world or the worst, you can still run hard to first base.' You reap what you sow, Damon."

"You're kinda philosophical today, Bill."

"Aw, that's just another way of saying 'fuck you, Danny Tarantino. Don't let the door hit you on the ass on your way out.' Either respect the game or don't. Bring me the big breakfast, Damon."

Billy sips his coffee and reads the rest of the paper while he waits for his meal. There's a picture of Rounders owner Carroll Miller there, not in the sports pages, but in the front section under City News. He's shown at a podium between a wild-looking old guy with long grey hair and an attractive woman in a blue suit. The headline reads: "Developer Carroll Miller Falters in Debate."

Billy is aware that Miller is running for mayor, but he's not interested in politics in the least and has paid little attention to it. This is the first he's ever seen Kate Simmons, although he's been vaguely aware that she's running in her father's place. From what little Billy has heard, the old man has lost the strike zone and they're putting him out to pasture. Billy can relate to that. He has to wonder if the old boy had any say in the matter; Billy sure as hell did not.

He skims the article, which suggests that Miller had shown up unprepared, then had made what the reporter referred to as "some unfortunate comments." The piece also said that the Simmons woman had acquitted herself well. There is something about a bicycle mishap, but by then Billy's breakfast has arrived and he sets the paper aside.

After eating, he has a second cup of coffee, watching the morning goings-on outside the window. There's a park across the street, with playground equipment and skate ramps. A number of kids are playing there, while a bunch of parents sit on the benches nearby or stand around talking. When Billy sees one mother on her cellphone, he remembers that he has a voice message he hasn't heard and he goes into his phone to check it. He assumes the caller to be a telemarketer or scammer; most strange numbers are. When he listens though, the message is from a Dale somebody, saying that he was calling on behalf of Carroll Miller and asking that Billy call him back.

Billy deletes the message and sits there thinking about it as he finishes his coffee. What would Carroll Miller want with him? Billy thinks about the article in the morning paper. Is Miller looking for Billy to endorse him for mayor? Billy knows he has a following among diehard Rounders fans, but he doubts his opinion means a hell of a lot in the world of politics. Besides, he wouldn't piss on Carroll Miller if the guy was on fire. He puts the matter from his mind.

When he gets back home, he has a shower while he decides what he's going to do today, although he pretty much knows the answer to that. He'll end up at Shaky's at some point, drinking beer and shooting pool. Maybe Jessie will join him when she gets off work at the stadium. First, he'll check in with Lenny Drinkwater, to see if a job offer came in over the weekend. It's wishful thinking, he knows. If there was an offer, Lenny would have called.

Getting out of the shower, his phone is ringing. He sees it's the same number as earlier, the guy named Dale something. Billy hesitates, but curiosity gets the better of him.

"What's up?" he answers.

"This is Dale Gosling. Is this Billy Crawford?"

"Yup."

"Did you get my earlier message?"

"Yup."

"I wondered because you haven't called me back."

"Nope."

Dale Gosling hesitates. "I mentioned earlier that Carroll Miller would like to talk to you."

"I don't know when I would have the time," Billy says. "What does this concern?"

Dale Gosling tells him.

The CM Enterprises offices are downtown, in a high-rise building named Miller Towers. Billy knows exactly where it is because he's been there three times in the past month, looking for an audience with Carroll Miller, hoping to plead his way back onto the team. Each time he'd been turned away without even talking to Miller. When he arrives today, he realizes that the guy who'd done the turning away is the same guy who's been calling him this morning, Dale Gosling.

Dale is much more receptive today. In fact, he is downright friendly, and goes to great lengths to compliment Billy's accomplishments on the ball field. In short, the man is doing some serious ass-kissing, which makes Billy more than a little apprehensive. In his experience, ass-kissers almost always have ulterior motives, and he doubts Dale will be an exception to that rule.

Carroll Miller is waiting for them in his office, a huge glassed-in space on the top floor of the building. The carpet is as green as the outfield at Rounders Field, and there are golf clubs and balls everywhere. Miller himself is dressed like a golf pro – khaki slacks and a short-sleeved polo shirt with CM stitched on the breast pocket. He appears to be coming from, or going to, a golf course somewhere. But that's just speculation on Billy's part; maybe the man dresses like this every day. From what he's heard and seen of the guy, Billy has always assumed him to be a bit of a poser. But at least he's a poser who gets directly to the point.

"I want you back with the Rounders, Billy," he says.

Billy doesn't bother feigning surprise. After all, Dale Gosling had told him pretty much the same thing over the phone earlier. If he hadn't, Billy wouldn't be there. Now, Billy sits on the expensive leather couch in silence, waiting to hear more.

"The team never should have signed Tarantino," Carroll says. "I knew it all along, but I let Dale here talk me into it. The most important rule in life – always trust your own instincts, Billy. It's gotten me where I am today. But I trusted Dale and Tom Plunkett on this Tarantino bozo and look how it turned out. I assume you're aware of what happened Saturday night?"

Billy glances over at Dale, who stands leaning against the wall, arms crossed. If he's unhappy about being blamed for the Tarantino signing, he doesn't show it. Maybe that's his job, being Miller's whipping boy.

"I've been fielding offers from other teams, so I really haven't paid much attention to the Rounders," Billy says. "But I'd heard that this Tarantino is pretty much the second coming of Babe Ruth, Mickey Mantle and Jesus Christ. Is there a problem with him?"

"Not anymore there's not," Carroll says. "I sent him packing Saturday night. And that opens a spot for you, Billy. We never should have let you go. I can tell you I was against it."

"Didn't trust your instincts, eh?"

Carroll hesitates, wondering if he's being mocked. If he is, he has to let it slide, under the circumstances. "That's right. And it bit me on the ass."

Billy nods soberly, but inside he's doing cartwheels, as would any man who's being offered precisely what he wants.

"We feel as if the team has turned the corner, Billy," Dale says now. "They swept the Redbirds over the weekend. But with the new manager and all the young kids, they're missing your experience in the dugout and on the field. The good news is – we're still paying your contract. We're hoping you can suit up and step back into the lineup when they head to Columbus tomorrow. Can you be ready –"

"I think a raise is in order," Carroll interjects. "We've caused Billy some unwarranted stress here, Dale. Well, *we* haven't. You and Tom Plunkett have. So, I'm proposing a ten percent raise, pro-rated back to when you guys released Billy."

"Of course," Dale says, flinching just slightly under the tire marks up and down his back.

"Does that work for you, Billy?" Carroll asks.

Billy pretends to think about it. He's in an expansive mood, his cap tipped back, arms stretched along the back of the couch. "That works," he allows.

Carroll slaps his hands together. "Good. We look forward to seeing you back on the field, Billy. And I look forward to the team making the playoffs. I'm not giving up on them."

Billy gets to his feet, thinking how this day has suddenly turned his life around. He'd been convinced he'd find a job eventually; he never thought for a moment it'd be back with the Rounders.

"One more thing," Carroll says now. "I was hoping you could do me a favour, Billy."

Billy has started for the door and now he turns around. "Shoot."

Carroll turns to Dale, tilting his head toward Billy as he does. Dale takes the cue.

"We want you to run for mayor," he says.

Billy looks from Dale to Carroll and then back to Dale. "No problem," he says. "I was thinking maybe prime minister, but what the hell – mayor sounds good."

Carroll walks across the bright green carpet toward Billy. "We're serious."

Now Billy takes a long moment. "What am I missing here?"

"You're not missing anything," Carroll says.

"You want me to run for mayor?" Billy says warily. "Of Rose City?"

"That's right," Carroll says.

Billy pauses again, waiting for someone to let him in on the joke. "You do realize that *you* are running for mayor?" he says. Then he recalls the piece he'd read in the morning paper, about Carroll's performance at the recent debate. "Or are you saying you're dropping out?"

"I've never quit anything in my life," Carroll says. "And I'm not about to start now. I need you to do me this favour, Billy." He looks over at Dale. "Tell him about the Huey guy."

Dale, having no desire to get into the Huey Long story again, cuts to the marrow. He's been working on his pitch all morning. "Carroll's running on a progressive platform, which is just what this city needs. The problem is, his opponent – who frankly couldn't operate a convenience store – is coasting on her father's name, even though Uncle Joe Simmons has been living in the past for years. If his daughter gets elected, then it's just more of the same for Rose City. Now, she's guaranteed a certain percentage of the vote on name recognition alone. They could have put Uncle Joe's cat on the ballot and achieve that. It's the rest of the electorate that concerns us. In the best interests of this city, we need somebody to split that vote. Somebody who's popular and charismatic. That's you, Billy."

That's you, Billy. He thinks of his first impression of Dale Gosling and his ass-kissing. Billy had been right in assuming that the ass-kisser had ulterior motives. Him and his boss both.

"You can see what this is, Billy," Carroll says then.

Billy can see exactly what it is. This isn't his first rodeo, and besides, Carroll Miller and ass-kissing Dale aren't the most subtle people he's ever dealt with. The truth is that Billy couldn't care less about their motives. All that matters is that he's just been offered the one thing he wants above everything else – his job back with the Rounders. Whatever he has to do to make that a reality is okay with him. If it means he has to play ball in order to play ball, that's exactly what he'll do.

"Hey, if you guys want me to pretend to run for mayor, I can do that," he tells them. "Hell, I'll pretend to run for dogcatcher if you like. But I'm back on the team, right?"

"You have my word on it," Carroll tells him.

Your word isn't worth shit, Billy thinks, but as long as he has something Carroll Miller wants, he's willing to play along. Billy has been involved in publicity stunts before. How would this be any different? In his mind, he is already on the team bus with all the other players and coaches, heading for the three-game series in Columbus.

"All right," Dale says then. "Don't worry – I'll handle all the necessary paperwork to get this thing rolling. You'll be gone with the team until Friday so why don't we announce your candidacy on the weekend? We'll have to decide on a proper venue for that."

"I hang out at Shaky's bar a lot," Billy says.

"Well, we'll think of someplace," Dale replies uncertainly. "I'm not sure a neighbourhood bar works in this day and age. Let us worry about that. You needn't fret."

Billy laughs. "Do I look like I'm fretting?"

NINETEEN

"This all goes back to the debate," Ben says. "It's a panic move."

It's Sunday morning and they're sitting outside, in back of the Simmons house, on the flagstone patio overlooking the Chalk River. Ben is across the table from Kate, while Joe sits at the head, wearing a bulky cable knit sweater against the cold snap of the previous night.

They're discussing the events from the night before, when it was announced from an east end bar called Shaky's that Billy Crawford of the Rounders was throwing his hat – or at least his baseball cap – into the ring for mayor. The news is getting some play in the media this morning, but not in any serious fashion. Most outlets are looking at it as a joke and now they're just waiting for the punchline.

It's been a busy week for Crawford; not only has he rejoined the Rounders after being unceremoniously released earlier in the summer, now he's doubling down on that by saying he wants to be mayor, and even though his sudden candidacy is being regarded as whimsical at best, both the political and sports pundits across the city are having fun putting two and two together. The math is easy enough to do.

"Nothing new under the sun," Joe says. He has a cup of tea balanced on his stomach. "Carroll Miller has decided he needs somebody to split the vote, and they know that Zeb Zabrisky isn't the guy to do that."

"And this baseball player is?" Kate asks.

"He's a very popular guy," Ben says. "Fans were up in arms when he got cut from the team. What's the old adage – women love him, men want to be him? That's what we're dealing with."

"That's a pretty antiquated adage," Kate tells him.

"Isn't that the very definition of the word?"

"There are enough Rounders fans to make that big a difference?" Kate asks.

Ben shrugs. "The fact is that sports figures are heroes nowadays, never mind that most of them are either too dumb or too insulated from the real world to know how anything works."

"Keep in mind, a big difference isn't the goal here," Joe says. "Let's say, before this, you were on track to beat Miller by a count of say, fifty-five to forty-five percent of the vote. Now that's considered a landslide. However, if they can convince just ten percent of your voters to go for Crawford, then that puts you and Miller in a dead heat. Eleven percent and Carroll Miller is mayor."

"But that's assuming that Crawford supporters are my supporters," Kate argues. "What about Miller's people who end up voting for him?"

Ben shakes his head. "I suspect the plan is to position Billy Crawford as being anti-Miller. That's the whole point. Why do you think they made this announcement from some bar where he hangs out? They're already courting the blue-collar vote. Those are your people, Kate. They were Joe's and now they're yours."

"Why would the ballplayer do this?" Kate says. "Is he under the impression he can win?"

"I doubt Billy Crawford has a political bone in his body," Ben says. "He has a reputation as a shitkicker – beer drinker, skirt chaser. He got his job back, simple as that. They cut a deal with him. Like Joe says, it's the oldest trick in the book."

"So how do I deal with it?" Kate asks.

"You deal with it as it comes," Joe says. "Like everything else in a campaign."

"I suspect that people will see it for what it is," Ben says. "It could even hurt Miller, the whole thing being so obvious. In that case, the voters will basically ignore Crawford, or treat him as an oddity like Zabrisky. However, if he starts polling, we'll have to address it. If he gets up around five percent, he'll bear watching. If he gets to ten, that could be trouble. But he won't get to ten."

"Maybe I need to find a neighbourhood bar to call my own," Kate says. "The regulars calling my name when I enter, like the big guy from *Cheers*."

"Make no mistake," Joe says. "There have been more political careers born in bars than anywhere else on the planet."

Billy doesn't leave Shaky's until last call Saturday night and Sunday morning he sleeps until ten o'clock. The event at the bar had been a bit of a lark, as he'd expected. Dale Gosling had taken care of everything, from behind the scenes, of course. As Carroll Miller's campaign manager, he obviously couldn't personally be on hand at Billy's launch, but he'd arranged for a couple of college kids to be there, looking to earn a few dollars before going back to school while getting some real-life experience in the world of politics. They'd scrambled at the last minute to come with posters and caps and buttons, all proclaiming BILLY FOR MAYOR. The decision to omit Billy's surname had been made on the premise that it made him more familiar and accessible to the masses. He wasn't some career politician; he was just Billy, the guy next door.

The kids, named Seth and Sevah, are unaware of the machinations behind Billy's candidacy, and are under the impression that he really wants to be mayor. Dale doesn't deal with them directly; he has one of Carroll's secretaries, Daphne Lawrence, do that, posing as Billy's handler. Daphne's not especially thrilled to be saddled with these new, decidedly un-secretarial, duties, but she's a loyal employee, having been with Carroll Miller for seventeen years. She even shared his bed a few times a decade or so ago and hopes to do so again. Not that it will happen. She's the same age as Carroll, which means she's too old for him. Of course, she is typically blind to that bias and so hope springs eternal, or at least eternal enough that she allows herself to get roped into handling the fake election campaign of one Billy Crawford.

Daphne hires the two students by posting an ad on the university website. She assumes that everyone appreciates the frivolous nature of the run, so she is surprised when the pair take their jobs, and Billy's candidacy itself, seriously. If anything, they are rather perplexed to find out that Billy himself doesn't, but that minor detail isn't enough to deter them. They are friends, both taking political science, and are at an age when anything is possible, even this.

Billy has a good time at the launch. He is obligated to make a speech and since he has no clue as to what he is supposed to say, and no inclination to find out, he resorts to tossing baseball clichés around like they were Frisbees.

"We need teamwork to make our city prosper," he tries. "No one player is bigger than the team."

By night's end he's practically babbling, but nobody really cares at that point. If the vote could have been held at Shaky's around midnight, he'd have won by the largest margin in the city's history. When Billy finally leaves, even he acknowledges he is too drunk to drive, so Suzanne gives him a lift home. That's all she gives him. When she pulls into the driveway, he makes a clumsy attempt to kiss her while asking her inside. Neither move is met with any success.

"But I'm gonna be mayor," he tells her.

"No, you're not."

Still, he's feeling pretty good Sunday morning, in spite of a slight hangover, as he walks over to Peg's for a late breakfast, his truck still being at the bar. His feeling fine has absolutely nothing to do with the so-called campaign launch the night before and has everything to do with the fact that he is now eight for fifteen at the plate since rejoining the team.

He mentions that fact to Damon when he walks into the diner. Sitting at a corner table, he reads the morning paper over breakfast. He skims the front section before going directly to the sports pages, where he reads how he had a single and a double in yesterday's game, sparking the Rounders to a 5–4 win over the Tigers. It might seem odd to be reading about what he himself had accomplished less than twenty-four hours earlier, but then that was the way with athletes. A golfer who shoots under par always keeps the scorecard, even though the numbers are seared into his subconscious forever. Same with ballplayers; the box score in the sports pages serves as verification of their deeds, as if the player's own recollection isn't enough.

There are two items in the paper about the game. The second, written by Scoop Sutherland, doesn't mention Billy's contribution at all. Scoop is apparently taking a long time to get over his involuntary shower that day in the clubhouse.

As he studies the box scores, Billy becomes aware that Damon is standing over his shoulder. Billy has no idea how long he's been there. Damon comes round the table to sit opposite, a cup of coffee in his hand.

"Billy Crawford eating breakfast and reading about himself in the newspaper," he says. "The world is back on its axis."

"You never read about yourself when you played?" Billy asks.

"I surely did," Damon said. "Well, if I scored a touchdown or made a forty-yard run, I did. If I fumbled the ball on the one-yard line, I generally lost my reading glasses for a few days."

"That sounds familiar."

"Yeah, I read about myself off and on for years," Damon says. He has a sip of coffee, then places the cup on the table. "But you know, I never once picked up a newspaper to discover that I was running for mayor of a large city."

His attention on yesterday's stats, Billy had almost forgotten about that. He reaches for the front section of the paper. "Shit, I never even made the front page." He flips through the paper.

"Page seven," Damon says.

Billy finds the page and looks.

"At the bottom," Damon says.

The report is a single column, buried under the local news. The headline, inconspicuous as it is, is not without an element of flair: "Rounders' Player Hopes for Grand Slam in Mayoral Race."

Damon has another drink of coffee. "So what the hell is this about, Billy? They were talking about it on Sports Central this morning, acting like it was April Fools' in August."

"That's about the size of it."

"Then what are you doing?" Damon asks. "Since when do you want to be mayor? Have you ever even voted?"

"Sure, I voted before."

"When?"

Billy gives it some thought. "I think I voted for that guy who was going to give us beer for a buck a bottle. At least I intended to."

Damon shakes his head. "And now you want to be mayor."

"I don't want to be mayor," Billy says. "And I'm not going to be mayor. Nobody's going to vote for me. Would you vote for me?"

"I might."

"Well, don't." Billy laughs. He drinks off his coffee and puts a twenty on the table. "I have to motor. Afternoon game. Did I mention that I'm eight for fifteen since my return?"

"You did," Damon says. "About twenty minutes ago."

"That's an average of .530, my friend," Billy says. "Ain't no mayor in this city or any other ever hit .530. So fuck politics, I'm sticking with my strong suit."

Damon shakes his head. He's known Billy for years but this is one for the books.

"I'm back," Billy says. His smile is as big as the moon as he leaves.

Walking out into the bright August sun, he has a notion to jog to Shaky's to get his truck. He hasn't worked out much since being cut weeks earlier. Actually, he hasn't worked out at all, unless eight-ball can be considered an aerobic exercise. Driving the ball off the wall in right-centre yesterday, it was all he could do to chug into second base ahead of the throw. It wouldn't hurt him to work on his wind. But then he rationalizes that he can do some sprints when he gets to the field. Besides, Shaky's is a good three kilometres off; he needs to get his truck and head for the stadium. He calls a cab.

He takes a lot of grief when he arrives at the park. He neglected to tell anyone on the team about his alleged mayoral aspirations. The omission really wasn't on purpose. Billy has forgotten about it himself off and on over the past few days. He's been concentrating on staying back on his right foot, seeing the ball and driving it back up the middle, and it's been working. Small wonder that he hasn't thought to tell the other players about running for office. Especially since he really isn't.

"The mayor is in the house!" is the first thing he hears today. This from Jacob "Lefty" McQuire, the young loud-mouthed pitcher whose ERA is currently nudging seven. There are only a half-dozen other players in the clubhouse so far.

Billy goes to his locker and begins to get dressed. Lefty approaches, wearing just his jockeys, holding a water bottle like it's a microphone.

"Lefty McQuire for *Eyewitless News* here," he intones. "Let's see if we can get a word with hizzoner."

Billy strips down and pulls his uniform from the locker. "I got a word for you, Lefty," he says. "'Change-up.' Why don't you learn how to throw one?"

But Lefty isn't one to be deterred by a put-down. "So, you intend to change up the city? Is that what you're saying?"

The handful of others, also getting dressed, are enjoying the exchange, all except for N.K. Choi, the South Korean pitcher who doesn't speak any English.

Billy dresses quickly, then stands up to face Lefty. "The only thing needs changing around here is your diapers, rookie. Hey – you want to run some sprints? Come on, I'll show you how."

Lefty has no intention of running sprints. Since spring training, nobody had ever seen him run a step. With the designated hitter in effect, he isn't required to bat, so he wouldn't be obligated to run the bases in the unlikely event that he ever got a hit. He declines the offer but continues his commentary as Billy heads out onto the field. Billy ignores him; he isn't about to let a pitcher with an earned run average around his hat size and no change-up ruin his day.

He starts to jog the perimeter of the field but doesn't get very far. Jessie is standing by the machine shed in right field, talking to two employees who are preparing to chalk the foul lines for the game. Billy spots her and approaches, just as the two head off with the markers.

Billy smiles. "Eight for fifteen, darlin'."

She gives him a look. If Billy was more observant, he'd notice it's a look she's never shown him before. "What?" she asks.

"Eight for fifteen since Columbus. I'm staying back, waiting for the ball. I'm actually doing what you told me."

Jessie's having none of it. "Mayor?" she says. "You're actually running for fucking mayor?"

Billy waves the question away. "Never mind that," he says. "It's just a lark. What I'm trying to tell you is that you're a bona fide hitting coach, Jess. I changed my whole way of –"

"It's in the fucking newspaper," Jessie says. "It's on TV. How is it a lark?"

"It's something that Carroll Miller cooked up," Billy tells her. "Some publicity stunt. I don't even know what it's about."

"So you're not running for mayor?"

"Well, technically I guess I am," Billy says. "But realistically I'm not."

"You sound like an idiot," Jessie says.

"Then maybe I'm qualified for high office after all," Billy laughs. "You sound as if you're pissed at me. Are you pissed at me?"

"I can't believe you're doing this," Jessie says. "Elections matter, you know. Why would you get involved when you couldn't care less about it?"

Billy shrugs. "Because I got my job back."

She looks at him for a long moment as she removes her sweat-stained Rounders cap and pulls her hair back in a ponytail, fastens it with an elastic, then puts the hat back on. At that point, she seems to decide that she's had enough of the conversation. She begins to walk away but turns back.

"What does one thing have to do with the other?" she asks. "What does getting your job back have to do with you running for mayor?"

"I guess we're done talking about my batting average?"

"You were the only one talking about your batting average," Jessie says. "Answer my question."

Billy exhales. He should have kept running, right past her. She seems determined to ruin his buzz.

"There's this guy Gosling, right?" he says. "He's like Carroll Miller's right-hand man or something."

"Dale Gosling is Miller's campaign manager," Jessie says. "And full-time bootlicker."

"See – you already know more about this shit than me," Billy says. "So the two of them sit me down and offer me my job back. Because they know I can hit blindfolded better than that fucking Tarantino. So they offer me my job back and then they say they want me to pretend to run for mayor. I'm thinking it's some sort of publicity stunt, so I go along. What do I care?"

"You're not *pretending* to run for mayor," Jessie says. "The papers have been filed, unless the media has it wrong. You're running for fucking mayor, Crawford."

Billy shrugs again, growing tired of the conversation. He

thought she'd be proud of him, the way he's hitting the ball. "Well, maybe I am. But I'm not going to win so why does anybody care? By the way, I did text you last night and invited you to my big party at Shaky's. Did you get that?"

"I got it," she says. "I just assumed it was a joke."

"That's what I've been trying to tell you," Billy says. "It *is* a joke."

"It's more than that," Jessie says. "And we might as well quit pretending. A blind man could see what's going on here. You made a deal with Carroll Miller to get your job back. Which means he figures your candidacy is going help him with the vote." She hesitates. "Nothing Carroll Miller does surprises me, but you're a different matter, Billy. Why would you get into cahoots with him? I wouldn't trust that fucker as far as I could throw a grand piano."

"I'm not in cahoots with anybody." Billy smiles. "What is a cahoot anyway?"

Jessie stares him down and makes no response. Billy is growing more uncomfortable by the minute. Why can't they forget about the goddamn election and talk about something more important? Like baseball, for instance.

"All right, I have to do some sprints," he says. "Who knows – I might have to leg out a triple or two today." He looks at Jessie, hoping for a smile that doesn't come. "Come on, Jessie, don't worry about this. It's all just make-believe. It's not as if it's going to catch on."

TWENTY

It catches on.

Not right away, of course. Something as far-fetched as Billy Crawford running for office required time for fermentation. For the first week or so, Billy's campaign for mayor is regarded as a novelty, much like that of Zeb Zabrisky's. Of course, Billy's profile, at least among the city's sports fans, is bigger than Zabrisky's, who for years has been regarded as a somewhat lovable but eccentric nut. Billy is a different story. Not only is he known to a significant number of people, he's also generally admired by them. That admiration stems mainly from the fact that he's adept at playing what many consider to be a kids' game, but such admiration only goes so far. There is a fringe element in the city that actually believes that Billy can be elected mayor, just as they believe that Billy wants to be elected mayor. Other than that group though, nobody thinks that Billy's run is anything more than a prank.

Billy himself belongs to that camp.

Somebody forgot to inform Billy's skeleton campaign staff of that. Dale Gosling knows he's working on a shoestring. Carroll Miller isn't interested in financing his own campaign to any great extent; he's even less likely to pony up any cash for Billy's. Dale tapped Daphne Lawrence as manager because she's already on Carroll's payroll, and they hired the two college kids at minimum wage to do the day-to-day work. Daphne, unhappy with the assignment yet eager for any opportunity to please Carroll, has been taking to the task in earnest. If nothing else, it beats the drudgery of being a secretary for a development company that really isn't developing much these days, not with the lack of building lots available.

If Daphne appears grudgingly enthusiastic, due to her unrequited fealty to Carroll, it's really the two kids who come through. Neither one of them has ever heard of Billy Crawford prior to being hired, but they consider themselves to be political junkies and so are basically looking at the unorthodox campaign as a school project, one that they intend to write a paper about when it's over and they're back in class that fall. Typical of the times, they also record everything on their phones. The lack of a real budget doesn't faze them, not in the age of social media. It doesn't matter to them that Billy himself doesn't own a laptop or a personal computer and can barely operate his own cellphone, and they come to accept the fact early on that he, for some unexplainable reason, isn't all that interested in his own campaign. They realize they can make a fair amount of noise without him; it might even make for a better paper in the end.

Within days, BILLY FOR MAYOR has its own Facebook page, Instagram, Snapchat and X account. The kids use pics scoured from the web, most of which have Billy in one baseball uniform or another, and a few from the night of Billy's launch, taken early on when he didn't look as if he was four sheets to the wind. There's little actual content in anything posted, but Seth and Sevah don't see that as much of a detriment. It's politics in the twenty-first century, after all.

A week after Billy announces he's running for mayor – or, more specifically, a week after Billy stood and watched Daphne Lawrence announce it for him – he doesn't register at all in the Rose City *Standard* poll, but then the kids go to work. Seven days later, he's at 6 percent.

"I don't know what you're paying those two," Carroll tells Dale after seeing the numbers, "but maybe you should double it."

"I was thinking that," Dale says.

"Nah, fuck 'em," Carroll retreats. "When I was that age, I worked for my old man six days a week and never made more than five bucks an hour."

Dale has known Carroll Miller since high school, so he knows that Carroll's "job" at that age was driving around with his father all day in a beat-up Buick sedan. Percy Miller's "business" was finding building lots he could flip. He never bought anything already on the market. His skill, if it could be called that, was finding lots that were abandoned or forgotten, sitting overgrown beside houses or warehouses or on farms. Then he would, with young Carroll in tow, appear hat in hand at the owner's door, armed with a concocted story of poverty and woe. Father and son were about to lose their current residence, always due to some vague but nefarious government mandate, and were now in desperate need of a cheap piece of land where they could erect a modest home. In the telling, Carroll's mother was either dead from a tragic accident or had run off with some rich guy. While Percy talked, Carroll's job, such as it was, entailed standing there looking forlorn. Oftentimes the scam didn't work, but occasionally it did. When it did, Carroll's old man would then, crying about his destitute state, nickel-and-dime the price of the land in question down to almost nothing. After the purchase, he'd have the property on the market within a month, asking anywhere from twice to ten times what he paid. The original owners were of course outraged by this double-dealing, but Percy Miller didn't care. He had a thick hide, and a preternatural lack of empathy, two elements that turned out to be hereditary.

"Billy's merely registering isn't enough, in and of itself," Dale says. "We need to position him."

"What does that mean?" Carroll asks.

Dale once again is required to point out the obvious. "We need him to present as the alternative to Kate Simmons, not the alternative to you. Otherwise this doesn't work."

They're in the car, heading for a meeting with Billy at Shaky's. It's early afternoon. When Dale had called a couple hours earlier, he realized he'd awakened the ballplayer. Who sleeps until eleven o'clock?

Billy is there when they arrive, sitting at a corner table, with a glass of beer and a half-eaten BLT in front of him. His hair sticks out every which way and he hasn't shaved. *He looks like a guy who sleeps until eleven o'clock*, Dale thinks.

They sit across the table from Billy. When the waitress comes, Carroll orders fish and chips and a beer, Dale chicken fingers and iced tea.

"Well?" Billy says. "Five in a row. How do you like me now, gentlemen?"

"What's five in a row?" Carroll asks.

"The Rounders," Dale hurries to explain. As usual, he's somewhat embarrassed that the owner of the team doesn't actually follow the team. "They've won five in a row."

"We're going to turn this thing around," Billy says. "We still got a month to go. And we have the momentum now. If we had one more starting pitcher, and maybe a lefty out of the pen, that would make a big difference."

"We'll see what we can do," Carroll says.

Billy can tell by the tone that his words went in one ear and out the other. He's aware that Carroll Miller knows nothing about the game of baseball, and cares even less. For some reason, Billy gets an odd satisfaction in making him pretend otherwise.

"I assume that's why you guys wanted to see me?" he says. "To talk about the team. The playoff push."

"That's one reason," Carroll says.

"We're here to talk about your campaign," Dale interjects. Billy is fucking with Carroll and Dale wants it to end. Not that he minds what Billy's doing. He'd love to do it himself, if he had the nerve. But they are there for a reason, and that reason has nothing to do with baseball.

Billy laughs. "Oh, that. How am I doing anyway? I hear I'm hell on wheels on social media, whatever that means."

"You're polling in the right direction," Dale says.

"Whatever *that* means," Billy says again.

Dale glances at Carroll, who says nothing, content for Dale to carry the ball.

"We have some ideas," Dale says, "with regards to your platform."

"I didn't know I had a platform," Billy says. He drinks off his beer and signals to the waitress for a refill.

"Why not wait until our friend arrives," Carroll tells Dale.

Billy wonders who this friend might be and, as if on cue, the front door opens and Scoop Sutherland walks in, wearing a maroon track suit and a charcoal grey pork-pie hat. His daytime attire, apparently. He takes the empty chair beside Billy and shows his too-white teeth.

"What the fuck is this?" Billy asks.

"Mr. Sutherland has agreed to help with your campaign," Carroll tells him.

"Mr. Sutherland is a fucking horse's ass," Billy says. "I don't want him around me."

Scoop smiles at Carroll. "Didn't I tell you?"

Dale steps in. "Your differences with Mr. Sutherland are all related to the ball team. This is another matter altogether. Scoop has agreed to help you out." He pauses. "Scoop, did I give you Billy's cell number?"

Scoop smirks in Billy's direction. "You sure did."

"Send him a text so he has yours."

Scoop does as he's told. Billy hears his phone ping a few seconds later. He's not going to look at it. He doesn't want Scoop Sutherland's phone number, or anything else the little prick might provide.

Dale continues. "We need someone who can monitor the ins and outs of Kate Simmons's campaign. Scoop is known as a sportswriter with an abiding interest in city politics. A significant number of people read his column every day. We're talking about sports fans, people who might not read anything else in the newspaper. He can help you, Billy."

"What about the part where he's a horse's ass?" Billy asks.

"My feelings are this close to being hurt," Scoop says. "How do I get a cup of tea around here anyway?"

"This is all about teamwork," Carroll explains to Billy. "I'm sure over your career you've played with men you didn't see eye to eye with. But that never stopped you from doing your job, right? Well, you need to look at this as being on a team. I mean that in more ways than one, Billy. Not just on the baseball field."

Billy can take a hint, especially one as broad as the Chalk River. The waitress interrupts the conversation, bringing their meals and Billy's refill. He has a long drink as Carroll and Dale begin to eat. Scoop Sutherland orders tea from the waitress. Billy isn't comfortable sitting elbow to elbow to the guy. Scoop smells of cologne or aftershave or something, a heavy, sweet aroma that clogs Billy's nostrils.

"What's he going to do?" Billy asks.

Dale has a bite of chicken. "Pretty simple. We need to follow the Simmons woman's lead. She's for something in particular, so are you. Whatever she's against, you're against. Scoop will make sure that info makes its way onto the sports pages. Your demographic, Billy."

Billy has a drink and wipes his mouth. The team has an off day, so he doesn't have to worry about his intake. Not that he ever really has. He has no problem playing with a couple of Buds under his belt.

"Tell me again how this is supposed to work," he says.

"Simple," Dale says. "We want people to vote for you instead of Kate Simmons. You can see what she is, Billy. Spoiled rich kid, practically grew up down at City Hall, silver spoon in her mouth. Goes to law school and then leaves the city because it's too small for her. But now she's back, and for some reason she thinks she's entitled to the mayor's job. People need a choice, Billy. They can vote for her, or they can vote for a genuine, blue-collar, beer-drinking boy like yourself."

Billy looks at Carroll. "And you reap the benefits."

Carroll smiles but says nothing. It's the smile he reserves for waiters and drivers and delivery people. People whose names he never bothers to learn.

"Carroll's the best choice for the city," Dale says. "The progressive choice. You can help make that happen. Look at it this way – you've been contributing to the fabric of Rose City for years now, as a star player of the Rounders. Now you're in a position to contribute further."

Billy sits back as he listens. Dale is very smooth, more so than the man he works for, and he speaks fluently in the kind of platitudes that sound profound at first but are essentially as hollow as a drum.

When Dale's done, Billy jerks his thumb toward Scoop in the chair beside him. "And where does this lilac-smelling fucker come in?"

"Lilac-smelling?" Scoop repeats. But he isn't offended. Maybe he likes being disliked by Billy.

"Scoop will steer the conversation," Carroll says. "We're talking on a subliminal level. Just enough that people know that you're aligned with Simmons."

"And the *Standard* is okay with this?" Billy asks. The question is really for Scoop but Billy is loath to even speak to the little shit, so he directs it across the table.

"The paper knows nothing about it," Carroll says. "Hence the word subliminal. And they are not to hear about it, you understand?"

Billy has another long drink of draft before setting the glass on the table. "I get it," he says. "I wouldn't go so far as to say I understand it, but I get it."

TWENTY-ONE

Kate's "office" at campaign headquarters is nothing more than a corner of the rented space, which is in fact the entire floor of the building. There are no walls and little in the way of furnishings – a scarred veneer desk that was already there, and a few slat-back chairs from the same era as the desk. The place smells vaguely of linseed oil, probably used on the worn flooring at some point.

Tuesday morning, she is sitting behind the desk, looking at her laptop, when Ben Craig comes in through the rear door, carrying a box of assorted donuts and muffins for the crew. He sets the box on a table in the middle of the room, selecting a jelly donut for himself before approaching Kate's corner.

"Want one of these?" he asks.

She shakes her head, her eyes on the screen. Ben sits opposite and begins to devour the treat, holding a napkin under his chin for a catchall. Kate checks one more site before closing the laptop.

"The good news is," she says, "Carroll Miller's numbers haven't moved."

"He's done nothing or said nothing to make them move," Ben says.

"But we can't say the same for the ballplayer," Kate says. "For somebody who's practically invisible, he keeps gaining momentum."

"It doesn't hurt that he's been on a tear at the plate lately," Ben tells her. "Two more hits last night, according to my son. He says Crawford is basically carrying the team."

Kate smiles. "So happy your boy isn't old enough to vote. Are you telling me that I need Billy Crawford to go into a slump if I have any chance of being elected mayor?"

"Wouldn't hurt."

"You have jelly on your chin," she says, then indicates the laptop. "He's pushing ten points in the polls. Isn't this where we said I should start to worry?"

"Keep in mind that the practical-minded voters out there don't take his candidacy seriously," Ben tells her. "They might love him as a baseball player but not as an elected official. There's a huge gap between the two."

Kate smiles. "East is East, and West is West, and never the twain shall meet."

"What's that from?"

"Rudyard Kipling," Kate says. "But I doubt old Rudyard is going to help us out here. Like my father said, if it's a close call between Miller and me, then Crawford's ten percent could seal the deal for Miller."

"Keep in mind that sometimes people lie to the pollsters," Ben says. "Claim one way and then vote another." He pauses. "And don't forget you have another debate coming up."

"Yes, and how is that going to look?" Kate asks. "Does Billy Crawford even show up? And if he does, what can we expect from him? He hasn't said a goddamn thing so far. And it's working."

"I'm thinking a debate just might expose him," Ben says. "Him and his calculated silence."

Kate opens the laptop then and begins to type. "I'm not sure about that, not when all he's been doing is mimicking me. Look here. He's for affordable childcare, more money for nurses and PSWs, inexpensive housing and added security for those living in tent cities. And of course he's against developing the greenbelt. Any of that sound familiar?"

"Imitation is the sincerest form of flattery, Kate."

"Oh yeah? And what is plagiarism?"

"Do you think he's actually tweeting any of this himself? I've been hearing that his entire campaign – if you want to call it that

– is being run by a couple of grad students from McCrae University. I'd be surprised if Crawford is hands-on with this stuff. Given the nature of his bogus campaign, he might not even know what his positions are. His alleged positions, that is. That alone should make him vulnerable in any kind of interview."

Kate sits staring at the screen. "On the other hand, he's a good-looking guy. He apparently has a certain charm. And he's at home in front of the camera. All that counts for something."

"That stuff's all on the surface," Ben says. "What do you get when you dig a little deeper?"

"I don't know," Kate says.

"Nobody knows," Ben says. "He's been a mute."

"Better to remain silent and be thought a fool than to speak and remove all doubt," Kate recites.

"Kipling again?"

"Mark Twain," she tells him. "Try and keep up, sport. But it's true. I mean – has he done a single interview?"

Ben shakes his head. "Not that I've seen. Lisbeth Seville has been trying, she tells me. Then again, she can't get Carroll Miller to sit down with her either. He's been talking mainly to John Comstock from *Rose City Review* and the *Jack Murphy Show* over on 98.6 FM. Jack's about as neutral as Sean Hannity these days."

Ben finishes the gooey donut and wipes his hands on the napkin, which he then tosses in the trash.

"What about this?" he suggests. "Why don't we call Crawford out? Ask his campaign why he hasn't appeared anywhere? The guy's running for mayor. Or so we've been told. Why doesn't he want to talk about it?"

Kate considers it. "We said we wouldn't go negative. I really hate that brand of politics. As popular as it is these days."

"Asking the man what he thinks isn't going negative," Ben replies. "If we go out and tell people he regularly has carnal knowledge of sheep and goats, *that's* negative."

"All right," Kate says after a moment. "How do we call him out?"

"We'll put it on your website. And just so we don't seem too focused on the ballplayer, we'll challenge Miller and Zabrisky too. You've been willing to talk to everybody. Why haven't they?"

"And we'll keep that thing with the goats under wraps?"

Ben nods solemnly. "Well, until a goat actually comes forward."

Kate closes her laptop again and gets to her feet, taking her jacket from the back of the chair.

"What's on your schedule this morning?" Ben asks.

"Nothing, for a change," Kate says. "But it's Tuesday, farmers' market. I think I'll take a stroll through there and see what's being said among the ordinary folks."

She drives to the market and as she parks in the lot, she realizes she's in an expansive mood today, being out and about on her own for a change. She's felt hemmed in of late, as if she's being pushed or pulled in one direction or another at all times. She knows it comes with the territory, but she sometimes feels as if she's losing control of her own life. Of course, she readily signed up for it, so she can't complain too much. Still, she doesn't like the sense that she's being constantly told what to do and – more to the point – what to think.

There was a time when she might have walked through the market and recognized the majority of the people there, both vendors and shoppers. That's not the case anymore, but she remains on a first-name basis with a number of people. She meanders through the grounds, shaking a few hands and accepting some compliments on her campaign. She's noticed over the past few weeks that people are treating her differently. They approach her somewhat cautiously, as if she is no longer just Kate Simmons, Rose City local. She chalks it up to the vagaries of seeking office, but even so she doesn't enjoy the feeling of being somehow different. How is an elected official any different than the neighbourhood plumber or carpenter?

When she reaches the stall of Ken and Lucy Lynch, they offer her a glass of cider and a chair to sit in. She accepts both. The cider is freshly pressed, the first of the season, Ken tells her. Kate sits in the shade of the canvas awning the Lynches have set up and sips the tart juice.

"Pressing the flesh, are we?" Ken asks. He's dressed in denim coveralls and work boots, a John Deere cap on his head.

Kate wipes her mouth with her fingertips. "I've always thought there was something unsavoury about that expression," she says. "It suggests some distasteful scenario, a nineteenth-century den of inequity or some such thing."

"I agree," Lucy says. She's on the far side of the stall, taking tomatoes from an overflowing hamper and placing them in quart baskets. "It brings to mind Robert Mitchum in *The Night of the Hunter*."

Lucy is also wearing faded coveralls. Her hat is a battered straw Stetson. Kate has been coming to the market for more years than she can remember and has known the Lynches the entire time. She doesn't recall the couple dressing this way in days of yore, and she suspects the current choice of rustic haberdashery is an affectation, the couple playing old-timey farmers for the new generation of customers. Some American Gothic for the youth market.

"Would you prefer – 'out wooing your constituents'?" Ken suggests.

"That comes across as manipulative," Kate says. "And again – a tad nineteenth century, with the wooing and all."

"Beating the bushes?" Ken says. "Testing the air?"

Kate has another drink. "How about wandering aimlessly through the farmers' market, seeking and receiving free applejack?"

"Do you want people to think that their next mayor is aimless?" Ken asks.

"Leave the girl alone," Lucy advises him. She comes around and pours some cider for herself, then sits beside Kate. The Lynches always have a half-dozen lawn chairs outside their stall, for socializing.

Ken shows his hands in mock surrender. He leans against the makeshift plywood table that supports the baskets of fresh produce. "How's it going anyway?"

"Fairly well, I guess," Kate says. "I mean, if you disregard the notion that I'm an opportunistic lightweight, sledding along on my father's coattails. According to Carroll Miller anyway."

"Speaking of lightweights," Ken scoffs.

"You cleaned his clock in the debate," Lucy points out.

"Low-hanging fruit," Kate says. "I assume he'll be better prepared next time out."

"You definitely got to him," Ken says. "And what a coincidence that Billy Crawford threw his hat in the ring a few days later?"

"The day after the Rounders brought him back," Lucy adds.

Kate smiles. "You two are so cynical. Surely you're not suggesting those things are connected?"

"Seriously, what the hell is Crawford thinking?" Ken asks.

"Come on, old man," Lucy says. "He just wanted his job back. He'd play centre field wearing a dress if they asked him to."

"Be less embarrassing than this phony run for mayor," Ken replies.

"Oh, you don't think he wants to be mayor?" Kate asks.

"He would shit a brick if he ever got elected," Ken tells her.

"Not that he has to be concerned," Lucy says. "He's not there to get elected. He's there to ensure that you *don't*, Kate. Anybody with half a brain can see that. I have to wonder though – what does he really think about it all? He has a reputation as a good guy. What does he think about sticking his nose in this? Making a deal with the devil just so he can keep on playing?"

"I get the impression he's not giving it a whole lot of thought," Kate says. "He got what he wanted."

"He's knocking the cover off the ball," Ken says. "Two more hits last night."

"So I hear." Kate smiles and sighs theatrically.

"Do you really think he can make a difference in the outcome?" Lucy asks.

"Ben Craig thinks so," Kate says. "And so does my father. We'll just have to let it play out and see what happens." She gets to her feet, placing the paper cup on the plywood table. "Thanks for the cider."

"Keep in mind you have one thing going for you," Lucy tells her.

"What's that?"

"You're the best one of the whole goddamn bunch," Lucy assures her. "By a country mile."

Kate takes that with her as she leaves, making her way among the other stalls, heading for the parking lot. She's had moments of self-doubt since her campaign began. She still wakes in the night and finds herself forgetting for a few moments that she's running for mayor. That she's actually running for office of any description. It's not something she ever considered doing, even as a little girl, when she used to spend summer afternoons at her father's office at City Hall, riding her tricycle up and down the corridors of power. She has doubts remaining as to whether or not she's qualified. Lucy Lynch considers her the best of the bunch though. That has to count for something, and when Kate looks at the bunch in question, she likes to think that Lucy is right.

There's been something else on her mind since this all began, and that is whether or not she wants the job. Is she just running out of some vague feeling of obligation toward her father, or is she running because she's at loose ends after her marriage dissolved? Or is it a combination of the two? She finds consolation in the realization that it really doesn't matter why; what matters is whether or not she wants the job.

In the past few days, she has decided that she does.

TWENTY-TWO

When it comes to a breeding ground for nicknames, there's nothing quite so fertile as a professional sports team. It's ever been thus. George Herman Ruth was the original Babe, Lou Gehrig was forever "The Iron Horse," Maurice Richard "The Rocket," Muhammed Ali self-proclaimed as "The Greatest." Some nicknames make sense, while others defy logic. Where did "Oil Can Boyd" come from? Some just sound right, like James "Cool Papa" Bell. If nothing as colourful as those monikers is available, then simply adding a "Y" to a surname will suffice. Jones becomes Jonesy, Dobbs morphs into Dobbsy, and so on.

Since signing a single-A contract when he was just eighteen and fresh from the grain fields near Zelma, Saskatchewan, Billy Crawford has always been known to his teammates and fans alike as either Billy or simply Craw. These tags have followed him for nearly twenty years. Now, a couple of weeks into Billy's unlikely mayoral campaign, he's become known as Hizzoner. It started with Lefty McQuire in the clubhouse, was picked up by a few of the other players, and was then adopted by the fans, particularly the bunch in right field, the raucous contingent that consider themselves Billy's private fan club. They are convinced that it was their loud and insistent lobbying – not some dubious political machinations by Carroll Miller – that prompted Billy's return to the team.

Billy doesn't really care what they call him. All he knows is that he's on the hottest streak at the plate that he can recall. It's a rare night when he doesn't get two hits. Sometimes there have been three, and one night in Toledo, he has a single, two doubles and a triple. Granted, the triple split the left and centre fielders, and the two players collided going after the ball. Billy could have sauntered into third base. The local scorer called it a triple, presumably because he didn't know which outfielder to saddle with an error. Besides, both were slightly injured on the play and the scorer didn't like to kick a player when he was down, especially one from the home side.

The Rounders are back home now for an extended stretch. Billy is still walking around on a cloud. He doesn't know why he's seeing the ball so well, but he's not going to overanalyze it. That would be poison. Does a man on a hot streak at a blackjack table demand to know why he keeps getting the perfect cards? Of course not; he holds his breath and rides it out, knowing that all good things must end. Likewise, Billy is riding out his resurgence at the plate and quite purposefully wearing blinkers in the process. He's been around long enough to know that there will come a day when his hot streak ends, when those screaming line drives will end up in someone's glove, when the seeing-eye groundballs don't quite sneak past the shortstop or the third baseman. Billy knows this but, for the time being, he's going to enjoy the ride, and he doesn't mind that there are now as many signs in right field reading HIZZONER as there are proclaiming GO CRAW and WE LOVE YOU BILLY. Why would he?

In spite of his accomplishments at the plate, there are certain negatives to his everyday life, negatives that might ordinarily affect his sense of well-being if that sense wasn't so inflated by his success in hitting the ball. Jessie wants little to do with him since their conversation about him running for mayor. She ignores most of his texts and they haven't been to bed together since his so-called candidacy was announced. Not only that, but Billy is saddled with having Scoop Sutherland hovering over him like an annoying and poorly dressed drone. Scoop has always been a fixture in the clubhouse, an unwelcome one for the most part because he rarely writes anything positive about the team, but now it seems to Billy that he is always within earshot when Billy is talking to . . . well, pretty much anybody. Snooping for Carroll Miller, of course, and ostensibly keeping Billy in line. Billy doesn't care to be spied on, and he particularly doesn't care to be spied on by a clown-suited little puke like Scoop Sutherland. As for keeping him in line, better men than Scoop have tried.

Wednesday is a rare afternoon game, and the Redbirds are back in town. The Birds haven't gotten any better since they last played the Rounders a few weeks earlier and are still mired in last place, while the home nine has risen to third in the standings, just a game and a half out of second. The matinee holds to recent form, as the Rounders win going away by a score of 8–1. Billy, uncharacteristically (of late anyway), is held to a first-inning single, although he does draw two walks in the game as well.

"A measly single for Hizzoner," Lefty needles him in the clubhouse afterward. "Call a fucking ambulance!"

"Reached base three out of four," Billy tells him. "That works out to a .750 on-base percentage. You can do the math, Lefty. Well, you could – if you'd ever made it past nursery school."

"Ouch," Lefty says.

Scoop Sutherland is across the room, talking to the rookie Diaz, who'd started the game and thrown six stellar innings, allowing just the single run on a long ball. Of course, the eternally negative Scoop is focused on that run, suggesting to the young pitcher that he'd made a mistake in throwing the pitch that had ended up in the left-field bleachers.

Billy, heading for the showers with a towel wrapped around his waist, hears the conversation and veers over to extend his hand to Diaz.

"Nice game, kid," he says. "Don't worry about that dinger. If the wind wasn't blowing out to left to beat the band, that ball is a can of corn. A man would have to be a fucking idiot not to realize that. Oh, hello, Scoop."

Message delivered, Billy smiles and walks on.

Later, as he's dressed and pulling on his Frye boots, he's aware of a sudden and significant drop in the noise level in the clubhouse. Billy looks up to see Lisbeth Seville standing in the doorway, looking quite fetching and a little lost. Billy recognizes her from TV. Indeed, she's a bit of a celebrity, and seeing her in the Rounders clubhouse is akin to spotting a swan in a cornfield full of crows.

Lisbeth looks around until she spots Billy, and heads over. Several players are still in their underwear, or out of it. She never reacts, keeping her cool, her gaze at eye-level.

"Mr. Crawford," she says, offering her hand. "Lisbeth Seville."

Billy briefly takes the firm, manicured hand in his own. Lisbeth Seville smells great, and she looks even better in person than on TV. In Billy's experience with media types, usually the opposite is true.

"I work for Rose City TV," Lisbeth tells him. As if he doesn't know this.

"I know who you are," Billy says. "I didn't know you were covering baseball now."

"Oh, I finagled a pass from our six o'clock sports guy," she tells him. "What I know about baseball, you could fit in a thimble. But you know that's not why I'm here."

Looking past her, Billy sees Scoop Sutherland beetling over, intent on hearing whatever it is Lisbeth has come to say. Billy nods toward him as he nears.

"Hell, when it comes to sports, Scoop here don't know shit from wild honey, yet he hangs around like a bad smell, day in and day out."

Lisbeth glances briefly at Scoop, then ignores his presence. Either she doesn't know who he is but doesn't care for an introduction – or she does and doesn't want one. Scoop takes up a position several feet behind her and pretends to busy himself with his cellphone.

"I've been trying to contact you for days," Lisbeth tells Billy.

"Team's been out of town," he replies.

"Am I to assume your cellphone doesn't work when you're on the road?" she says, smiling.

Lisbeth Seville has a terrific smile. It's somewhat disarming and Billy is sure she knows it. "I never know where that damn thing is," he alibis.

Lisbeth points to the lost phone in question, on the bench a foot away from where Billy sits. "Would that be it?"

Billy feigns surprise. "Sonofabitch."

"I've been talking to your campaign people," Lisbeth presses on. "The Katzenjammer kids. They suggest that they have trouble getting in touch with you too."

"Team's been out of town," Billy repeats.

"Right – and you lost your phone," Lisbeth says.

"That's my story and I'm sticking to it," Billy says. He's been ignoring any numbers he doesn't recognize for a week or more now. "How'd you like the game anyway?"

As he speaks, he's watching Scoop, who has moved closer now, ears perked like a bird dog while he pretends to read a text.

"I wasn't here for the game," she replies. "I just arrived. Although I've been hearing that you're a big success lately. The team's been winning because you've been scoring a lot of goals."

"Runs, not goals," Billy says. "It ain't hockey."

"Hey, my mother was born in Portugal and my father is from Spain. I grew up watching football, which you probably call soccer. I didn't particularly like it, but it was on all the time, so I had no choice."

Billy finds himself liking Lisbeth. Of course, he's seen her on TV any number of times, but her usual beat is politics and as a rule Billy goes channel-surfing when anything political comes on. But she obviously has a sense of humour, along with the smile and the somewhat intoxicating perfume. She's probably about fifty, he guesses, and extremely attractive. She's sexy too, something Billy attributes to her humour and her confidence. Billy has always found confident women sexy.

"You know why I'm here," she says then.

Billy grins. "Why, to talk about soccer, I assume."

"Yes," she says. "I want you to come on my show and talk about soccer." She pauses and shows him the smile again. "If you don't feel like talking soccer, I'm sure we can find other things to discuss."

Scoop Sutherland, still lurking, now takes another step forward. Behind Lisbeth's back, he begins to shake his head emphatically at Billy, urging him to bail from the conversation. Billy regards him briefly before turning back to Lisbeth.

"I don't know when I'd find the time," he says. "I'm a full-time ballplayer, ma'am."

"You're going to play the good ol' boy card with me?" she asks. "Aw shucks and ma'am and all that? Good luck. I'm aware that you're a full-time ballplayer but I keep hearing that you are also running for mayor of Rose City. Is that not true?"

"I suppose it is."

Scoop is still shaking his head wildly. Billy half expects the man's hat to fly off.

"Your opponent, Kate Simmons, is wondering on social media why you haven't done any interviews," Lisbeth says. "Is that due to your oh-so-busy schedule, or is it due to some philosophical bent, some belief that politicians, like unruly children, should be seen and not heard?"

"The first thing, the schedule." Billy smiles. "Although I kinda like how you put the second part."

"Oh, I have a way with words," she tells him. "Let's book your interview and I'll show you."

Scoop can no longer hold his tongue. "Billy," he says, stepping into the conversation. "Good game today, my man. Can I get a quick word for the paper?"

Scoop has all but shoved Lisbeth aside. She turns to give him a long cool look. He won't acknowledge her but glares at Billy, further warning him off. Does he think that Billy hasn't picked up his signals yet?

"Nah, I'm good," Billy says. "Why don't you go tell Diaz again how you would never have given up that home run?"

Scoop tries again. "Just hoping to get a quick interview."

Billy ignores him and turns back to Lisbeth, who is still watching Scoop with a baleful stare. Billy suspects the woman could crush Scoop beneath her heel like he was a dung beetle. He likes the very idea of that. And, as much as he has enjoyed talking to the woman, he has no interest in appearing on her show. Why would he agree to go on TV to talk about politics when he knows nothing about politics?

It will be easy enough to tell her no. He would do just that, if it wasn't for the other fox in the henhouse. It's quite apparent that Scoop Sutherland, carrying Carroll Miller's water, doesn't want Billy to appear on TV to talk to Lisbeth. He seems downright frantic that Billy might say yes.

Which makes it easy for Billy to do just that.

"Let's do it," he says to Lisbeth.

She shows that wonderful smile again, while Scoop grimaces like a man passing a kidney stone.

"Excellent," Lisbeth says. "I'll be texting you the details, so hang onto that phone, Mr. Crawford." She wags a forefinger at him. "Don't make me come looking for you again."

"What the fuck was I supposed to do?" Scoop asks.

He's in the back of the limo with Carroll and Dale. Scoop had called Dale from the stadium, minutes after the exchange between Billy Crawford and Lisbeth Seville. The limo was returning to the city from Toronto, where Carroll had met with some investors who were interested in one of his proposed developments, a golf course slash condo layout north of Oakville. The meeting had been rocky. The investors, a consortium originally from Hong Kong but now based in Canada, hadn't been aware that Carroll had yet to acquire the land for the project. This was due to the fact that he'd been suggesting all along that he had.

After Scoop's call to Dale, the limo took a detour to pick the sportswriter up in front of Rounders Stadium. While waiting, Scoop has been rehearsing his story, emphasizing the part where he was in no way responsible for what had just happened. Seville had approached Billy for an interview and Billy had agreed. In spite of his efforts to rein Billy in, Scoop had been left out of the conversation altogether. What was Scoop supposed to do?

"You just tell him he's not appearing on TV," Dale says. "That's what you're supposed to do."

"The woman is standing right there," Scoop replies. "How's that going to look? A journalist from the *Standard* telling the mayoral candidate what he can and can't do?"

"I didn't know you considered yourself a journalist," Carroll says. "Where'd you get that idea?"

"It would require some finesse," Dale tells the morose Scoop. "We thought you were aware of that."

"For fucksakes, did you hear me? The woman was standing right there."

Dale dismisses the whine with a look, and turns toward Carroll, whose phone has just pinged. Dale waits while Carroll returns the text, then waits some more while Carroll reads the reply.

"What do you think?" he asks.

"These fucking Hong Kongers," Carroll says. "They're looking for paperwork on the property. Don't they trust anybody?"

They don't trust you, Dale thinks. He knew that the group would be googling Carroll's name the moment they left the meeting, and he also knew that they were savvy enough to figure out that the reason Carroll hadn't yet officially acquired the land in question was that he planned to use the Hong Kong group's money to do so.

Dale clarifies. "What do you think about Crawford going on TV?"

Carroll sends another text, then sets his phone aside. "Who cares? Let him talk to the woman. What harm can it do?"

"Plenty, if he gets to jabbering and happens to mention that little quid pro quo connection between you and him. Are we going to trust him with that? The guy's half in the bag most of the time."

Scoop, feeling left out, speaks up. "It's not as if it's a big secret. I mean – you give him his job back and suddenly he's the third-party candidate for mayor. Even those idiot fans in right field can put two and two together."

"Fourth-party candidate," Dale says. "If we count Zabrisky. And I'm not sure those fans are idiots."

"Nobody counts Zabrisky," Scoop says lamely.

"You guys are looking at this all wrong," Carroll says. "I actually look pretty good in all this. Think about it – who else would allow one of his employees to run against him for a position as powerful as mayor? Shit, I look like the ultimate square dealer."

"You make a good point," Scoop says, eager to find some common ground.

Dale hesitates a moment. "I'm just saying we don't need this backfiring on us. Crawford is a loose cannon. I mean, the guy is only sort of aware of what's going on here. Who knows what he might say to Seville? And let's keep in mind that she's a lot smarter than the average bear. She might get him in that chair and play him like a yoyo."

"She has never impressed me as being all that intelligent," Carroll says.

"Me neither," Scoop agrees. Again.

Dale knows that a few years earlier Carroll developed a crush on Lisbeth Seville, after watching her on-air every night, and had asked her out more than once. He'd even donated money to a charity she was involved in at the time. In his fertile mind, she would take note of his sizable donation and agree to attend the annual banquet with her. She wasn't buying it. So now Carroll is no longer impressed with her. Neither is Scoop Sutherland, but only because he has his lips glued to Carroll's posterior. If Carroll said he thought Lisbeth Seville was an extraterrestrial, Scoop would go along with that too.

Dale shakes his head. "We know goddamn well she's going to turn on the charm and get Crawford all comfortable, talking about baseball and apple pie and whatever – and then she's going to ask what happened between the two of you. The juxtaposition between him getting his job back and then announcing for mayor."

Scoop snorts. "As if Crawford knows what juxtaposition means."

"So he tells her nothing happened," Carroll says. "Simple as that."

"You're assuming he knows enough to lie," Dale says.

Carroll laughs. "I would hope so, if he's running for office." His phone pings again and he reaches for it and reads. "These fucking people are getting on my nerves. How do they get this info so quick? Scoop, you don't have an extra three point seven million you can lend me?"

"What?" Scoop laughs nervously. "Well, not on me I don't."

"Didn't think so," Carroll says as he begins to type a reply. "How do you say kiss my ass in Chinese?"

Dale waits until Carroll finishes and puts the phone in his pocket.

"So what's the plan?"

Carroll thinks about it. "Talk to Crawford," he says. "Tell him what he can and can't say. Write it down if you have to. We can make this work in our favour. Tell him to toe the Kate Simmons line and he'll be fine. He likes more childcare, the LRT, save the greenbelt, those bums living in tents, blah blah. This isn't fucking rocket science. You know what to do, Dale. It's sort of what we're paying sad Sam here to do."

"I resent that," Scoop says. "I did everything but gag him when that woman walked in the clubhouse." He pauses, seeking other words to exonerate himself. "And what the fuck is she doing in the Rounders clubhouse anyway? She's not a sports journalist."

"They let *you* in, don't they?" Carroll says.

Scoop resents that too, but he decides not to mention it. Mentioning stuff just gets him in deeper today, it seems.

Carroll looks at Dale. "Talk to the man. I get the sense he's very happy these days with the way his baseball career is going. Especially when you consider that a month ago, he was out of the sport altogether, and his prospects were dimmer than his intellect. You might want to figure that into the conversation."

"I'll talk to him," Dale says.

"Good."

"Talking to him is easy," Dale adds. "Getting him to listen might be another matter."

TWENTY-THREE

Jessie has the big mower on jack stands outside the equipment shed beneath the right-field bleachers. She pulls on a pair of coveralls and crawls beneath the machine with a ratchet in her hand to loosen the bolts holding the blades in place. Sharpening the mower blades is usually a job for Big John, the Rounders Field maintenance man and jack-of-all-trades, but Big John's wife had a baby two days ago so he's home with her.

It's immediately apparent that the last person to tighten the bolts in question was Big John himself. Jessie can't loosen them with the ratchet and has to return to the shed to fetch a Johnson bar. Walking out again into the brilliant afternoon sunshine, she sees Billy Crawford as he emerges from the clubhouse and begins to stretch in front of the home team dugout. He is about to run laps, Jessie knows. He's been running every day since returning to the team. Before he'd been cut from the team earlier in the summer, Jessie couldn't recall ever seeing him run. Now it's become part of his daily regimen.

Jessie suspects that the change in routine has more to do with superstition than with any notion of staying in shape. Billy has been scorching the ball and so he's going to stick to whatever habits he thinks might be responsible for that. She's seen it often enough over the years to recognize it for what it is. Some players refuse to change their socks or underwear while on a hot streak. She's heard of players refusing to have sex with their wives for fear it might jinx the roll they're on. Others resort to strange OCD behaviour, like rubbing a certain teammate's head before walking to the plate or avoiding the chalk lines while running off the field.

So, compared to some players' odd obsessions, Billy Crawford running laps every day, while uncharacteristic for him, can hardly be considered eccentric behaviour. As activities go, running was healthy, a damn sight healthier than refusing to change one's underwear. Jessie walks back toward the mower, as Billy finishes his perfunctory stretching and begins to jog along the first base line. Not eager for a conversation with him, she drops to the ground and slides under the machine again.

She still hasn't been able to reconcile herself to Billy's ridiculous run for office. Jessie comes from a less-than-comfortable upbringing. Her father was a chronically unhappy man who became even more miserable whenever he was drunk, and he was drunk nearly every day that Jessie can recall. He would infrequently go on the wagon and when that happened the family, instead of being relieved to see him sober, simply waited around in dread for the time when he started drinking again. They never had to wait long. However, drunk or sober, her father was a political junkie who believed that the right to vote was the greatest privilege a citizen had, and that anyone who chose not to vote was nothing less than a blight on society as a whole. Jessie took those sentiments to heart. Maybe, on a subconscious level, she needed to take something of value from her fractured relationship with the mean alcoholic bastard she now sarcastically referred to as "dear old Dad."

Since reaching voting age sixteen years ago, Jessie has never failed to cast her ballot, whether the election in question be municipal or provincial or federal. She voted when she felt strongly about one candidate or another and she voted when she felt nothing, always finding some small rationalization to support her choice, however lukewarm her feelings might be.

Which is why she's not happy with Billy Crawford and his half-baked mayoral run. How can it be that Jessie, a solitary vote in the process, takes the election seriously while Billy, an actual candidate, does not? He either treats the whole hodgepodge as a prank or acts as if it doesn't exist at all. Sometimes Jessie thinks it's a good thing that she's seeing his true colours. She was developing real feelings for him, although she did her best to conceal them. She'd told herself early on that he was a rounder – no pun intended – who had no interest in commitment. Like most rounders, he is charming and amusing and fun to be with, a rounder's stock in trade. She had no intention of allowing herself to be hurt by a guy like that and now she's been thinking she can look at this election nonsense as her way out.

The Johnson bar works on the bolts. Nothing like a little leverage to make this hundred-and-thirty-pound woman as strong as Big John, who is at least two-fifty. She removes the three blades and comes out from under the mower with them. As she heads toward the maintenance shed to hone them, she glances back to Billy again. He isn't running now; he's standing outside the dugout, talking to a guy in tan pants and a polo shirt. Jessie watches them until the guy in the polo turns and walks away, heading for the exit on the first base side.

She is still there, leaning against the mower and wiping her hands on a rag, when Billy starts his laps again. When he draws near, she calls to him. He'd seen her, obviously, but she's been so standoffish of late, Billy has assumed she doesn't want to talk to him. Now he slows down, then stops. He stages a little pantomime, looking behind him as if to see who it is she's really calling to. She doesn't smile at the joke.

"Hey," he says, approaching and indicating the blades. "You a mechanic now?"

"Big John had a baby."

"Wow," Billy says. "What does the medical profession think about that?"

Jessie points her chin toward the dugout. "Who were you talking to?"

Billy shrugs. "Ah, some guy. How's it going?"

"Some guy," Jessie says. "Wasn't that Dale Gosling?"

"Yeah, I think that's it," Billy says. "Why – you know him?"

"We talked about him the other day, remember?"

"Not really."

"You're full of shit."

"I remember something about it."

"I told you that he's Carroll Miller's campaign manager."

"That's right," Billy says. "You did tell me that. How do you know this stuff?"

"I watch something called the news," Jessie tells him. "It's on television regularly. And in the daily paper. You know – the part you throw away when looking for your name in the box scores. You should check it out – if you ever get tired of watching *Andy Griffith* reruns."

"Floyd the barber had a girlfriend the other night," Billy says. "That's not really in Floyd's wheelhouse."

"Look who's talking," Jessie says. She can see she's making Billy uncomfortable. "Back to the subject at hand. Why would you be talking to Dale Gosling?"

"He just stopped by for a chat," he says.

A chat, Jessie repeats to herself. When did Billy Crawford ever use a word like chat? "So I assume you were talking baseball?"

"Yeah," Billy says. "He's a fan."

The mower blades are getting heavy; Jessie turns and places them on the seat of the tractor, then wipes her hands with the rag again. "I figured that. I mean, why else would Carroll Miller's campaign manager want to talk to you? Seriously, Billy – what possible reason could he have?"

Billy turns and looks into the bleachers. He twists his neck back and forth to get rid of the kinks before turning back to Jessie. "So how often do you have to sharpen those mower blades?"

"You are too fucking much," she replies.

"What do you mean?"

"You really don't know how this looks, do you?" she says. "Or do you not care? Do you realize that you, Billy Crawford, are suddenly in a position to sway a mayoral election in this city?"

"Come on," Billy says. "I ain't going to sway shit. Everybody knows this is nothing but smoke and mirrors. Okay, I said I'd play along. What's it going to hurt? Do you really think it makes a difference, who wins the election? Politicians are all the same, talking out of both sides of their mouths. Slap you on the back with one hand while the other is in your pocket."

"Sounds like you don't have much respect for them in general," Jessie says.

"None."

"Then why do you want to be one?"

"Fucksakes, Jessie," Billy says. "I'm *not* one. I'm a ballplayer. All I've ever been and all I've ever wanted to be."

"But you're only a ballplayer now because you made a deal with Carroll Miller."

"You don't know anything of the damn kind," Billy says. "I told you the other day. They gave me my job back and *then* asked me to run. There was no trade-off."

"You're not stupid, Billy. We both know that's nonsense."

"You can believe anything you want," Billy says. "My job is to play baseball. And in case you haven't noticed, I've been pretty damn good at it lately." He hesitates. "The rest of it is all bullshit as far as I'm concerned."

"If it's all bullshit, why was Dale Gosling here?" Jessie asks. "What was that about?"

In that instant, Billy decides he might as well tell her the truth. On one hand, he's sick of the conversation and he's tired of being evasive. On the other, he finds that he's thrilled that Jessie is actually talking to him again. She's not being overly friendly but at least she's no longer shunning him outright. The fact is that he misses her company. He misses her knack for knocking him down a peg, he misses shooting pool with her and he misses her being in his bed. He's aware that there's a big leap from no longer being shunned to shooting pool or fucking, but for the time being he'll take what he can get.

"I have to be on this woman's TV show tomorrow," he says. "You know who Lisbeth Seville is?"

"Everybody knows who she is."

"Well, I got roped into going on her show," Billy says. "Old Dale whatshisname is worried I'm going to go on there and shit the bed. How many times does he think I've been interviewed in the past twenty years? I know how to do an interview."

"That's because you guys only talk in clichés," Jessie tells him.

"What guys?"

"Pro athletes," she says. She pauses, then lowers her voice a couple of octaves and her IQ by fifty points. "We gave a hundred and ten percent out there today. I was just looking for a pitch I could drive. There's no I in team. And a big shout-out to my homeys in Buttfuck, Alaska."

Billy grins. "Is that how we sound?"

"Pretty much," Jessie says.

"And you say there's a town in Alaska called Buttfuck?"

She ignores that. "How's that shit going to fly with Lisbeth Seville? She'll roast you like a Christmas goose."

"That's sort of what the Dale guy wanted to talk about. He thinks she's going to have a lot of questions about what went down between me and Carroll Miller. You know – sort of like you."

"And he wants you to lie about it."

Billy shrugs. "Seems like."

"So you're going to go on TV and lie your ass off," Jessie persists.

"I never said I would," Billy replies.

"Really?" she asks doubtfully. "You told him you wouldn't lie?"

"I never actually said that either. There's such a thing as deflection. You might think us ballplayers are a bunch of dummies, but I can tell you that I'm pretty good at changing the subject."

"You're not a dummy," Jessie says after a moment. "That's the thing that pisses me off in all of this."

Billy begins to speak then stops, not knowing where he stands. He exhales heavily. "I wish you wouldn't take it seriously, Jessie. I sure as hell don't."

"That's another thing that pisses me off."

TWENTY-FOUR

They gather in the den at Joe Simmons's house to watch the interview. Joe is there, of course, with Kate and Ben and Maria. For something as serious as the matter at hand, there's a festive mood in the room. Not quite the Grey Cup or Superbowl, but not a dirge either. Ben brings beer and Kate makes popcorn. Joe has a Scotch on the rocks at his elbow. The anticipation of what they're about to see is high. Up until this point, Billy Crawford has been the invisible candidate, and everyone is eager, if somewhat apprehensive, to hear what he has to say for himself.

"And all it took was a couple of barbed tweets," Ben says.

"The power of social media," Maria says. "For good or bad, I still haven't decided. I'm surprised he took the bait."

"I'm not," Joe says. "Not when it was Lisbeth setting the hook. She could sell fudgesicles to an Eskimo."

"You can't say Eskimo," Kate corrects him.

Joe has a drink and snorts. "Hey, I figure I can say whatever I want these days. I'm the one who got pushed out onto an ice floe." He grins at Kate. "Like a damn Inuit."

She smiles and shakes her head.

The show starts at seven. It's in studio, the same space where Kate talked to Lisbeth Seville a few weeks earlier. Billy Crawford wears a sports jacket with a blue dress shirt and no tie.

"What – no baseball cap?" Ben cracks. "How will his supporters even recognize the man?"

"Welcome to the show," Lisbeth says to begin. She sits across the glass-topped table from Billy, wearing a navy sheath, her hair tied behind her neck. She wears her trademark horn-rimmed glasses, which she removes periodically for effect. "I'm happy you could fit us in. I know how busy you are."

Billy nods seriously. "Big series this weekend against the Swamp Angels. You should come down and watch. I can fix you up with tickets if you like."

Maria is lifting a beer to her mouth, and she nearly spits it out. "What the hell? Did a candidate for mayor just offer a gift to the journalist interviewing him? Ooh – this is going to be fun."

Lisbeth throws Billy a lifeline. "Always good to start things with a joke," she says. "However, I wasn't referring to the baseball team. I was talking about your run for mayor in the upcoming election. We're just a month away. How's it been going?"

"Pretty good," Billy says. He thinks about the notes he'd been given by Daphne Lawrence. Not physically; they'd arrived at his house by Fedex. Billy hasn't seen Daphne since the night of the announcement at Shaky's. "The fans have been responding to our message."

"By fans, you mean voters, I assume?"

"Yeah," Billy says. He realizes the gaffe and takes a moment before smiling. "Fans can be voters and voters can be fans."

"And what are you hearing from them?" Lisbeth says. "What do they like about your campaign?"

Billy pauses. The only thing he's actually heard has been the crowd chanting his name whenever he gets a hit. That doesn't seem like a proper response now. "Well, they like the idea of new blood," he decides to tell her. That isn't in his notes, but he likes the sound of it.

"New blood," she repeats.

"You know – somebody from outside the world of politics. Somebody new to the game."

"I know what new blood means," Lisbeth says. "You're saying that you are that candidate?"

Billy nods. "Yes, I am."

Lisbeth regards him a moment before commenting. "Well, it's true that Zeb Zabrisky is a perennial candidate for mayor, but both Carroll Miller and Kate Simmons are running for the first time. If I'm not mistaken, they're both running for the first time for any position of power. Wouldn't that put them in the 'new blood' category as well?"

It's a valid point, Billy thinks. Apparently that's why that particular phrase isn't in his notes. Well, he can't take it back now. "Yes, it would. It means that the fans have a choice. We have three new candidates running. That can be a good thing. Options are a good thing."

"Again, when you say fans, you mean the voters."

"Right," Billy says. "It gives the voters options. And I know a little bit about options. I've been a professional ballplayer for nearly twenty years, so I've signed a lot of contracts. And options are usually a part of that. I'll give you an example. When I signed with the Redbirds back in '15, they offered a standard contract, X amount of dollars for the season. I could have gotten more, given my record, but I took it. But then I asked for bonuses based on a few things – number of plate appearances, number of hits and number of runs scored. If you check my stats for that season, you'll see I did pretty damn good with that particular contract."

Ben snorts. "Lisbeth has no idea what he's talking about. She doesn't know whether to shit or wind her watch."

Lisbeth does neither as she attempts to corral Billy. "I don't really understand how that relates to your campaign."

"Well, you brought up options," Billy says.

"Actually, I didn't," Lisbeth says. "Okay, let's move on from this. From what we're hearing from your people – and it's not a whole lot – it would seem that you are pretty much in lockstep with Kate Simmons on most of the bigger issues. Would you agree?"

"I have my own opinions on things," Billy says. "I really don't know what her views are. My ideas are –"

"Hold on," Lisbeth says. "Did you just say you don't know what your opponent's views are? How can that be possible? How can you suggest that you are the more viable *option* when you don't even know what she thinks?"

Billy shifts in his chair. "I didn't say I didn't know what her views were."

"You did," Lisbeth says. "That's exactly what you said."

"Well," Billy begins, "what I meant was that my views might be different from hers. We need more affordable childcare, we need the LRT, and I'm against the greenbelt thing. I mean I'm *for* the greenbelt staying . . . well, green."

"Those are precisely Kate Simmons's views."

Billy smiles. "Well, she sounds like a smart woman."

Maria whoops, spilling popcorn on her lap. "I can't believe we don't have to pay for this!"

"What the fuck is he doing?" Ben asks.

"Digging a hole," Joe says. "Like a mad gopher."

Lisbeth shifts gears. "Let's talk about one of your other opponents. Carroll Miller happens to be your boss on the baseball team, correct?"

"I wouldn't say that," Billy says. "That's not how it works. The general manager is the boss up in the office, and the manager is the boss on the field. Carroll Miller is just the owner."

"You're splitting hairs."

Billy shrugs and smiles again.

"For a guy who's basically sinking in quicksand, he sure smiles a lot," Maria says. "Then again, he has a good smile."

"Okay," Lisbeth says. "The fact is you're a member of the Rose City Rounders and you're running for office against the *owner* of the team. Have you talked to Carroll Miller about this?"

"About the Rounders?" Billy asks.

"Her head is going to explode," Kate says, watching Lisbeth.

"About the election," Lisbeth says patiently. "Since you

announced your candidacy, have you talked to Carroll Miller about the fact you're running against him?"

"No," Billy says truthfully. "I haven't seen the man since I announced."

"And he never asked you to run for mayor?" Lisbeth persists.

"Here we go," Joe says.

"He never asked me to run for anything," Billy says. It's true, if barely so. It was Dale Gosling who first did the asking. He was obviously doing Carroll's bidding but Billy manages to convince himself that wasn't the question.

Lisbeth leans forward. "I'm asking because there's a theory out there that you got your job back with the team because you agreed to run for mayor on a platform that strongly resembles that of Kate Simmons, ostensibly splitting the vote and opening the door for Mr. Miller to win the election."

"Wow, that's a crazy theory," Billy says. "Where did you hear that?"

"Frankly, everywhere," Lisbeth says. "Is there any truth to it?"

"I'll tell you what's true," Billy says. "I got my job back with the team because I'm a pretty good player. Since returning to the lineup, I'm hitting .392 with an on-base percentage of nearly .500 and a slugging percentage of almost .700. *That* is why I got my job back."

"You're saying there is no quid pro quo with Carroll Miller?" Lisbeth asks.

"Hell, I don't even know what that means," Billy says. "I'm from Saskatchewan, lady."

Lisbeth actually smiles at that. "One more question, Billy. Do you want to be mayor of Rose City?"

"Absolutely," Billy says.

Lisbeth wraps it up after that. Billy is relieved to be finished but his heart is heavy. He'd made it through the entire interview without lying, until the last question.

Sonofabitch.

At the Simmons house, Kate mutes the TV, then looks at the others.

"Well," Maria says. "That was . . . um . . . I don't even know what that was."

"A disaster," Ben says. "That's what it was."

It was a disaster. There is little disagreement about the assessment, not from the mainstream media, or the numerous social platforms. Virtually everyone agrees that Billy Crawford's only interview to date was a crash and burn not seen since the *Hindenburg*. In the words of one blogger, Billy's sit-down with Lisbeth Seville could not have gone worse if he had "taken a dump on her desk."

The next day his numbers go up.

In a poll conducted by the Rose City *Standard*, Billy's approval rating goes from ten points to twelve. Carroll Miller remains at forty, while Kate Simmons drops to thirty-eight. The rest of those in the survey are either undecided or in the Zeb Zabrisky camp.

"It's working," Dale tells Carroll the day the numbers are released. "I have no idea how or why but it's working. This guy might be the worst candidate in the history of the world."

"People are stupid," Carroll says. He's at his desk, his feet up, remote in hand as he surfs through the channels on the screen against the wall. The sound is muted.

"I don't think they're this stupid," Dale replies. "It's the whole pro athlete thing. Guy's a hero because he has a talent for hitting a baseball. How that translates into anything else is what has always baffled me. I wouldn't hire the guy to walk my dog, but people out there think he can run the city?"

Carroll laughs. "Apparently twelve percent of them do."

Dales shakes his head. "Used to be that our heroes were soldiers or statesmen or the like. Athletes were second-class citizens. There was a time when a pro golfer wasn't allowed in the clubhouse at St Andrews, even if he won the Open."

"How the fuck do you know this shit?" Carroll asks.

"I just do," Dale says. "I read a lot when I was a kid."

"You read about golf when you should have been playing golf," Carroll tells him. "Then maybe you wouldn't suck so bad at the game today." He watches something on the TV a moment before moving on. "I'd like to play St Andrews someday. Hey, if I get elected, maybe we can do some sort of thing with the mayor of St Andrews. He comes here for a round with me, and I go there to play the Old Course with him. What do you think?"

I think you should be focusing on getting elected, not playing golf in Scotland, Dale thinks. He gestures to the copy of the *Standard* on the desk. "Well, if those numbers continue, it won't be *if* you get elected. This is playing out better than I ever imagined."

"Hold on," Carroll says, looking at the screen.

There's tape of a reporter from one of the cable stations interviewing people on the street downtown. The subject, according to the scrawl beneath the video, is Billy Crawford and his candidacy. Carroll unmutes the set.

"He tells it like it is," a man in a Maple Leafs T-shirt is saying. "None of this double-talk."

"He's not in anybody's pocket," a woman says.

"He's a guy you could sit and have a beer with," a young man in a hoodie suggests. The man slurs his words; he appears to have been sitting with someone having a few already.

"He doesn't swing and miss," the last Crawford fan says.

"Whatever the fuck that means," Carroll says as he turns the TV off. "So – what's next?"

"Next I think you should reconsider doing an interview with Lisbeth Seville," Dale says. "After the shit show with Crawford, all you have to do is not fall off your chair and you'll look like the second coming of Wilfrid Laurier."

"Who?" Carroll glances at his watch, usually a sign that he's due on a golf course somewhere.

"You'll look good, is all I'm saying," Dale tells him. "Hit your marks. Keep in mind that a lot of people in the city are in favour of opening up the greenbelt. I'm talking about people who want to move out of the city and either can't find a place or can't find anything they can afford. These people aren't as vocal as those opposed, but they're going to vote. And as of right now, you've got the numbers in your favour. Why not burnish them by talking to Seville?"

"If the numbers are on my side, why do I need to talk to that snooty bitch?" Carroll asks.

There it is, Dale thinks.

"Listen, I know you have history with the woman," he says.

"What history?" Carroll demands.

Dale hesitates. "I know that at one point you were . . . interested . . . in her. On a social level."

"Bullshit," Carroll says. "If I wanted her, I would have had her. Truth of the matter is, she was calling me up." He warms to the idea; however false it is. "I eventually had to tell her that I wasn't into it. So you see why I don't want to sit down with her? Woman's got an axe to grind with me and she just might decide to grind it on TV."

Dale says nothing. He knows the story is false but then he's learned to live with that side of Carroll. Everybody has. Carroll looks at his watch again, then stands up.

"I have to run," he says.

"Where are you headed?"

Carroll gives him the look that says mind your own business. "I have a meeting."

"Hit 'em straight," Dale says.

TWENTY-FIVE

The Swamp Angels are in town for a four-game tilt, starting Thursday night. For the past few weeks, Billy has been showing up at the stadium around mid-afternoon for a night game. He likes to get his running in and then spend time in the batting cage. Once again, it's all about routine. But Thursday afternoon, he switches things up. He drives to Shaky's for lunch and a couple of beers, then goes home and has a nap. Rising, he dresses in track pants and runners and does a half-dozen laps around the city park located a few blocks from his house. Then he goes home and watches TV until half past five, when he heads for the stadium.

The change in regimen is no accident and is wholly due to his interview the previous night. Well, not the entire interview. What has him out of sorts this morning is the last question Lisbeth Seville had posed, and Billy's lie when answering. She'd set him up, asking if he wanted to be mayor, and Billy has no doubt she knew exactly that when she asked it. What is bothering Billy now is that he hadn't managed to avoid answering. He's done hundreds of on-camera interviews over the course of his career, and he's learned how to slip a punch like a good welterweight.

But last night had been different. Under the circumstances, it would have been impossible to tell the truth. How could a man running for mayor announce on TV that he had no desire to be mayor? In Billy's mind, he had no choice but to lie. There was no dodge that would have appeared as anything but just that – a dodge.

The lie itself isn't what's bothering him today. People lie occasionally and, when it comes to politicians, Billy is of the mind that they lie constantly. It comes with the territory. If he is a politician

– or at least pretending to be one – then isn't he allowed to play fast and loose with the truth? Presumably people take everything out of a candidate's mouth with a grain of salt anyway. No, what is eating at Billy today is not that he lied on TV about wanting to be mayor, it's that he did it after assuring Jessie that he wouldn't lie for Carroll Miller or anybody else. Billy doesn't know if Jessie was watching last night, but it didn't matter; surely by now she knows what happened.

It's Billy's anguish over what Jessie might think that leads him to run his laps in the park and show up late to the stadium. The hope, of course, is that he won't have reason to run into her. By the time he arrives, she and the crew will have the field ready for play. If Billy avoids batting practice, there's a chance he won't see Jessie at all. That's the plan for today, at least. He's not quite sure what he'll do tomorrow.

Or the day after that.

He's surprised that he's so torn about her, or more specifically over what he assumes her reaction will be. Since first hooking up with her in the spring, he's never considered whatever was happening between them to be anything more than a fling. Billy has had plenty of flings. One girlfriend had told him, as she was walking out the door, that he was the poster boy for non-commitment. It might have been a joke, but she wasn't smiling when she said it.

So why is this – whatever this is – with Jessie any different? Admittedly, she is the only woman he's ever known who can take the mickey out of him without him getting pissed off over it. She's also the first woman who has ever beat him at pool. She has a decent fastball, a tongue as sharp as a laser and she's tough as nails. Tougher than Billy, but he would never tell her that.

Billy tries to convince himself that she's just another woman. He's been with a number of women, and he guesses Jessie has been with a few men. Billy has assumed all along they would have their fun and then move on. He suspects she feels the same way. She's kept him at arm's length as much or more as he has her. She won't even tell him where she lives. So why is he so troubled about last night that he's avoiding her today? Why does he think she even cares? And since when did he begin to care about her caring?

Billy doesn't have any answers. All he knows for sure is that running for mayor is a pain in the ass, and pretending to run for mayor is an even larger pain.

He's the last player to walk in the clubhouse. That in itself is an oddity. The Rounders manager, Erskine, stands just inside the door, looking at a clipboard in his hand. Figuring out the lineup, no doubt. He raises his eyebrows when he sees Billy's late arrival but says nothing. There might have been a time when the manager would consider sitting a player who shows up late, but there's not a manager on earth who would sit a player hitting nearly .400 over the past six weeks. Besides that, Billy hasn't been late to a game all season. Erskine will cut him some slack.

Lefty McQuire is, naturally, not so circumspect.

"Look at the big TV star, dragging his ass in here at this hour," he says. "What – did your limo have a flat tire?"

"That's it," Billy says, not rising to the jab. He goes to his locker and starts to undress.

"I caught your little interview last night," Lefty presses.

"The Cartoon Network down again?" Billy asks.

"You looked like you were about to shit your britches," Lefty says.

"Nah, you done great, Billy," the reliever Scotty tells him. "Don't listen to this shitbird."

"Watch who you're calling names," Lefty snaps. "I'll hit you in the mouth."

"You can't hit the strike zone," Scotty tells him. "How you gonna hit my mouth?"

With bigger fish to fry, Lefty waves him off and wanders over to Billy. He has a baseball in his hand and he's tossing it in the air and catching it.

"So what's the deal with that Lisbeth chick? She's kinda hot, you know. She's gotta be, what, fifty or so? I don't usually go for older women but I'd give her a spin. That is, if she begged me." He looks around the room, smirking at the other players. "On her knees."

"I'm sure she'd be honoured," Billy says. "Young buck like yourself, willing to give her a thrill."

Even on his sharpest days, Lefty is somewhat obtuse.

"Seriously?" he asks. "Would you, like, be willing to give her my number? Tell her to hit me up."

Billy hangs his jeans in his locker and sits down to pull on his socks. He takes a moment, thinking about it. Telling himself not to do it. Let sleeping dogs lie and all that.

He does it anyway.

"I probably shouldn't tell you this, but she's a huge Rounders fan and she was asking about you. Why not fire her off a text? Take the bull by the horns, Lefty. Women like that."

"She was asking about me?" Lefty says.

Billy shrugs. "By name. Word is, she has a thing for younger guys. Hard on my ego, I have to tell you."

"Give me her number."

Billy goes into his phone and finds Scoop Sutherland's number. Billy hasn't called it since Dale insisted Scoop give it to him, and he never will. He shows the display to Lefty, who enters the number in his own phone.

"And she really asked about me?"

"Asked about you is an understatement, big guy," Billy says. "She actually said she'd love to see you with your shirt off. Big TV personality like that, I was kinda shocked. But – well, you know women."

Lefty is excited now. "Fuck, I'm going to send her a selfie."

He heads back to his locker. Billy is happy that Lefty isn't tonight's starting pitcher. He'd be lucky to hit the backstop, what with visions of Lisbeth Seville dancing in his empty head. Billy pulls his jersey on and then notices Erskine, watching him from a few feet away. Billy smiles sheepishly.

"I don't know whose phone number you just gave him," Erskine says. "But I know whose number it's not."

The Rounders eight-game winning streak comes to an end that night as the Swamp Angels pound them by a score of 12–2. It was bound to happen; all streaks must end. But the Swampers are a mediocre team this year. Befitting their name, they are mired in last place and their pitching staff is statistically the worst in the league. Tonight, they send a twenty-year-old rookie to the mound for his first start in Triple A, and all the kid does is shut down the red-hot Rounders offence for seven innings. A two-run homer by Scotty in the bottom of the ninth accounts for the home team's scoring, long after the contest has been decided and half the fans have left.

More significantly, Billy "Hizzoner" Crawford wears the collar, going zero for five at the plate, with three strikeouts. It's Billy's worst showing, by far, since his return to the team weeks earlier. Afterward, Billy writes it off as a bad night, at least initially. He's gone hitless plenty of times in his career. But then his mind gets to working and he wonders if there's more at work here. Being a typically superstitious ballplayer, Billy believes in karma, at least some of the time. He shouldn't have changed his routine, even if keeping with it might have meant running into Jessie. He should have done his running at the stadium, not the city park. And he should have taken batting practice. And maybe he shouldn't have played a trick on Lefty McQuire, although Lefty is basically a shit-disturbing dimwit who had it coming.

And maybe – just maybe – he shouldn't have lied to Lisbeth Seville.

He showers and dresses quickly after the game. Scoop Sutherland approaches, snidely looking for a comment on the oh-for-five and Billy asks the little shit if he'd like another shower. Scoop backs off but holds the smirk. Billy wonders if he'll still be smirking later when he receives a shirtless selfie on his phone from Lefty McQuire.

Billy gets into his truck and drives to Shaky's, at least maintaining this part of his routine. When he gets there though, sitting behind the wheel in the parking lot, he decides he isn't in the mood for Shaky's. The whole day has been a wash-out. Drinking beer under the judgmental eye of Suzanne and the rest of Shaky's gang isn't going to improve on it. Not only that, but lately he's been approached more and more frequently by people who want to talk to him about his political views, now that he's a bona fide candidate for mayor. Billy isn't interested in sharing opinions he doesn't have.

He decides to head home and to bed, even though he's not tired in the least. Maybe he'll see if there's anything on TV. He wants to call Jessie, or at least text her to see if she responds, but then he's afraid that she won't, which will make him feel even worse. All in all, he's had a lousy day, from the moment he got up this morning, and there's nothing at this late hour that will change that.

Running for mayor is a pain in the ass.

TWENTY-SIX

Jeremy's there when Kate returns from her run Friday morning.

She'd been up late with Ben and Maria the night before, at the campaign office downtown, trying to determine just what they might do to combat what was being referred to in the media as the "Crawford bump." They bought pizza and beer and sat around the plywood-topped table in the centre of the room. Ben was in a thirsty mood, outdrinking the women two to one. By midnight, he'd become morose and pessimistic.

"He's polling at fourteen percent," Maria said. "Since when is fourteen percent a bump?"

"When those fourteen points should be ours," Ben told her. He looked over at Kate. "You need to go back on Lisbeth's show. And talk a lot of nonsense when you get there."

"Why would I do that?"

Ben had shrugged. "It worked for the ballplayer."

After that, he opened yet another Bud Light and sat slumped in his chair, allowing the others to do the strategizing.

"The next debate is going to be key," Maria said. "You kicked Miller's ass the last time out, and you'll do it again. What we don't need is for Crawford to show up. Hopefully he won't. So far the two schoolkids running his campaign have been extremely non-committal."

"How can he refuse to appear?" Kate asked. "How can a debate be optional?"

"Keep in mind this guy isn't exactly a traditional candidate," Maria had replied. "They're promoting him as the *non-politician*. Not showing up to a debate dovetails perfectly into that whole outsider image."

"Jesus H. Christ," Kate sighed. "So showing up the first time gave him a bump and not showing up the second time might give him another? This guy has a horseshoe up his ass. He should be buying lottery tickets, not running for office."

"But we don't want him there," Maria said.

Ben came back to life then. "Maria is right about that. I mean, think about it. You got Carroll Miller on one side, and you and the ballplayer on the other. Isn't that just playing into their hands?"

They all fall silent for a time.

"I suppose you're right," Kate finally agreed. "But I hate to give the guy a free pass like that."

"Pick your poison," Ben said. "Is it better to have him there or not?"

Maria had sighed. "I swear, this fucking election is like nothing I've ever seen. I'm not sure about anything anymore."

Kate doesn't get home until two in the morning and so she sleeps in until eight o'clock, unusual for her. When she comes downstairs, Joe is sitting outside with his coffee and newspaper. The sun is up and shining bright, not a cloud in the sky. Kate watches him from the kitchen window for a bit, thinking about how normal he looks. Did he really need to quit the race? But as she watches, Joe lifts his coffee to his mouth, clutching the cup in both hands. He shakes so badly he can barely drink without spilling.

Kate has a glass of orange juice, then heads out on her run. She'd had enough beer the night before that she is a little groggy this morning. To clear her head, she takes the longer route, along the river to the Walden Bridge, across into the park and back, a distance of roughly eight kilometres.

She woke up feeling discouraged. Usually, a run helps to shake her from the doldrums, but this morning is an exception. Last night's strategy session had produced nothing of an encouraging nature. With all that has happened since she announced her candidacy, Kate feels that she should be in a good position. She's agreed to every interview, appeared at every venue and stated her positions over and over without contradiction. She has the name recognition, which is no small thing as it links her to the man considered the best mayor the city has ever known. Her opponents are a septuagenarian pothead who has virtually vanished from the public eye, a slippery developer with motives so obvious a toddler could spot them and a professional baseball player who is, frankly, somewhere out in left field.

She should be in the catbird seat, but clearly she is not. It's true that she's been called out for parachuting into the race, and that there have been the expected accusations of nepotism. But is the latter necessarily a bad thing? It worked for the Roosevelts and the Kennedys; the Trudeaus too.

In any case, that's not really the problem. The problem is Billy Crawford. For someone with a zero chance of winning, he's certainly thrown a monkey wrench into things, even if the man seems blissfully unaware of the fact. But maybe that's an act too; maybe he knows exactly what's going on. Maybe he even gets a kick out of tilting the field in Carroll Miller's favour. The man is his boss, after all. Maybe Crawford is not the shitkicker he portrays but just a garden variety ass-kisser. Either way, Kate has to wonder where her poll numbers would be if he wasn't in the race.

She's feeling both helpless and hapless as she nears the house at the end of her run. From the river path she can see her father, still in his Muskoka chair on the patio. He's not alone though. The man sitting a few feet away is all too recognizable.

The moment she arrives in the yard, Joe gets up and goes into the house, his body language suggesting he's been waiting for her return so he can do just that. He doesn't say a word to Kate, or to the man who was sitting beside him, the man who Kate had until a few months ago called her husband.

Jeremy stands when she crosses the patio, but she doesn't get close to him. He may have had notions of giving her a hug and that isn't about to happen.

"Well now," she says and afterward she kicks herself for it. That's the best she can come up with – *well now*? What would the feisty female protagonist in a movie say in such a situation? What would Rosalind Russell say to Cary Grant? Something pithy and cutting and funny, no doubt. *I got nothing*, Kate thinks.

She sits down a few feet away, keeping the table between them. After a moment's awkwardness, he smiles. *He looks good*, she hates to admit to herself. He's wearing suit pants and a shirt and tie. His jacket, she assumes, is in the car. His hair is carefully mussed.

"I swear your old man would like to gut me like a fish," he says. "I barely got a hello out of him. What have you been telling the old fart?"

"About you?" Kate shrugs. "I really can't recall the last time your name even came up around here. Been awhile."

"Oh, I just bet."

"You always were good at flattering yourself," Kate tells him. "Why are you here? Your girlfriend off at summer camp?"

Now that was more in line with Rosalind Russell.

It seems as if he hesitates, weighing whether or not to respond to the girlfriend jibe, but decides against. "I have a hearing at the courthouse this afternoon," he says. "Civil matter that I'll have thrown out. One of these nonsense suits but I have to make an appearance to get it tossed. Thought I'd stop and say hello. I've been reading about you."

Kate looks at him evenly but says nothing. She'd like a cup of coffee but she can hardly go inside to fetch herself a cup without offering one to him, and she's not exactly in the offering frame of mind, not when it comes to him. His appearance has done nothing to dissolve the negative thoughts she's been entertaining since getting out of bed.

"This election you people have going is a real clusterfuck, isn't it?" Jeremy asks then.

You people, she thinks. *Go fuck yourself.* "Aren't they all to some extent?" she smiles coolly.

"Yeah, but this one is a dog's breakfast. You got Donald Trump Lite, you got Casey at the Bat, and then you have Kate Simmons, the prodigal daughter. Oh, and the old dude with the beard who fell off his bike." He regards her a moment before laughing. "Are the film rights available?"

She debates for a moment challenging the word *prodigal* again, as she had done with Maria, but decides at once to let it go. It's nothing more than semantics and, besides, he's not worth the effort. "Not to sound like a broken record, but why are you here?"

"I told you. I have court this afternoon."

"That's why you're in Rose City. I asked why you are *here*."

Jeremy extends his arms, palms up. It's a gesture familiar to Kate, his go-to move when pontificating, whether in a courtroom or with his buddies at a bar. "I'm here because I'm concerned. This mayoral run is turning into an albatross for you. It's like that old song – you've got clowns on one side and jokers on the other. Do you really want to be part of that? Worse yet, do you want to be part of that and ultimately lose? That's going to follow you around forever."

"There are worse things to be known for," she says pointedly.

"Jesus Christ," he replies, but again won't engage in any conversation about his personal life.

"Besides, what makes you think I'm going to lose?" she asks.

"The most recent polls, for one," he replies. "The writing's on the wall. Miller has this Crawford character in his pocket and he's using him to split the vote. Which is going to fuck you in the end. My political friends in Toronto are watching this and they are amazed by what they are seeing. And they're telling me to advise you to bail now, while you can."

"Oh, your *political* friends in Toronto are worried about me," Kate says.

"Don't be like that," Jeremy says. "People care about you."

"For fucksakes. Listen to you."

He shakes his head in annoyance, as if he's miffed that he's telling her something for her own good and being ignored for his effort. He looks out over the river for a moment before turning back to her. "Would you have any coffee around here?"

"I think we're out."

"Sure you are," he says. "Okay, you want to know why I'm here. I'll tell you. We are swamped at work. Sheryl just went on mat leave and Jeff took a job in Calgary. We've been talking about you. I think we have an idea that can serve the firm and at the same time allow you to bow out of this calamity here and save face while doing it. You've no doubt heard that Micro-Tech is doing that merger with Spirit. We want you to come back and take the lead on it. Connie Weston over there asked for you."

Whatever Kate had been expecting, it wasn't this. "You're here to ask me to come back?"

"Yes," Jeremy says. "But as a partner. Before you say anything more, I can tell you that I know what the mayor's job here pays and you'll be making three times that at the firm. And let's keep in mind that the mayor's job pays absolutely nothing if you don't get elected mayor."

Kate feels her blood rising. "You do realize that I just quit the firm a few months ago. And you do recall why, right?"

"You have to let that stuff go," Jeremy says. "People get divorced all the time, Kate. They grow apart. They develop different interests. The fact is, most couples remain on good terms, and yes, some couples even keep working together."

"Does she still text you pics of her tits?" Kate asks. "I heard you liked to show them to the boys down at Hannigan's Pub. Well, before you decided she was the love of your life."

"Let it go," he says sternly. "I'm here with a business proposition. A very good business proposition. You've always been the smartest woman I know, Kate. You should take it."

Kate gets to her feet. "The problem is, Jeremy, I have a business proposition here. I made a commitment to a bunch of people, and one of them is my father. You know – the man who taught me that it's important to keep my commitments. That overrides everything else. If you came here thinking you could charm me back into the firm, you'd have to be Cary Grant. And you sir, are no Cary Grant."

She leaves him sitting at the table, looking confused.

Inside, she pours herself a cup of coffee and sips it while looking out the window. Jeremy remains seated at the table for a few minutes. He might be thinking that she'll regret her attitude and return to the conversation – and the offer. There was probably a time when she would have done just that, but those days were in the rearview. When he finally stands and makes his way out of the yard, he glances toward the window, and she raises her cup to him.

Farewell, motherfucker.

For the rest of the day, though, her thoughts keep returning to the offer. She attempts to look at it without bias. What if somebody other than her cheating ex-husband had come to her with an identical proposal? It was pretty appealing, and even more appealing now that the latest polls show her losing the election to the slippery eel Carroll Miller. It's unfortunately true that in a month or less, Kate might very well be standing in the unemployment line. At that time, handling a merger like Micro-Tech and Spirit would be extremely appealing.

Around four that afternoon, she walks out to the patio with her phone and brings up Connie Weston's number. Connie answers on the first ring; Kate's number is obviously still in her contacts.

"Kate Simmons," she says. "How are you?"

"I'm okay. How are you, Connie?"

"Ah, you know, plugging along," Connie tells her. "I've been reading about you and your mayoral campaign. Pretty exciting stuff."

Kate laughs. "At this point, that's not the first word that comes to mind." She hesitates. "Your name came up today, Connie."

"How so?"

"I had the pleasure of a visit from my ex-husband. He was telling me that the firm is handling your big merger and he offered me a promotion to come back and manage the deal. He said you requested me?"

Connie falls quiet.

"You there?" Kate asks.

"I'm here," Connie says. "You don't mind if I speak frankly, Kate. Your ex-husband is playing fast and loose with the facts. I did ask for you, but it was three months ago, before you announced for mayor. I would never interfere with that."

Kate considers this. "But why would he show up here today, if someone else there is handling things?"

"I'll tell you why," Connie says. "It's because I told him I wanted you, and if I couldn't have you, I'd be taking it to another firm. Which is exactly what I'm going to do. I don't have any more use for Jeremy than you do at this point."

"Fuck," Kate says. "He knows he's losing you, so he comes here with his desperate little pitch."

"That's about the size of it."

"That sonofabitch," Kate says. "Okay, thanks for the info. We need to have dinner sometime."

"Sounds good. Get yourself elected mayor, girl," Connie says. "You'll be good at it."

I hope so, Kate thinks as she quits the call. Her other post-election option just flew out the window.

"Good riddance," she says.

TWENTY-SEVEN

Carroll calls Dale at home the night before, waking him at a quarter to midnight, to tell him they're going to Brownsville the next morning. Dale is out like a light when his cellphone rings, but he comes to and answers it in the dark. He is used to the late calls. Carroll Miller is a nighthawk, while Dale likes to be in bed by ten o'clock. Maggie has given up on suggesting he turn his cell off when he goes to bed. He has tried it, and it only serves to infuriate Carroll when he can't reach Dale on his whim.

They meet for breakfast at a place called the Country Café on the highway. Carroll is there when Dale walks in, drinking coffee and reading the paper. When Dale sits down opposite, he notices that it's yesterday's edition of the *Standard*, meaning there must be something of a positive nature regarding Carroll inside. Otherwise, he wouldn't be carrying it around with him.

Carroll has already ordered. Dale asks for coffee and an egg white omelette. Carroll's pancakes and sausage arrive a few moments later.

"What's with this egg white omelette shit?" Carroll asks, slathering his stack with syrup. "You got something against yolks?"

"I have to watch my cholesterol," Dale tells him. "I've told you that."

"Shit, you tell me so many things," Carroll says. "You think I remember them all?"

"My father died of a heart attack when he was forty-seven," Dale says.

But Carroll is finished with the egg white discussion. He shovels a forkful of pancakes in his mouth and pushes the newspaper over to Dale. "If we can believe this editorial, I'm going to be mayor."

Dale had seen the piece twenty-four hours earlier. He reads the *Standard* online over coffee every morning. What Carroll says is true, or at least partly true. The op-ed basically says that if the trend in the polls continue, Carroll will be elected. What Carroll, typically, hasn't noticed is that the piece is intended as an urgent call-to-arms to the citizenry. Rather than extolling the possibility of a Carroll Miller victory, it's warning against that outcome. Indeed, the last line urges voters to "wake up" or suffer the consequences. Dale suspects that Carroll, given his severely crimped attention span, never read that far.

"I saw that," Dale says. "Not a surprise. The election is a couple weeks away and you're leading in the polls." He pauses, wondering if he should point out the obvious. With Carroll, it's usually necessary. "You realize that this isn't any kind of endorsement, right? The *Standard* has already endorsed Kate Simmons."

Carroll spears a sausage with his knife and puts it in his mouth whole. "Fuck 'em," he says around the mouthful. "They might have endorsed her but they're telling people I'm going to win. I'll take it."

Dale begins to reply but then doesn't. He has followed Carroll down the op-ed rabbit hole as far as he wants to this morning. Carroll has decided that the piece is a feather in his cap, and he won't be dissuaded in that. He's a master of picking and choosing what he wants to believe. Dale sips his coffee and waits for his meal. The place isn't busy; presumably the early-morning crowd has come and gone. None of the remaining customers or wait staff seem to have recognized Carroll Miller. It seems odd to Dale that the leading contending for the mayor's job in a place like Rose City wouldn't be recognized but he guesses that's the way of the world these days. Pop singers and movie stars get recognized; municipal leaders do not, even if calling Carroll Miller a leader is a bit of a stretch.

Dale's omelette arrives and he picks up his fork and begins to eat. Carroll has inhaled his own meal by now. He sits back, wiping his mouth on a napkin as he watches Dale.

"Does that even taste like eggs?" he asks. "With no yolks, how can it even taste like eggs?"

Dale gestures to his plate. "Try a forkful."

"No fucking way."

Dale shrugs his indifference to Carroll's palate. "So what are we doing out here this morning anyway?"

Carroll leans forward to tap the newspaper with a forefinger. "We're not the only ones reading this. If people begin to see me as the next mayor, then they know the greenbelt surrounding Rose City is going to open up wide. I want to visit our three farmer friends to make sure they haven't been entertaining offers from anybody else. I have no intention of going through all this fucking aggravation just to have them sell out to some speculator. Some fucking opportunist."

Dale looks up, thinking that Carroll has just described himself. "But I thought you had them locked in. They've received down payments, right?"

Carroll coyly tilts his head back and forth, as if deciding whether or not to share. "Not exactly."

"What does that mean?" Dale asks. "I thought these properties were locked in."

"There are letters of intent," Carroll says. "We've agreed on the bare bones of the transactions." He pauses. "But no money has changed hands."

"Are you saying these three farmers can sell to somebody else if they want?"

"Technically, yes," Carroll says. "Hey, we're looking at a cost of over two million a farm. Did you really think I was going to shell out six million dollars on some fucking farmland and then find out I can't develop it? I was born at night, but it wasn't last night."

Dale looks around to signal the waitress for more coffee. He waits until she pours refills for them both.

"So what's your move now?" he asks.

"Now?" Carroll replies. "Now I'm feeling good enough to lay down some cash. A hundred thousand apiece, I'm thinking, should keep them happy. Promise them the rest when the rezoning goes through. Which should happen within the year, once I'm the deciding vote on council. Maybe sooner than that. It's going to be priority number one once I take office."

"Are you sure the owners are open to that? A hundred grand to hold two million at large?"

"Why wouldn't they be?" Carroll asked. "They're farmers. A hundred grand to them is like winning the fucking lottery."

Dale isn't convinced of that, but again he sees little point in mentioning it. For some unknown reason, Carroll considers modern-day farmers to be stereotypes right out of the Waltons, bartering eggs and butter for trade goods down at the general store. Of course, nothing could be further from the truth, but once Carroll has convinced himself of something, that's it. Dale sips his coffee in silence for a bit, then glances over to the newspaper again, still folded open to the op-ed, the title of which is "Carroll Miller's Inside Track."

"We need to talk about the debate next week," he says. "Last time out, it did not help your numbers. We can't have that happen again. Have you given any more thought to going on Seville's show beforehand?"

"I'm not fucking doing that so stop asking me," Carroll snaps. "I might even skip the debate. I'm leading in the polls. Let them come after me."

"You can't skip the debate." Dale taps a forefinger on the newspaper. "This op-ed is based on one thing: the polls. You skip the debate and your numbers will drop, I guarantee you."

"You guarantee me, do you?" Carroll asked, mockingly. "You really think you know everything, don't you? If you're so fucking smart, then how come I'm a billionaire and you're still a fucking flunky?"

I'm not a flunky, Dale thinks. *And you're not really a billionaire.*

"I know this," Dale says. "You fail to show and it looks like you don't care. Or worse yet – you're afraid to face Kate Simmons a second time. That could finish you. You have to be there. But this time it will be easier."

"And why's that?"

"Because this time Billy Crawford will be there," Dale tells him. "All you need to do is keep it to a minimum, push your main talking points early on, then hit the mute button while you sit back and watch Crawford and Kate Simmons take each other down, basically by agreeing with each other. You might wake up the next day with a ten-point lead. And that's game over."

Carroll stares across the table, his hand stroking his chin. Dale can see him imagining the scene. Carroll has always had a fertile imagination, especially when it features himself in scenarios where he is the hero. The star. The fact that he lives inside his head so much of the time is what makes it so difficult for Dale to get through to him.

Carroll finishes his coffee and gets to his feet. "I do like the sound of that," he says. "Grab breakfast, will you? I left my wallet in the car."

They leave Carroll's Mercedes in the parking lot and take Dale's car into the valley. The sky is clear as they crest the hill, overlooking to the south the farms in question. The fields are sun-soaked, the corn eight feet high, the fields of soybeans lush and beginning to turn colour. Halfway down the sloping two-lane highway, Carroll orders Dale to pull over.

"I want a look at what I'm about to buy."

Dale parks on the gravel shoulder and kills the ignition. The farmland that is the object of Carroll's schemes and desires covers half the little valley, reaching from the bottom of the escarpment to the west and almost to the Chalk River to the east. Carroll studies the landscape, nodding his head slightly as he envisions the future of the valley. Dale watches him, wondering what he sees. Thousands of new housing units? A shopping mall? Maybe a park to contain the untold number of kids who will eventually live here? Not a park, Dale realizes. That's not Carroll's style. There's no money in a park.

Carroll glances to the east, to the fifty-acre piece that separates the object farms from the river. There's a Jeep parked in front of the rundown house. Carroll gestures to the place.

"What's the status on that shithole?"

"Last I heard, the owners still won't budge," Dale says.

"Last you heard?" Carroll replies. "Have you even talked to them again?"

"Jocko's been handling it," Dale says. "I've been busy with your campaign; in case you haven't noticed."

Carroll gives him a look. "Kinda touchy today, Dale old man. Those egg whites upset your delicate tummy?"

Up yours, Dale thinks.

"So what are these people saying?" Carroll asks. "I assume they're holding out for more money. Maybe it's time we upped the offer, given my poll numbers. I really want that river property. Those would be prime lots."

"Like I said, Jocko has the reins," Dale says again. "I haven't touched base with him in a while."

"Maybe we should drive down there and knock on the door," Carroll suggests.

"That won't do any good," Dale tells him. He's told Carroll this before, but the information obviously didn't take. "The owner died, remember? One of the grandkids is in charge of the probate and he's in Vancouver."

"What's his fucking problem?" Carroll asks. "He doesn't like money?"

"From what I was told, he wouldn't mind selling but he's being cagey. My assumption is that he's aware of what's going on here, and he knows that a zoning change in this valley will jack the property prices sky high. He's playing a waiting game."

Carroll shakes his head in disapproval. "So who owns the Jeep?"

"No idea. Maybe they rent the place out."

"Who would rent a dump like that?"

Dale doesn't have an answer and doesn't attempt one. "What is the plan here? Do these owners know we're coming?"

"No," Carroll replies. "I figure it'll be more impressive if I show up at the door with a hundred grand in hand. That's a good start to anyone's day, don't you think?"

"You have the money with you?" Dale asks.

"Not exactly," Carroll says. "I make the offer and then you step in and tell them what a great thing it is they're doing. You know, how they're about to be a part of progress and growth. That's why you're here; you have the gift of gab. These dumb fucks will eat it up. We'll get them the money within a week."

Dale sits silently. It seems that his gift of gab is a positive when Carroll needs it to help seal a real estate deal. The rest of the time that gift is as often as not the object of Carroll's ridicule. Dale is used to it by now, or at least as used to it as he will ever be.

"Hey, I have an idea," Carroll says. "We tell these people we'll name the new subdivision after them. I bet they'll love that idea, having their name out there for all time."

"But there are three families," Dale reminds him. "You can't use all their names."

Carroll scoffs. "Wake the fuck up. We're not going to do it. We're just going to say we will. Any development will be named after me."

Of course it will, Dale thinks.

Carroll considers the idea further. "We'll give it a classy name. Miller Heights or something."

"Heights?" Dale repeats. "It's flat land."

"So I'll build some fucking hills somewhere."

Dale sighs, but decides to allow the notions of future names and future hills to pass.

Down in the valley, the door to the farmhouse on the river opens and someone emerges and walks to the Jeep. Carroll powers down the window for a better look.

"What do we have here? Not the grandson, is it?"

The house is a far piece off, five hundred yards or more. Dale's eyesight is better than Carroll's, primarily due to the fact that Carroll's vanity won't allow him to wear eyeglasses.

"It's a woman," Dale says.

The woman wears jeans and a T-shirt, a baseball cap on her head. She climbs into the Jeep and pulls out of the yard onto the river road, heading toward Rose City.

"You want to talk to her?" Dale asks.

"Not if she's not the one calling the shots," Carroll says. He gestures to the farmhouses to the left. "Come on, let's go make Ma and Pa Kettle happy."

TWENTY-EIGHT

Billy wakes up Friday morning thinking about Jessie. He has already put last night's performance behind him. It's an old cliché that pro athletes need to have short memories and – like most clichés – there's more than a smidgeon of truth in it. A field goal kicker who misses a twenty-yard chip shot had better forget about it before his next attempt, a golfer who lips out a three-foot putt needs to get that hiccup out of his head before teeing off on the next hole and a ballplayer who goes oh-for-five with three K's needs to wake up the following day with his mind a clean slate.

Billy Crawford can do that, as well as anybody and better than most. He's been doing it for nearly twenty years. Confidence in his game has never been an issue for Billy. He'll arrive at the stadium this afternoon knowing full well that he'll knock the cover off the ball in tonight's game. It might not happen, but until it doesn't, he's going to believe it will.

For a change, he doesn't go to the diner for breakfast. He has cereal and coffee at home instead, sitting out back on the deck. The day is crisp and clear; the humidity of the past week took its leave overnight. Billy eats a bowl of Cheerios and then sits in the sun with his coffee, wondering what to do.

He's not wondering what he wants to do, at least not in a general sense. All he's ever wanted is to play baseball. It's been his sole aspiration since he can recall and until recently a very simple one. But it's not all that simple anymore. It's not some kids with a tattered ball and a cracked hickory bat playing scrub in a field behind the church in small-town Saskatchewan. Now it's complicated. Billy always suspected that life would get more complex as the years passed. He never thought that baseball would. It seems the game has somehow betrayed him. It is no longer a bat and a ball and a field of weeds. It's no longer Babe Ruth, hitting towering moonshots into the stands, fuelled not by steroids, but by hot dogs and beer. It's not even Casey striking out, to the eternal dismay of the fans in Mudville. No, now it's about nefarious backroom agreements and deals with the devil and one hand washing the other. Now it's about pretending to run for office in order to run out onto the field.

That part Billy thought he could live with. In truth, he still thinks that. The election is in two weeks and after that, he can go back to being just a ballplayer. It seemed a small price to pay.

But he woke up thinking about Jessie.

And not for the first time. It seems he's been thinking about her more and more lately. More to the point, thinking about what she thinks. When did he start caring about other people's opinions? Billy has always considered himself to be a good person. Well, an average person at least; not quite a sinner yet definitely not a saint. He believes that of most people and so he's never spent much time judging himself.

But now it seems that Jessie is his judge, and in her eyes, Billy has come up short.

And that bothers him, more than he would like to admit. Whether it's because he suspects Jessie might be right, or because it's Jessie doing the judging bothers him even further. If it was Lefty McQuire or Scoop Sutherland questioning his character, Billy wouldn't give it a second thought. Neither Lefty nor Scoop is particularly thoughtworthy.

But Jessie – well, Jessie is a different matter.

And that is the meat of the thing, Billy decides. Jessie is a different matter. That's the part that snuck up on him. There have been times in the past when Billy thought he was in love and maybe he was. He knows he's done strange things in the name of love – or whatever the feeling was. But never before had he skipped his running and batting practice, as he had yesterday, just to avoid a woman. His baseball life and his personal life did not overlap, and not by accident. He had never changed his routine to impress anybody, not even a woman who was unhappy with him, and there had been more than a few of them over the years.

If he hadn't acted that way before, then why now? He doesn't have an answer for that, but he decides that whatever the reason, today it stops. He isn't about to let Jessie or anybody else control how he lives his life. Which means first off, he would return to his routine today. He has managed to forget about last night's poor showing at the plate, but he hasn't forgotten about it completely. Nobody's memory is that selective.

So he'll go to the ballpark mid-afternoon, as usual. He'll run his laps and take batting practice and maybe have a massage or steam before the game. Business as usual. He's a ballplayer, first and foremost, and it's time he started acting like one again. Besides, there's a good chance he won't even run into Jessie.

When he gets to the stadium, the first person he runs into is Jessie.

Actually, he doesn't even get inside. Parking in the level beneath the field, he gets out and starts to walk to the tunnel leading to the clubhouse. Jessie's white Jeep is parked there, with the hood up. She's leaning against the front fender, her back to Billy, talking on her cellphone.

"How long?" she asks.

As she listens, she catches sight of Billy in her peripheral vision. Her eyes narrow and she looks away.

"Two hours doesn't work for me." She quits the call and turns to Billy. "I need a boost."

"You got cables?"

"Yup," she says and walks around to the rear of the Jeep.

"You sure you want help from a bad person like me?" Billy asks.

She retrieves the booster cables and returns. "Hey, I need to get to TSC to pick up a wheel bearing for the big mower. Right about now, I'd take a boost from Lucifer."

Shit, Billy thinks. *Now I'm being lumped in with the devil.*

Even with a boost, the Jeep won't turn over. There's a loud clicking noise from beneath the engine, but nothing else. Billy shuts his truck off and walks around to look under the hood of the Jeep.

"Sounds like a bad solenoid," he tells her.

"How would you know that?"

"I grew up on a farm," Billy says. "I know stuff. I'm a pretty smart guy, to tell you the truth."

"You hide it well," she says.

Billy digs his truck keys from his jeans and tosses them to her. She catches them without thinking as he turns and starts to walk toward the tunnel to the stadium.

"I don't need your charity," she calls after him.

Billy doesn't break stride. "It ain't a charity, it's a Ford."

Billy doesn't exactly knock the fences down that night, but he does have a walk, a single and a sac fly. It's enough to convince himself that the previous night was an anomaly. Not that he required any convincing of that. He's not back; he never left. His only problem has been allowing outside interests to muddy his concentration and the time for that is over. It's mind over matter and he proved that tonight. He's a ballplayer, not a politician, and from now on he's sticking with his strong suit.

And the crowd remains in his corner. That's important to Billy and always has been. If ever he wonders about the fact that he's dedicated his entire adult life to playing a kids' game, he just looks to the fans for validation. Tonight, there are plenty of the now-commonplace HIZZONER and CRAW FOR MAYOR signs, but there are just as many non-political displays of support, leading Billy to suspect that the fans for the most part are no more interested in Billy's political career than he is. When Billy singles up the middle to drive in a run in the fourth inning, the ovation is as if he'd hit a grand slam to win the World Series. As Damon had mentioned, the world was turning as it should.

After the game, Scoop Sutherland approaches Billy as he's getting dressed and informs him the Carroll Miller wants to talk to him. Tonight.

"He's at the CM offices downtown," Scoop says. "He's expecting you."

"Then he's going to keep expecting me," Billy says. "I'm heading for Shaky's."

Carroll Miller shows up at Shaky's a half hour behind Billy. He has his sidekick Dale in tow, of course. If Carroll is upset over having to come to Billy, he manages to conceal the fact. When they arrive, the bar is uncharacteristically quiet, and Billy is shooting pool by himself. He has a mug of draft beer on the rail. He sees the two of them approach as he leans over the table, eyeing a bank shot. He hammers the cue ball and drops the twelve ball in the side pocket. A perfect carom.

"You up for a game?" he asks Carroll.

Billy doesn't know that Carroll is not inclined to play any game where there's a chance he might lose. Billy wouldn't care if he did know. When Carroll declines, he offers the challenge to Dale.

"We're not here for pool," Dale tells him disdainfully.

"Shit, it's not like I asked you to slow dance," Billy tells him.

They sit at a table along the wall. Carroll orders a Scotch on the rocks. Billy has another beer and Dale asks for a cup of coffee. Billy gives him a look. Who drinks coffee in a roadhouse at midnight?

"We need to talk to you about next week's debate," Dale says.

"That'll be a short conversation," Billy says. "I'm not doing any debate."

Dale glances at Carroll for a moment. Carroll, of course, says nothing. Billy wonders if the man ties his own shoes, or does Dale do it for him?

"We need you there, Billy," Dale says. "If it's any consolation, this is our last big ask of you. Our last ask of any kind, in fact. But it's key to our strategy that you're there."

"Why is it key?"

"A couple of reasons," Dale says. "According to the polls, a solid fourteen percent of the voters are in your camp. Which pretty much accomplishes what we set out to do. But if you don't show up to the debate, that fourteen percent might decide you're not serious about this."

"I'm not serious about this."

"Yeah, well your supporters think you are," Dale says. "And we need them to keep thinking that way, for ten more days. You just need to keep on doing what you've been doing."

Billy isn't happy with the conversation, but he's not overly concerned. He has no intention of debating anyone, on-camera or off. "This wasn't part of the deal," he tells them. "Was there anything else you wanted to discuss? You sure you don't want to shoot some stick?"

"It's part of the campaign and that makes it part of the deal," Dale tells him. "You agreed to run."

Billy starts to reply but he glances past the two of them as the front door opens and Lisbeth Seville walks in. She doesn't look their way but goes straight to the bar, where she waits for a takeout order. Both Carroll and Dale have their backs to her and don't notice. Billy continues to watch her and after a moment she glances over and sees the three of them. She reacts but just slightly before turning away.

Billy looks back at Dale. "I agreed to letting you put my name out there. But there was nothing said about going on TV and debating anything."

"It's part of the process," Dale says. "You can't just sort of run for mayor."

Billy laughs. "That's pretty much what I've been doing."

Before Dale can respond, Carroll takes a slug of the Scotch and bangs his glass on the table. "This is part of the fucking agreement. Now, either you're in or you're out. I've held up my end. Haven't I?"

"Yeah, and that's working pretty well for you," Billy says. "Have you seen my numbers?"

Carroll nods. "Yeah, yeah . . . fourteen percent. You want a fucking parade?"

"Not those numbers," Billy says. "I'm talking about the really important numbers – my stats. You're getting your money's worth. Plus, we're a game out of first place."

"We're not here to talk about baseball, Billy," Dale says. "Let's stick to the matter at hand. This is about the debate. We need to position you and Kate Simmons on one side and Carroll on the other. And all you need to do is follow her like she's the Pied Piper. Do that, the polls stay where they are and we're in good shape come election night."

Billy has a drink of beer as he watches Lisbeth Seville, Styrofoam takeout in hand, head for the door.

"That's a hell of a plan, except for one thing."

"What's that?" Dale asks.

"I'm not going to any debate," Billy replies.

"Listen, Billy –" Dale begins but Carroll heads him off.

"When is the season over?" he asks. "The baseball season, not the election season."

Billy stares at him. The man owns a baseball team and has no idea when the season ends. "End of September."

"And then what?" Carroll asks.

"What do you mean?"

"You're signed until the end of the season," Carroll says. "But what about next year?"

Billy isn't sure if the question is rhetorical or not. Again, a team owner would ordinarily know the answer to a question like that. But maybe not an owner like Carroll Miller.

"The team has an option on my contract for next year," Billy tells him. "Seeing as I'm hitting almost .400 the past two months, I would assume they'll be picking up that option."

"Yeah, well . . . that's a decision we'll make after the season," Carroll says pointedly.

So that's how it is, Billy thinks. He's been waiting for this since the two of them walked in. Actually, since Scoop Sutherland informed him in the clubhouse that Carroll wanted to see him. Maybe since his return to the team weeks earlier.

"Long term, this thing could go a couple different ways," Carroll says then. "What do you think of this guy Erskine? I have to wonder about him. I mean, the media made a big deal about the Rounders hiring their first Black manager, but I'm not so sure."

"He's a good man," Billy says. "Knows the game inside out and is good with the kids. He preaches fundamentals, and they listen to him. Most of them anyway."

Carroll shrugs. "I'm not sold on the guy. Those people are inherently lazy. It's in their blood."

That raises Billy's hackles. "You mean people from Michigan?"

Carroll laughs. "Yeah, that's what I mean. But what I'm thinking, Billy, is that the manager's job is going to be available, whenever you quit playing. You could be a Rounder for life. Does that appeal to you?"

It does appeal to Billy. It's something he has considered in the past, on those rare occasions when he has admitted to himself that he might not be able to play forever. But he's not taking the bait, not tonight.

"Like I said, Ron Erskine is a good manager," he says. "And you want to know something else? He's a good man."

Dale cuts in then, obviously uncomfortable with Carroll's racist slant. "We can discuss the manager's job another time. Right now, we're talking about whether or not the team is willing to pick up your option for next season. You're making a lot of money, Billy. I mean, this isn't the major leagues, but you're still making a very good living."

"Like I said, look at my numbers."

"Enough of this shit," Carroll snaps. He gets to his feet and leans over the table, towering over Billy. "We both know this isn't about your fucking numbers, dipshit. This is about you showing up at the debate this weekend. The way I see it, you're going to be one of two places Saturday night. Either at the debate or at the stadium, clearing out your locker. Questions?"

Billy looks away, toward the pool table, where the balls are scattered across the felt. The eight ball hangs precariously over the corner pocket. It seems as if the slightest breath of air would cause it to fall.

"I asked if there were questions," Carroll presses.

Billy exhales. "Nary a one."

TWENTY-NINE

Billy goes to Peg's for breakfast the next morning, a return to routine. Cheerios are okay once in a blue moon but in the grand scheme of all things breakfast, they aren't a patch on ham and eggs at Peg's.

He's done eating and finishing his second cup of coffee when he glances out the plate-glass window and sees the white Jeep pull into the lot outside and park beside Billy's truck.

When Jessie enters the diner, she stops at the counter and embraces Damon.

"How are you, kid?" he asks. "Where you been lately?"

"You know," she replies. "TCB and all that."

"You want a coffee?"

"I'm good."

"He's sitting over there."

"I see him."

She turns and approaches Billy at the table. She's wearing jeans and a faded Rounders T-shirt. Her hair is usually in a ponytail beneath a baseball cap but today it hangs to her shoulders. Billy watches her cross the floor, loose-limbed and confident and real. He has been trying to convince himself that he didn't care what she thinks about him. It would help if she wasn't so damned attractive. And smart. And not inclined to fall for anyone's bullshit, including Billy's. At the end of the day, looks don't mean a whole lot, but when combined with brains and sass and common sense, it made for a hard combination for a man to ignore.

As hard as he might try.

"You got your car fixed," Billy says.

"It was a bad solenoid," Jessie tells him.

"Imagine that." Billy drinks off his cup. "How did you find me?"

"You're about as unpredictable as gravity, Crawford," she says. She doesn't sit down. "Come on, we're going for a drive."

They take the Jeep at her insistence. She drives across town and gets onto the highway, heading north toward Brownsville. The day is overcast, with rain threatening. Billy hopes it either rains before tonight's game, or afterward. He doesn't need a day off due to inclement weather. The only place his mind is clear these days is on a baseball field.

"Where are we going?" he asks once they're out of the city proper, where the road is two lanes, running parallel to the river.

"For a drive," she says.

Billy already knows that much. He watches her profile as she drives. He likes how serious she is, even when she's not. "You're not about to kill me and toss my body in the river?"

"Saving that for plan B," she tells him.

On the outskirts of the city, she turns right, heading into a newer subdivision situated between the main road and the river. The area is called Hawk's Landing. It's a couple hundred acres of condos, apartment buildings and townhouses. The residences are jammed together so tight it appears that a person couldn't walk between them. There is a mini-mart as well, with a convenience store and a pizza joint and a place selling computers and software.

Jessie drives through the subdivision and down to the river, where there's a pier and marina and a restaurant called The Docks. She turns around in the parking lot there and then stops, facing back into the congested assortment of homes that make up the neighbourhood.

"You ever been here?"

"Nope," Billy says.

"Five years ago, this was farmland," she tells him. "Look at it now."

Billy doesn't say anything for a bit. "It seems a little cramped."

"Kate Simmons calls these subdivisions ant farms," Jessie says. She looks over at Billy. "Kate Simmons is right."

They leave Hawk's Landing in the rearview mirror and get back on the highway, driving north again. The road runs straight through the village of Brownsville and then out again, into the valley. Descending, they take a side road, which curves along the escarpment before dropping down into the flatlands. They pass several lush farms, then Jessie pulls into a laneway leading to a story-and-a-half frame house, situated a hundred yards or so from the river. The house is fading to grey and has obviously seen better days. A steel-sided machine shed and a small barn with a gambrel roof are tucked in between the house and the river. The boards on the west end of the barn are mostly missing, exposing the interior to the elements.

A dozen or so brown hens hunt and peck in the yard. There's a mailbox mounted on a post at the end of the lane. Jessie eases the Jeep alongside and retrieves a couple of letters and some flyers from inside. She glances at the letters before tossing them on the centre console.

"Stealing somebody's mail is a crime, you know," Billy tells her.

"So I've heard," she replies, driving up to the house.

Billy looks the place over as she shuts off the ignition. The house sits square and level, but the paint is peeling and the windows are ancient. There's a narrow porch with a mismatched pair of rocking chairs sitting there, and a small vegetable garden off to the side, maybe twenty feet long and half as wide. Billy can see tomatoes and peppers and squash among the dying vines.

"Okay," Billy says. "You've decided to show me where you live. What brought this on?"

"I want you to know who you're working for," she replies. "Or should I say what you're working for."

She gets out of the car and Billy follows as she walks toward the line fence to the west and stops there, propping her forearms over the top rail. She gestures to the adjacent farm.

"Being a bona fide candidate for mayor, you know everybody's talking about the urban boundaries in this election. Yeah, the greenbelt. Well, this is it, cowboy. You and me and everybody else knows the only reason Carroll Miller is running is to open up farmland for development. What you don't know is that he's already made offers on that farm there, and the two on the other side of it. Over three hundred acres in total."

Billy looks at the property next door. Past a large field of ripening soybeans, the house is of red brick, with prominent dormers in the front and porches along three sides. The barns and outbuildings are painted green, with red trim. The place looks like a postcard.

"He would tear that place down?" Billy asks.

"In a heartbeat."

After a moment, Billy turns toward the house behind them. "Why hasn't he offered on this place? I mean, it's on the river."

"Oh, he's trying."

"But you won't sell," Billy says.

"I don't own it," Jessie says. "Not outright anyway. It belonged to my grandfather, on my mother's side. He died about a year and a half ago. There're two grandkids – me and my cousin Rory."

"So you and Rory don't want to sell."

"Rory would sell in a New York minute," Jessie says. "He couldn't care less about the place. But he's a smart guy. Not as smart as he thinks, but pretty smart. He's waiting to see how this plays out. If the city rezones the valley, then this fifty-acre piece of river property will be worth a lot of money. And I mean a *lot*. So Rory figures, why sell now when we can just wait?"

Billy continues to look at the rundown house as he considers this, trying to piece it together. "I don't get it. You're pissed because I'm supposedly helping Carroll get elected, but you're hoping he does, because then you're going to sell this place for a shitload of dough."

"Oh Billy," she says. "I don't want to sell. Rory wants to sell."

"You don't want to sell?"

"This is my family farm," Jessie says. "We came here in 1847 from Ireland. The Potato Famine, right? There's history here. I can show you a little graveyard on that rise by the riverbank where my great-great-grandfather and his wife are buried. Maybe I'm an unrealistic sentimentalist, but I want this place to stay in the family."

"Won't cousin Rory want to sell whether the greenbelt opens or not?" Billy asks.

Jessie nods her head. "He will. That's all he cares about, the money. But if the area isn't rezoned, I think I can buy him out. I've been squirrelling away every nickel these past few years, since Granddad went into the home. That's why the house looks like it does. I don't even want to splurge on a gallon of paint until I can raise enough for the downpayment."

"You really need to close in the end of that barn," Billy tells her.

"I'm aware of that," she says. "But there's not much I can do while things are still in the air. Am I going to fix a barn that some developer is just going to bulldoze in a year or two?"

Billy walks toward the old house and steps up onto the porch. He sits down in a rocking chair and looks over the place. A narrow lane curves from the house to the river. A cedar strip canoe is pulled up on the bank there.

"This is where you learned to fish," he says.

Jessie walks over to sit on the porch steps. "My old man was a drunk. I think he was a drunk from about fourteen years old. He left us when I was ten and I came here with my mother to live with Granddad. Yeah, this is where I learned to fish. And to throw hay bales and weed a vegetable patch and shovel poop."

She's looking at the clucking, roving hens as she talks. Billy watches her for a while, wondering why it's taken her this long to tell him all this. Maybe she's been as uncertain about him as he has about her. Or maybe she's considered him to be one of the enemy, working against her in this. If that's the case, it seems she's right.

"You obviously don't have a lot of use for Carroll Miller," he says. "And I can see why now. So I have to wonder – why are you working for the man?"

"Good question," she replies. "I didn't start out working for him. He bought the Rounders seven years ago. I'd already been with the team five years before that. I started out selling beer and snacks in the stands. One day one of the grounds crew didn't show up and they put me on a mower."

"And the rest is history."

"If you like your history boring," she says. "Thing is, it's a good job and it pays well enough. And I've never had to deal with Carroll Miller. I doubt he even knows my name. You and I both know he's not much of an owner. The story is that he bought the team because he wanted to tear down the stadium and develop the river property. Well, he should have done his homework before he bought. The city put the kibosh on that plan because the old riverfront is considered historical. He's been pouting about it ever since. And now he decides he's going to be mayor."

Which brings it full circle back to me, Billy thinks. Nothing is ever as simple as it seems. There's something to be said for good old-fashioned ignorance, and while it could be argued that knowledge is a good thing, it could also be argued that the less a person knows, the better off he is. It's a theory that Billy has subscribed to most of his life, even knowing that there's something inherently selfish about it. It seems he has learned more in the past thirty minutes than he has in the previous three months, about Carroll Miller and election campaigns and the ulterior motives therein.

About Jessie too.

He looks at her, sitting on the lower step, diligently picking away at the peeling paint there. Her fingernails are cut to the quick, befitting someone who works with her hands all day. She's quiet yet restless in the same moment. Billy realizes that he's rarely ever seen her still.

"What will you do if you lose the place?" he asks.

She hesitates for just a second then shrugs, too quickly. "Keep on keeping on. It's just a piece of dirt. No big deal."

"Nice try," Billy says.

THIRTY

They meet at the Simmons house Saturday afternoon. The debate is scheduled for seven o'clock that night, at the Rose City convention centre. Kate leaves early that morning to do a walking tour downtown. Shaking hands and asking for support, the regular routine. She isn't required to kiss any babies, which is fine with her. She's always thought that to be an odd thing for a politician to do, if indeed any politician has ever done it. Maybe it's just a cliché, a hackneyed throwback to another time. Who would want a stranger kissing their infant?

Maria goes with her this morning. It has rained off and on for the past two days and it remains overcast, but dry. Kate's reception among the citizenry is by this point typical. Some people recognize her and offer encouragement; some recognize her and do not. Others clearly have no idea who she is and don't seem to care. She knows they won't be voting for her but that's okay because she also knows, in all likelihood, they won't be voting at all.

There are quite a number of Carroll Miller signs in evidence in the core, all with the word PROGRESSIVE stamped prominently across a photo of Miller standing defiantly in front of various backdrops, his fists raised in the air, as if he's leading an insurgence somewhere.

There are just as many KATE SIMMONS signs to be seen. Kate in her shirtsleeves talking to "ordinary" people in different neighbourhoods. Kate riding on a city bus. Kate in full stride along an urban street, heading for somewhere with a great deal of purpose.

Smoke and mirrors, of course. All of it.

"But that's the way the game is played," Kate sighs.

"I beg your pardon?" Maria asks.

They're on King Street, heading back to the car, their little walkabout concluded. It's doubtful that they nudged the needle much today, but every little bit helps, as Joe has told Kate repeatedly.

Kate looks at Maria. "Did I say that out loud?"

"You did."

"I'm losing my mind, Maria."

Maria laughs. "Luckily that doesn't preclude you from holding office these days."

Back at the house, they find Ben with Joe on the patio overlooking the river. Joe is huddled in his chair, with a blanket over his legs, even though it's warm enough for September. He's slipped a bit in the past week, Kate has noticed. His shaking is worse, and his short-term memory is even more ragged than usual. His long-term memory is intact; the previous night he recited the results from the 1992 mayoral race down to the percentage point.

Ben has burgers and corn ready to go on the grill. He's been waiting for Kate and Maria to return. He's drinking a beer and snacking on peanuts, talking to Joe while they wait.

"Beer?" he says to them.

"I have a debate tonight," Kate reminds him.

"It's one o'clock," Ben says. "A beer won't hurt."

"A couple won't hurt," Joe tells her.

So Kate has a beer. Maria opts for a cooler of some kind. Ben had arrived with an assortment of drinks, hard and soft.

"Zabrisky is out," he says as he lights the grill. "Lisbeth Seville texted me an hour ago. He's still not getting around very well."

"What about Billy Crawford?" Kate asks.

"We haven't heard anything, one way or the other," Ben says. "I guess we'll find out tonight."

"Shit," Maria says. "The mystery man."

"There's really nothing mysterious about the guy," Ben replies. "He's too obvious and about as deep as a mud puddle."

"Fourteen percent think otherwise," Kate reminds him.

Joe shifts in his chair. "If nothing else, he will certainly add to the entertainment value of the evening."

"Thanks for that, Dad," Kate says.

"I call 'em as I see 'em."

Kate shakes her head. "You really need to use a baseball analogy? Whose side are you on?"

Joe smiles.

"Crawford could work to our advantage," Ben says. "We know he's going to follow Kate's lead. That's the only reason he's in the race. Maybe voters will see that and decide that they both make a lot of sense, but that Kate is the only electable one of the two."

"You really believe that?" Maria asks.

"I will if you will," Ben replies as he arranges the burgers over the fire.

Kate has a drink of beer. "You're a discouraging bunch, the whole damn lot of you."

By the time the food is ready, the sun has come out. They gather at the glass-topped table to eat. As the day warms, Joe leaves the blanket on the chair. His appetite seems better today than recently, Kate notices.

"Where'd you get the corn?" Joe asks after trying an ear.

"Craddock's," Ben says.

"What's wrong with the farmers' market?"

"I was at Craddock's buying hamburger," Ben says.

"That doesn't answer my question," Joe says. "I would never buy corn at a supermarket."

Ben falls silent then. He glances sheepishly from Kate to Maria, like a schoolboy caught in a lie.

"What's the matter?" Joe asks then. "Afraid of a little debate?"

Ben laughs at that.

The first beer manages to settle Kate's nerves a little, so she decides to have a second after eating. Joe has a couple fingers of bourbon. The four of them sit in the sun, quietly but nervously, like a regiment about to go into battle.

"So this is it," Kate says after a while. "To quote Joe Simmons, 'Tonight we find out where the bear shit in the buckwheat.'"

"What does that even mean?" Maria asks.

"I really don't know," Kate says.

"Nobody knows," Ben says.

"It means exactly what it says," Joe tells them.

THIRTY-ONE

Saturday is an afternoon game. The Rounders won again Friday night, for the ninth time in ten games. Billy hit an eighth-inning ground rule double that bounced over the fence in left field, scoring two runs to put the home side up by a run. He also had two singles and a walk, another perfect night.

He can't identify how he feels. He's never been more relaxed at the plate. The ball seems to be coming at him in slow motion. He doubts that Bob Gibson or Sandy Koufax could get him out these days.

Well, maybe Gibson or Koufax, but nobody in this particular league.

Saturday morning, he follows routine and goes to Peg's for breakfast. He grabs a sports section from the newspapers by the front counter and sits at a table in front. He's reading about last night's game when Damon approaches and pours him a cup of coffee.

"We're going to the playoffs, Damon."

"Looks that way," Damon says. "You got the momentum. Trickiest damn word in sports – *momentum*. Better not try to analyze it, or even admit you got it, for that matter. It'll bite you on the ass every time."

"Oh, I know all about that," Billy says. "I'll have the usual."

"Like you have to tell me."

Billy reads the standings as he waits for his eggs and ham and home fries to arrive. The Rounders are in first, up by one over the Tigers. A win today and the division is theirs. Peg's is busy, the usual Saturday morning crowd. People eat breakfast later on Saturday, and furthermore are more inclined to go out for breakfast than on a weekday. Finishing his meal, Billy savours his second cup, looking out the window to the new day. A day, maybe, like no other.

But isn't that true of all days?

He's still sitting there, watching the passing pedestrian traffic outside, when Damon comes over with his own coffee to join him.

"What's going on, Billy?"

"You mean what's going *up*," Billy smiles. "As in, my batting average."

"Jesus, you got a one-track mind, son," Damon tells him. He has a drink of the hot coffee. "There's a persistent rumour that you'll be attending tonight's debate after all?"

Billy has been trying not to think about the debate. He has a ball game to play, after all. Priorities.

"I guess I am."

"What made you change your mind?"

Billy exhales heavily. He should have left after one cup. "Just something I got to do."

"Why is that, Billy? Why do you have to do it?"

Billy does not want to get into it, not with Damon or anybody else. It's a conversation he refuses to have with himself; why would he want to have it with anyone else? But he can't shut Damon out; the two go back a long way.

"I guess I made a deal with the devil, bud," he says. "And tonight I have to pay the bill. But this is the final instalment. So praise the lord and start the goddamn playoffs."

"Pretty sure I know who the devil is in this scenario," Damon says. "He who would be mayor. And if this deal pays off, maybe he will. I assume you're okay with that?"

"Hey, all I did was hold up my end. Didn't I? When I came back, we were in fourth place and the post-season was a pipe dream. Now we're about to clinch."

"I asked you one question, and you answered another," Damon says. "Congrats – you really are a politician."

"Fucksakes," Billy says. "I said I would do this and so I'm going to do it. My word is worth something. Why don't people understand that? All I wanted was my job back. If this asshole gets elected mayor as a result, so what? Who's it going to harm?"

"Do you think he's a man of character?"

"Nope."

"And that doesn't matter?" Damon persists.

Billy is getting frustrated. "Ordinarily it would, I guess. Come on, I usually don't pay any attention to this shit. You know that. This is just a – what do you call it – unique situation. What do you want me to say, that I was looking out for me? Well, you're right. I got what I wanted and if Miller gets what he wanted, then that's the way of the world."

"End of story?"

"End of story," Billy agrees. "Like I said – who's it going to hurt?" He pushes his empty cup away and gets to his feet to leave.

Damon stands as well. "Jessie was here last night. Stopped for takeout."

Billy hesitates. "Yeah?"

"She thinks she's going to lose the farm. If Miller gets elected, that is. Sounds to me like she's resigned herself to the fact."

"If that happens, she's going to make out very well financially, Damon. And I mean *very* well."

"You think Jessie cares about that?"

"She damn well should. Hell, with that money, she can go buy another place somewhere."

"She doesn't want another place."

"Well then, that's her problem." Billy heads for the door, but Damon follows.

"She doesn't care about the money either, Billy." Damon pauses a moment. "Isn't it funny? You guys are on the opposite sides of this thing, and yet that's the one thing the two of you have in common. You don't care about the money either."

"Nope, and I never have. I care about the game."

"And Jessie cares about the land. Wouldn't you agree, Billy?"

"That's enough, Damon," Billy says. "I told you – I said I would do this and that's it."

"Do you think Jessie will vote for Caroll Miller?"

"Hell, no."

Damon nods. "But what if Carroll Miller made a deal with her? What if he said he would allow her to keep the farm if she supported him? Would she vote for him then?"

"Jessie would never vote for Carroll Miller."

"Why not?" Damon asks. "What if there *was* something in it for her? Then she might vote for him. There's nothing wrong with that, is there, Billy?"

Billy scowls as he opens the door to leave, then stops and turns back to point his finger at his old friend. "You're a fucking asshole, Damon. You know that? You're a fucking asshole."

Billy leaves the diner and gets into his truck and starts to drive. He heads south along the river, aimlessly, but after five minutes he turns around and goes north. A half hour later he's parked on the ridge that overlooks the valley where Jessie lives. Her Jeep is in the driveway, meaning she hasn't left for the stadium yet. Billy studies the rundown farmhouse a while, then glances to the left, to the other farms slated – in Carroll Miller's master plan anyway – for demolition. When he turns his attention back to Jessie's, he sees her come out of the house with a galvanized pail in her hand. She begins to scatter feed to the brown hens in the yard. Finishing, she walks over to sit on the bottom step of the porch. She remains there for several minutes, not moving, just sitting and watching. Billy wonders what she's thinking.

He knows exactly what she's thinking.

Why would she go to Damon with her concerns? After what she and Billy have shared these past months, why would she go to Damon?

Billy knows the answer to that too.

Now Jessie gets to her feet and walks to the Jeep. Before getting in, she turns back to take a long look at the house and the barn and the lane leading to the river. She stands there motionless for several moments. Then she gets into the truck and drives off. Billy watches as she pulls out of the driveway and heads for the city.

"Well, all right," he says.

An hour later Billy is heading for the stadium. Today's game starts at two o'clock. He has his running and batting practice to do. He'll stick to the routine, at least for this part of his day.

Something has come over him. He feels a calm he's never known before. He doesn't know what it is, but he knows exactly when it started. It began a few days earlier after the visit to Jessie's little patch of land on the river. Maybe it began when he realized that she trusted him enough to take him there. That she liked him enough to do that. He shakes his head at the notion. What is this – high school?

Whatever the root cause, he's suddenly feeling as tranquil as he has in months. Maybe that's what happens when a man finally makes up his mind. But it's like what Damon said about momentum. Best not to overthink it. That might encourage self-doubt, and Billy is finished with that.

Or so he hopes.

While he's jogging around the field, he sees Jessie, standing by the machine shed, talking to one of the crew. When she spots him, she stops and turns in his direction, as if expecting him to come over. But he doesn't. He smiles and points to her with two fingers, a sort of salute. He can tell she's puzzled by the gesture, as if she doesn't know what it means. But that's okay.

She can't know what it means.

The Rounders win again, this time a romp. The final is 14–3 and Billy comes to the plate five times. He gets a hit the first four appearances – two singles, a double and a first-inning home run with two men on. His final at-bat is in the bottom of the eighth and he crushes a change-up to straight-away centre field. It's maybe the hardest ball he's hit all year and as it leaves the bat, Billy thinks it might actually clear the fence in centre, and the stadium itself, and end up in the Chalk River. But a huge gust of wind comes up at the last moment, knocking the ball out of the air like it's a wounded mallard. It ends up in the centre fielder's glove.

Billy laughs as he trots off the field.

In the clubhouse afterward, Billy showers and dresses, keeping mainly to himself. The Rounders are officially in first place now and the mood is buoyant. The beer is flowing freely in the locker room and the players are planning a blowout at one of the local bars.

"Billy!" Scotty hollers from across the room as Billy heads for the showers. "You coming to Roscoe's?"

"Can't tonight," Billy says. "Got a debate."

"Shit, I forgot about that. Come afterward then."

Billy nods without commenting. He has no idea what afterward is going to look like. When he's dressed and ready to leave, he stops and sticks his head in the manager's office. Ron Erskine has finished talking to the media and sits behind the desk, puffing on a Havana and looking content. The cigar is verboten in the clubhouse, but they just clinched; exceptions will be made. Billy extends his hand.

"First place," he says. "You did it, Skip."

"We did it," Erskine says.

Billy nods. "We did it."

Erskine taps the cigar ash into an empty takeout cup.

"I've been in this game for thirty-five years," Erskine says. "And I can honestly say I have never seen a hotter hitter than you are right now, Billy. And the weird thing, the ball you hit the hardest was an out."

"That's baseball."

"It's sort of surreal," Erskine says. "To be hitting the ball like Ty Cobb in his prime, at your age. Don't take that the wrong way, Billy. You know what I mean."

"I do."

"It's almost Faustian."

The statement gives Billy pause. Of course the manager has heard the theories surrounding Billy's return to the team. Everybody in the city has heard the theories surrounding Billy's return to the team. But this is the first time the subject has come up between the two.

"What do you figure, Skip – that I made a deal with the devil?"

"Did you?"

"No, but I came awful damn close."

Billy has a blue suit he hasn't worn in a couple of years. It's for funerals and weddings, and he's been lucky enough to avoid both of late. Saturday night, he pulls it from his closet, along with a white shirt and a red tie. He looks at himself in the mirror before leaving the house. He's not sure whether or not he looks like a mayor but then he will never have reason to look like a mayor.

Daphne Lawrence and the two college kids – the trio comprising Billy's entire campaign team – meet him at the convention centre. The students are amped up. In spite of the fact that they have been "running" Billy's campaign for weeks now, it's only the second time they've been in his presence; the first was the night at Shaky's when he'd announced his candidacy and then gotten roaring drunk. Tonight – still with the goal of turning Billy's campaign into a school project – the two intend to film the debate and everything surrounding the debate with their iPhones. They set up on opposite ends of the stage. If Billy does well, they'll have it all recorded to use in the documentary they plan to make about the campaign. If Billy falters, then it will be even more grist for the future doc. After Billy's last on-air interview with Lisbeth Seville, the smart money is against Billy doing well. But that's all right with the two students. When does anyone ever look away from a train wreck?

Daphne greets Billy enthusiastically enough, playing along as if she fully expects him to be elected the city's next mayor. But after a while, Billy notices that she mainly has eyes for Carroll Miller, who has arrived with Missy Hemphill on his arm. Missy is dressed to the nines in a little black dress, her lustrous blond hair piled high, a string of pearls around her neck. As Daphne glares at her from across the room, Dale appears from somewhere backstage and quietly approaches. He gestures to Billy.

"How are we doing here?"

"What?" Daphne says, reluctantly shifting her gaze from Missy. "Oh fuck, who knows?"

There are three moderators tonight. Lisbeth Seville is joined by John Comstock, the anchor from *Rose City Review*, and a woman from some other cable network; Billy doesn't catch her name as he walks out onto the stage with the others. Carroll, of course, doesn't so much as make eye contact with Billy, but Kate Simmons comes over and introduces herself.

"My father used to take me to Rounders games," she says as they shake hands. "Before your time, of course."

"You should go to a game this fall," Billy tells her. "They're going to the playoffs."

The statement gives Kate pause. "They" are going to the playoffs?

The candidates are called to order shortly. Lisbeth takes the lead and makes the introductions, after which each is given two minutes for opening remarks. Carroll Miller talks for nearly twice that long and uses the word *progressive* fourteen times. Kate gives a more concise account of her vision for what she terms "the city going forward," a hybrid combination of the status quo and measured progress. Then it's Billy's turn.

"Hell, I'm just happy to be here. Let's do this thing."

And so the discussion begins. At this late stage of the race, there are only so many topics to discuss, and they've all been covered again and again. Affordable childcare, more money for nursing homes, the light rail proposal, the homeless encampments. An unending loop, with nothing new to report. Carroll toes his line and Kate hers, while Billy uses as few words as possible to follow Kate's lead. The issue of the greenbelt is last and once again Kate and Carroll Miller square off.

"One of my opponents would build condos in the Garden of Eden," Kate says.

"You're damn right I would," Carroll replies to laughter. "The ads would write themselves."

Lisbeth waits for the crowd to settle, then turns to Billy. "Mr. Crawford, you're on record as saying that you, like Ms. Simmons, want the greenbelt to remain untouched."

"I said that?" Billy replies. "Well, I must have meant it then."

There's more laughter, albeit somewhat uncomfortable, from the audience.

"Amusing as that is . . ." Lisbeth prompts.

She's staring a hole through Billy, as if challenging him to step up. Billy feels his pulse quicken. All right, it's time to show the devil a thing or two. He's been pushing Billy around for too damn long.

"No, I did say that," Billy goes on. "And at the time, I meant it. But I've been doing my homework on this thing. There's a side to this particular issue that I never really considered. And the funny thing is, it's my opponent here Carroll Miller here who schooled me on it."

Billy can actually feel Carroll stiffen at the podium, a dozen feet away. Billy won't look at him, nor at Dale Gosling, suddenly twitching nervously in the wings.

"I had the opportunity to meet with Mr. Miller and his manager Dale Gosling the other night, at a bar called Shaky's," Billy said. "Hey, you folks should check it out. They have great wings and the coldest Guinness in the whole damn city."

"The topic, Mr. Crawford," Comstock reminds him.

"Right," Billy says. "Well, we had a good confab about this greenbelt issue, and it opened my eyes. Mr. Miller told me that these days there are literally thousands of young people who can't find a home. Couples with young families, or about to start families, whatever. The cold fact of the matter is – Rose City just isn't big enough anymore. And the reason for that? One word: immigrants. The inner city is now chock full of all these new Canadians. I have to admit I was ignorant of that fact until Mr. Miller laid it out for me the other night. It's like he told me – you got your Orientals and your curry eaters and your camel jockeys, people from all over the world. And don't get me wrong – that's fine. They have their own customs and ways, these people, and they get to have their own neighbourhoods. I have no problem with that."

"Hold on," John Comstock says, beating a stunned Lisbeth to the punch. "You're not suggesting that Carroll Miller used that language?"

Carroll begins to make excited noises as Billy feigns confusion. "What language?"

"The language you yourself just used to describe our quote, unquote, new Canadians."

"You mean about the camel jockeys and Chinamen and all that?" Billy asks. "Yeah, he did. I mean – what else are you going to call them? People from other countries call me a Canuck and I'm okay with that."

"Hold on now!" Carroll snaps. "This is a complete fabrication. I will *not* stand for this."

Billy stays with it. "Wait now, I'm agreeing with you here, Mr. Miller. Open up that greenbelt so these real Canadians have a place to live. Well, I don't mean real Canadians, but you know what I'm saying. I'm with you on this."

Billy glances toward the wings and sees the sap running out of Dale Gosling. He manages to refrain from smiling.

"This is a set-up!" Carroll shouts. "This is entirely fabricated. I never had any such conversation with this man. I never met with him and we never had this discussion."

Lisbeth leans into her mic. "You're saying this meeting at Shaky's bar never happened?"

"Never happened."

"I happened to be there that night," Lisbeth says. "Picking up an order of those chicken wings Mr. Crawford just mentioned. And I saw the two of you talking."

Carroll sputters. "Okay, we did meet. I didn't mean to suggest otherwise. That part is true. But the rest is complete nonsense. This is a fucking set-up."

"You'll watch that language," Comstock says.

Billy, feigning confusion, gives Carroll one last volley. "Hell, I'm trying to agree with you here, man."

With that, Billy looks to the wings again, just in time to see Dale turn on his heel and head out of the building. Daphne is close behind him and smiling now, not scowling. She'll leave gussied-up Missy Hemphill to deal with Carroll's mood tonight. Billy watches as the two of them disappear out a steel door. The two students remain, filming the theatrics from different angles while gleefully smiling like it's Christmas morning.

Billy turns back to the moderators. "So – is there anything else?"

There is nothing else.

At least, there is nothing else to debate. Carroll raises such a racket that the network turns off his microphone while Lisbeth announces that the debate is finished. But Carroll Miller is not. He yanks off his mic and follows the moderators into the green room backstage. Billy is leaving and he stops to shake Kate's hand. She has been nearly speechless since his greenbelt monologue and now looks at him as if he just fell from the sky.

"Who in the hell are you – the Lone Ranger?" she asks.

Billy smiles. "Hi-yo Silver, ma'am."

"Look at those two!" Carroll barks. "They're in on this, I fucking knew it."

Billy waves at Carroll as if they're best friends and leaves. Kate corrals Maria and follows shortly. Carroll, in a state, looks as if he wants to chase after them but instead turns back to Lisbeth and the others.

"You hear me?" he demands. "They're in on this together. Any idiot can see that. I demand an investigation!"

"In on what?" Lisbeth asks calmly.

"You know what," Carroll snaps at her. He takes a moment then, his muddled yet fertile mind working overtime. "Sonofabitch. You're in on it too, aren't you? You set this up. Well, this is election interference. I'm going to sue you and this fucking network. You'll never work again, you fucking bitch."

Lisbeth laughs. "I could use some time off. You know, you have a vein the size of a garden hose popping out of your forehead. I hope the kids are getting it on camera."

Carroll turns, realizing that Billy's campaign workers are diligently recording him even now.

"Turn those phones off!" he shouts. "Do it! You're working for me, you little shits. Turn 'em off *now*!"

John Comstock perks up. "Did you just say that Billy Crawford's team is working for *you*?"

Carroll catches himself, but too late. "I didn't say that. I just told them to stop filming. I'm a private fucking citizen."

"Who's at a public debate while running for mayor," Comstock reminds him.

"Keep talking, Carroll," Lisbeth says. "The good news is you're going to get your wish. You're going to be all over social media tomorrow."

"The hell I will," Carroll says. "I'll file a fucking injunction first thing tomorrow morning to seize any video; I don't care if it's from the network or those fucking kids over there. I will do it. I have the best lawyers in the goddamn city."

"You may have the best lawyers, but you don't have a very good grasp on modern technology," Lisbeth said. "Their video will be in the cloud quicker than you can say 'Bill Gates.' And it'll be there forever."

This fact doesn't sit well with Carroll Miller. "I will fucking sue all of you!" he threatens again. "You think I'm joking? Do you know who I am?"

Lisbeth smiles as she puts on her coat. "Oh, Carroll. After tonight, everybody knows who you are."

At the Simmons house across town, Ben has watched the debate with Joe. He and Maria intended to accompany Kate to the convention centre, but Kate had asked Ben to stay with her father. Not that he wasn't all right alone, it was just that she knew the debate could get heated and she didn't want his blood pressure to boil over. Ben might be a moderating influence.

The two sit in the den, drinking Irish whiskey and watching things unfold on the TV against the wall. Up until the last five minutes or so, it has been as uneventful a night as either could recall. Ben has his doubts that anything has occurred that will sway public opinion a centimetre either way.

Until, of course, the grand finale.

Ben's mouth is agape as Carroll Miller storms across the stage to rant at the moderators while they rather quickly and clumsily wrap things up. Even they are shocked by what just happened, and don't quite know how to deal with it.

Ben turns to Joe. "Can you believe that Crawford? That stupid sonofabitch has no idea what he just did. He just handed the election to Kate."

Joe is smiling as he sips from the rock glass of Jameson's. "You're half right."

"How's that?"

"He just handed Kate the election," Joe replies. "But he's as far from stupid as anybody I've ever seen."

THIRTY-TWO

Billy waits until Monday before driving out to Brownsville. Skirting the village proper, he stops at a lumberyard and buys twenty lengths of one-by-twelve rough pine boards and ten pounds of three-inch nails. There's a coffee shop across the road where he picks up a couple cups of takeout from the drive-thru.

When he gets to the farm on the river, he finds Jessie walking up from the river, talking on her phone. She smiles when she sees him and ends the call as he gets out of the truck and approaches.

"Cream only," he says, handing her the coffee.

"Aw, you remembered." She takes the cup from him and has a sip. The two of them walk over to sit in the mismatched rockers on the porch.

"So, I saw you on TV the other night," she says. "You're a walking hand grenade, Crawford."

"I don't know what that means."

"You know exactly what it means," she tells him. She has another drink, then sets the cup on the step beside her. "I hear you lost your job. Again."

Billy nods and he shrugs his shoulders to show his indifference.

She gestures to Billy's truck. "What's with all the lumber?"

"Thought I'd close in that barn," he says.

She falls silent a moment. "Why would you want to do that?"

"So your chickens don't freeze this winter."

As if on cue, a clucking brown hen wanders close, high-stepping past them before moving on to scratch for gravel in the driveway.

"I don't need you to fix my barn," she says.

"God, but you're stubborn."

"Like looking in a mirror, Crawford?"

Billy smiles and drinks his coffee.

"What are you going to do now?" she asks.

Billy shrugs. "Wait for another team to call, I guess. Too late for this year but I hope to get an invite to spring training somewhere." He pauses. "Well, unless I get elected mayor next week. That's gonna change everything."

"I think that ship has sailed," Jessie says. "And you ain't on it, bud. And neither, from what I'm hearing, is Carroll Miller. Kate Simmons is suddenly polling at around seventy percent. Carroll Miller's numbers are down around Zeb Zabrisky's. And yours."

"Ain't that a shame?" Billy stretches his legs out on the steps. "So what's your next move with this place?"

"I'll wait until after the election," Jessie says. "If Kate Simmons gets in, I'm going to call cousin Rory and offer to buy him out."

"Can you swing the money? He might want to list it and sell to the highest bidder."

"I've thought about that," she admits. "If he does, I'm pretty much fucked. I won't be able to compete with some rich couple from Toronto who want to come here on the weekends and play farmer."

Billy watches the hen in her quest for the fine pebbles in the drive.

"We had chickens on the farm back home," he says. "We'd kill a couple dozen at a time. My old man would handle the axe and my mother and us kids would do the gutting and plucking. I hated that job. The plucking especially."

"There's none of that here," Jessie says. "I have these birds just for the eggs. I intended to butcher a few, thinking they'd be healthy eating, but I let myself get to know them and now I'm too soft-hearted to lop their heads off. These girls will die of old age."

Billy finishes his coffee and places the cup on the worn planking of the step. He takes a few minutes, thinking of what to say and how to say it. He feels her watching him.

"The Rounders owe me a buyout for next year's option," he begins. "It's a decent piece of change."

"I'd love to see Carroll Miller's face when he has to sign that cheque. I wouldn't expect a Christmas card from him this year if I was you."

"Life is full of disappointments." Billy hesitates again. "Thing is, I could help you out with the down payment."

Jessie grows quiet again. Billy glances past her, down to the river's edge. The canoe has been pulled up and overturned, to keep it from getting swamped from the recent rain, he guesses.

"You're going to fix my barn and then help me with the down payment," she says. "Why would you do that?"

"I don't know," he says. "I don't always know why I do the things I do."

"Sometimes you do," she says. "Sometimes you know exactly what you're doing."

"I guess maybe this is one of those times."

She leans over to slide her arm through his. Neither says anything for a long time.

Award-winning author **BRAD SMITH** is a novelist and screenwriter, born and raised in southern Ontario. *Billy Crawford's Double Play* is his fifteenth novel. His 2019 novel – *The Return of Kid Cooper* – won the Spur Award for Best Western Traditional Novel from the Western Writers of America. His novels *One-Eyed Jacks* and *Copperhead Road* were shortlisted for the Dashiell Hammett Prize. He adapted his book *All Hat* to feature film, starring Keith Carradine and Luke Kirby. He now lives in a ninety-year-old farmhouse near the north shore of Lake Erie, where he tinkers, respectively, on his vintage cars and his golf swing. Visit his website at www.bradsmithbooks.com.